FLYNN

THE SERIES

A WESTERN STORY COLLECTION

BY

TELL COTTEN

DUANE BOEHM

KEN FARMER

BUCK STIENKE

BRAD DENNISON

T.C. MILLER

DEDICATION

We dedicate this anthology to all western fans. Thank you for being such dedicated readers. Happy Trails

COVER ART:

Ken Farmer & Adriana Girolami

Publisher's note:
This novel is a work of fiction...except the parts that aren't. Names, characters, places and incidents are either the products of the author's imaginations or are used fictitiously and sometimes not. Any resemblance to actual persons, living or dead, business establishments, events or locales is entirely coincidental, except where they aren't.

TIMBER CREEK PRESS
www.timbercreekpresss.net
ISBN: 978-0-9984703-6-8 - E
ISBN: 978-0-9984703-7-5 - Print

CONTENTS

MEN OF FEW WORDS

BY

TELL COTTEN

CHAPTER ONE

Their main problem was money. They didn't have any and they needed some. It was just too difficult to get by without it.

A simple solution presented itself when an eastbound stagecoach was spotted in the distance.

There was no need to discuss anything. They glanced at each other, and the four outlaws nodded as a silent understanding passed between them.

They were a trail-weary, filthy bunch. Their clothes were stained with sweat and they hadn't shaved or bathed in weeks.

These men were seasoned outlaws who never hesitated to kill. They were also desperate and on the run, and that made them even more dangerous.

Lester was the leader. He was tall and he had a leathery face with a hard jaw. He didn't talk much, but when he did his voice had a hard ring of authority and no one questioned his leadership.

Cad was second in command. He was thin with high shoulders and a bony face. His eyes were cold and cunning, and there was no kindness in him.

The last two outlaws were brothers. Hank was the oldest sibling. He was light built and wiry, with the marks of a lot of hard, mean years on his face.

Then there was Ned. He was the youngest of the bunch, and perhaps the meanest. He always looked pale, and his face was tight-drawn and controlled. He didn't respect anything or anybody, except for his brother.

Cad knew the country. He pointed towards a steep hill to the east and explained that the stage would slow down while climbing it.

The outlaws kicked up their horses. They arrived at the hill in plenty of time and they tied their horses in amongst some trees.

The terrain was covered in brush and catclaw and the road was narrow and rocky.

"This is a likely spot," Lester commented as he glanced around. "Should work just fine."

"Do you want us to pile up some brush in the road?" Hank asked.

"What for?" Lester looked at him.

"So they'll have to stop."

"They'll stop just fine when we shoot the horses," Lester replied.

No one seemed bothered by the thought and they nodded in agreement.

"They'll be here soon. We'd best get ready," Lester said.

They covered their faces with neckrags and scattered. Lester and Cad hunkered down behind a fallen log, and the two brothers hid behind a big boulder on the other side of the road.

Time passed slowly. However, this wasn't their first robbery and they remained calm.

They finally heard the sounds of the stagecoach, and anticipation built as they palmed their revolvers and pulled back the hammers.

"Here they come," Lester called out softly.

§§§

CHAPTER TWO

Many miles to the south, a Conestoga wagon made its way north. A team of mules was pulling the wagon and the pace was slow.

"We're lost, aren't we?" Karen McKee asked.

She sat on the wagon seat beside her husband. She was almost thirty, and she had a tall, lean figure with fair skin.

Her two children sat behind her. Sam was ten years old, and Suzan was eight. Their eyes were wide and attentive as they listened to their parents.

"Not lost." Jack McKee smiled reassuringly at his wife. "Just misplaced."

Jack looked like a storekeeper. He had stooped shoulders, white hair, and the makings of a belly. But his face was kind and gentle.

Karen uttered a disgruntled grunt.

"What's the difference?" she demanded.

"We'll be fine," Jack replied, then, more to himself than to Karen, he added, "As soon as we find Jacksboro…that is."

Karen didn't reply. Instead, she smoothed her dress over her knees, as she took in the view.

A vast openness loomed in front of them. There were also several rolling hills, with rugged limestone rocks and some trees scattered about.

"It's so big and empty," she commented.

"Not like back east," Jack said.

"Nothing like *home*," Karen agreed, and he frowned at the way she said that.

"This *is* our home now," he reminded, a bit stern. "There's nothing to go back to."

"I know that."

"Do you?"

Karen turned and looked at him, it was silent a moment. Then she sighed and looked back at the countryside. "Do you think we missed it?"

"Missed what? Jacksboro?"

Karen nodded.

"No, we haven't crossed the Brazos yet."

"And where is the Brazos?" Karen challenged.

"In front of us somewhere."

Karen bit her lower lip and said no more. A few minutes passed, and Jack cleared his throat and tried to look cheerful.

"We'll travel another hour." He decided. "Then we'll make camp. How does that sound?"

Karen nodded, but her mind was elsewhere.

Jack watched her. He started to say something, but decided against it. Instead, he focused on the mules and yelled words of encouragement.

§§§

6

CHAPTER THREE

The stagecoach struggled up the hill, and the horses strained against the weight as they fought for footing.

Lester waited until the stage reached the top and leveled out. Then he breathed deeply, took aim, exhaled, and pulled the trigger. There was a loud thumping sound as his bullet hit flesh and a horse squealed in terror.

More shots exploded from all around. All the horses screamed and kicked out as they went down and the stage came to an abrupt halt.

The shotgun rider uttered a surprised grunt. There wasn't time to think, and instincts took over. He spotted movement behind a boulder, and he swung his shotgun up and fired. There was a thumping sound, followed by a scream.

The shotgun rider dove towards cover, but Lester filled him with lead before he hit the ground. His body twisted from the bullets' impact—he landed face first and didn't move.

Lester, Cad, and Ned sprang forward and surrounded the stage. Meanwhile, Hank thrashed around on the ground, moaning and clutching at his shoulder.

The stage driver sat frozen, still holding the reins and Lester trained his Colt on him.

"Don't try anything foolish," he warned.

"I won't." The driver lifted his hands.

"Hank, you all right?" Ned asked, his voice anxious.

7

"No! I've been shot!" came the curt reply.

"You hang on," Ned said.

Hank muttered a muffled reply. Meanwhile, Lester approached the stage driver.

"Toss the gun belt," he commanded.

"I will. Just don't shoot," the driver replied.

Being careful not to make any sudden movements, he reached down and unbuckled his belt. He pitched it into the bushes and raised his hands again.

"Get the passengers out," Lester told Cad.

He nodded, moved to the door, and swung it open. "You heard him!" Cad said gruffly.

Six passengers stepped out and Cad lined them up beside the stagecoach.

"Throw the Wells Fargo box down," Lester told the driver. "There isn't one," the driver replied.

"What?" The outlaw glared at him.

"Just mail on this trip."

Lester stepped up and peered down. There was only the mailbag, and he scowled at their misfortune.

Cad searched the passengers while Ned covered them. He took their wallets, jewelry, and a few watches. He pocketed the loot and looked at Lester.

"All done," he said.

Lester nodded and looked at Ned.

"Get Hank on his horse," he said.

Ned nodded and hurried off while Lester and Cad covered everyone. They waited a moment, and then Lester looked at the passengers.

"Get back inside, and don't come back out until we've gone," he said roughly.

The passengers obeyed with somber faces. Once they were inside, Cad stepped up and slammed the door shut.

Lester glanced at the driver. "You just sit there and be quiet."

"Yes, sir."

"Let's go." Lester beckoned at Cad.

They hurried over to their horses, untied them, and climbed on.

The two brothers were already mounted. Hank looked pale, and he was hunched over the saddle.

"How is he?" Lester asked.

"He can ride," Ned replied.

"He'd better."

"He won't slow us down."

Lester grunted at that and kicked up his horse. He rode south in a brisk trot, and Cad was right behind him.

Ned grabbed the reins to his brother's horse and encouraged his own mount forward. He followed after Cad, and he led Hank's horse behind him.

§§§

CHAPTER FOUR
JACKSBORO, TEXAS

The stranger had the look of someone who'd been in the saddle for days, perhaps even weeks. He was in need of a bath and shave, and he displayed a tired, weary look.

However, his eyes were thoughtful and sharp and he didn't miss a thing as he walked his horse down the main street of Jacksboro, Texas.

The stranger was looking for something, and he nodded and uttered a slight grunt of satisfaction when he spotted the sheriff's office. There was a man sitting on the porch, and he wore a sheriff's badge.

The man was Mason Flynn. He was forty, tall, and wide-shouldered. He had brown hair, sky blue eyes and a full mustache.

The stranger captured and held Flynn's attention. He rode a horse well, and there was a hard, experienced look about him. He was smaller than most, spry, and in good shape.

This was not a man to take lightly and Flynn understood that at first glance.

Mason shifted slightly in his chair, making the revolver on his hip more accessible.

The stranger rode toward him, and Flynn spotted a circle and star Texas Ranger badge pinned on his vest pocket. Flynn relaxed slightly, but stayed alert.

The man pulled up in front of the jail, and several seconds passed while they studied each other. No words were spoken, but neither one seemed uncomfortable with the silence.

"You must be Mason Flynn," the stranger finally said in a soft, Texas drawl.

"I am."

"Heard of you," the man said. "I'm Yancy Landon."

Flynn nodded his admiration. "Heard of you too," he said. "You've quite the reputation."

"As do you," Yancy returned the compliment.

"I've been around."

"So, we both know each other," Yancy said.

"Appears so."

"Well, that saves time," Yancy looked pleased.

"Does." Flynn smiled pleasantly.

Yancy nodded and changed the subject.

"I've been all over Texas, but this is my first trip to Jacksboro."

"Personal reasons, or business?" Flynn asked.

"I'm here as a Texas Ranger."

"I was afraid of that," Flynn said. "Urgent?"

"Not particularly."

Flynn nodded. "Hungry?"

"I could eat."

Flynn gestured down the street. "I know a good café."

Yancy didn't think for long. "Lead the way." He dismounted.

§§§

CHAPTER FIVE

Lester rode south in a brisk trot.

A few hours passed, and he finally slowed their pace. He glanced back at Hank, and a thoughtful look crossed his face.

Hank was pale, and his brow was beaded with sweat. Blood dribbled from his shoulder, and his shirt was stained red.

"You gonna make it?" Lester asked.

"Don't know," Hank muttered.

"He's lost a lot of blood," Ned spoke up, concerned.

"That's 'cause his shoulder's full of holes," Lester replied, and he asked Ned, "You any good at digging out buckshot?"

"Never done it before."

"Cad?" Lester looked at him.

"Not me." He shook his head.

Lester pinched his face in thought as he considered their options.

It would be a shame if Hank died. It wasn't that they were close—Lester didn't even consider him a friend. However, the four of them had been together a long time, and they worked well together.

Lester was still pondering things when they rode up to some wagon tracks. He grunted in surprise, pulled up, and squinted.

"Lookie there." He gestured.

Cad was the best tracker of the bunch. He dismounted, squatted on his heels, and studied the ground with care.

"What do you think?" Lester asked after a moment.

"Fresh," Cad commented. "Ruts run deep too."

"Wagon must be loaded heavy," Lester observed.

"I'd say so," Cad replied. "And, they're traveling alone. Besides the mules, there's no other tracks."

"What do you suppose they're hauling?" Ned spoke up.

"Whatever it is, it'd be worth *something*," Cad replied, and added, "There's also the stock."

"Mebbe they could help Hank," Ned added.

"Perhaps," Lester said. He thought it over a moment more, and then nodded. "Let's go find out."

Cad grinned and stepped back into the saddle. Lester gestured at him to take the lead, and they left out in an easy trot, following the tracks.

§§§

CHAPTER SIX

Yancy followed Flynn to Sewell's Café. They stepped inside, and were greeted with the pleasant aromas of home cooking and fresh pies.

"Smells good," Yancy commented.

"Tastes even better," Flynn said. "Come on."

They made their way to Flynn's regular table in the back. They sat and a slender, smiling waitress came over.

"I was getting worried," she said, glanced at Yancy and explained. "Sheriff Flynn comes in here everyday, same time. If he doesn't show, then something's bad wrong."

Flynn frowned at the waitress. "Yancy, this is Molly. She talks too much."

"My brother has the same problem," Yancy replied.

Molly made a face at Flynn. "Tea?"

"Be fine," Flynn said.

"I'll take coffee," Yancy spoke up. "With sugar."

"Be right back." Molly flashed a smile and took off.

"Friendly thing," Yancy commented as he leaned back in his chair.

"Oh, she is," Flynn grinned. "She worries about me every time I leave town."

"You close?"

"Naw, I owe her money," Flynn jested, and Yancy smiled wryly.

Molly returned with the drinks, she took their order and left.

Flynn was amused as he watched Yancy pour three spoonfuls of sugar in his coffee. He stirred, took a swig, and sighed in contentment.

"Having a little coffee with your sugar?" Flynn grinned.

"Good coffee." Yancy missed the sarcasm.

Flynn smiled faintly and let it go, and it fell silent. He waited for Yancy to explain why he was here, but he never did.

Several minutes passed and Flynn finally cleared his throat. "You don't say much."

"Always thought conversation was overrated," Yancy replied.

"Can't argue with that," Flynn agreed. "Feel the same way myself."

"My brother usually does the talking for both of us," Yancy continued.

"But you're alone on this trip," Flynn pointed out.

"I am."

"Must be difficult for you."

"Been getting along."

"Well." Flynn looked thoughtful. "That's good to know."

Yancy nodded somberly, and they each took a swig from their cup.

"Any strangers in town?" Yancy changed the subject.

Flynn thought a moment.

"None that come to mind," he replied. "How many strangers you looking for?"

"Four."

Flynn shook his head. "I'd have noticed that many."

Yancy frowned his displeasure. "I was hoping they'd be here," he said. "Lost their tracks to the west, but they were headed this way."

"What do they look like?"

"Not sure, exactly."

"Why are you after them?" Flynn pressed for information.

"They murdered a feller back home," Yancy said, and his voice turned bitter. "His name was Rick…Good man."

"Why'd they kill him?"

"Rick didn't say."

Flynn frowned at that. "But Rick is dead," he reminded.

"That is correct."

Flynn studied Yancy a moment. Before he could speak, Molly brought them two plates heaped full of pot roast, mashed potatoes, and a steaming bowl of peach cobbler.

"Thanks Molly." Flynn smiled at her.

"Enjoy." Molly returned the smile, and then she hurried to another table.

"This sounds personal," Flynn commented as they started eating.

"It is, but in a professional way."

"Meaning you want justice, not revenge?"

"More or less."

"I learned a long time ago to never hate your enemies," Flynn said quietly. "It affects your judgment."

Yancy thought on that. "You have a point."

"Why I said it," Flynn replied.

"How about strongly dislike?"

Flynn smiled. "That'll do."

Yancy nodded, and they ate in silence.

"I can see why you come in here everyday," Yancy commented as he finished, and carefully wiped his mouth with a napkin.

Before Flynn could reply, there was a noise at the door, and a smaller, straw-haired young man burst in. He stumbled and almost fell down. He recovered, spotted Flynn, and hurried towards them.

Flynn took in a deep breath and sighed.

"Friend of yours?" Yancy asked.

"My deputy, Gomer Platt."

The young deputy reached them, his face was flushed with excitement.

"What is it, Platt?" Flynn asked.

"Could be trouble," Deputy Platt replied, excited to be the one delivering the news.

"What sorta trouble?"

"Stagecoach hadn't showed up yet."

"How late is it?"

"Several hours."

Flynn nodded, and it was silent while he assessed the situation.

17

"Let's send a wire up the line," he suggested. "Find out when the stage was last seen."

"Already did." Deputy Platt beamed with self-importance.

There was an awkward moment of silence while Flynn waited for Platt to continue, but instead he just stood there looking proud.

"And?" Flynn prompted with a scowl.

"They left the last town right on time."

Flynn frowned his disappointment. "Let's not jump to conclusions," he said. "It could be a broken wheel, or a lame horse."

"*Or,* it could be something else," Deputy Platt replied, enthusiasm in his voice.

"Possible," Flynn replied. "We'd best ride out and take a gander."

"I'll saddle the horses," the deputy exclaimed as he turned abruptly towards the door.

Molly was coming up behind him, and they ran into each other. Arms and legs went everywhere as they tried to separate, and the dishes Molly carried crashed to the floor.

"Excuse me, ma'am," Deputy Platt apologized.

Before Molly could respond, Gomer went around her and hurried out the door. Molly just stood there, her hands on her hips and scowled.

"I declare," she said.

She glanced at Flynn, and a pained expression crossed his face.

"Sorry, Molly."

"He's worse than a kid," Molly replied, fire in her eyes.

"He *is* a kid," Flynn muttered.

Molly bent over and picked up the dishes. Flynn started to help, but she waved her hand at him.

"Go on, I've got this."

"You're the best, Molly."

"I know…You can leave me a good tip."

"Yes, ma'am," Flynn grinned, and he reached in his pocket, pulled out several coins, and placed them on the table.

"Your deputy seems eager," Yancy spoke up.

"He is," Flynn said sourly. Then, as a thought occurred to him, he glanced at Yancy. "You want to ride with us? I have a theory about your outlaws."

"Oh?"

"They might be hiding in the Palo Pinto Mountains," Flynn said. "It's mighty rough country. Only bad people and rattlesnakes live there."

"Sounds like a likely place," Yancy reasoned.

"It'd be the first place I'd look."

"Let's get going then," Yancy suggested.

Flynn nodded, and they stood and headed for the door.

§§§

CHAPTER SEVEN

"We'll make camp here," Jack McKee decided.

It was a likely spot. There was a small creek nearby and there was plenty of firewood scattered about.

They were between two steep ridges. There were oak trees all around them, and it made them feel sheltered and protected.

It was only mid-afternoon, and Jack knew it would be best if they pushed onward. However, he figured uplifting his family's morale was more important.

He could see the weariness in everyone's eyes, and he knew the same look was probably displayed in his own face. They were a fatigued bunch, and they needed rest.

"Is that the Brazos?" Karen gestured at the creek.

"No, but it probably runs into it," Jack tried to sound cheerful. "We'll probably come across the Brazos sometime tomorrow."

"I sure hope so," Karen looked wistful.

"Sam…" Jack suggested. "…why don't you and Suzan gather some firewood."

"Yes, Pa," Sam replied, and he and Suzan hurried off.

"Don't go too far," Jack called after them.

He watched them a moment, and then he unhitched the team and picketed them out so they could graze. Meanwhile, Karen went about the routine of setting up camp.

Once the horses were tended to, Jack built a fire. Karen put some coffee on, and then she turned her mind to supper.

"Do we need more wood, Pa?" Sam asked as he walked up and dropped an armful of wood on the pile.

"One more load will do." Jack smiled at his son.

Sam nodded and turned to go, but he stopped abruptly.

"Pa!" he exclaimed. "Look!"

Jack looked to where Sam was pointing. There, on top of the ridge, sat four men a-horseback. They made no attempt to hide, and it was obvious they were looking their camp over.

"Well! We're going to have company." Jack looked pleased. "Perhaps they can point us towards Jacksboro."

Karen walked up beside Jack, and she wasn't as enthused as she squinted up the ridge.

"What if they're looking for trouble?" she asked quietly. "We're all alone, Jack."

"Don't be so suspicious," Jack replied. "They probably just want to visit and drink some coffee."

Karen didn't look convinced as she turned and went back to the wagon.

Jack watched her a moment, and then he glanced back up the ridge.

The riders were gone. A few seconds passed, and Jack spotted them again. They were halfway down the ridge, coming toward them in an easy trot.

§§§

CHAPTER EIGHT

Until they knew for sure what had happened, Flynn saw no reason to assemble a posse. It would only worry folks.

Flynn and Yancy joined Deputy Platt at the livery stable. They climbed on their horses, and then waited as Platt hurried to the jail to fetch his shotgun.

Yancy was slightly amused as he watched Deputy Platt struggle to slide his shotgun into his scabbard.

"Shotgun's bigger than you are, son," Yancy observed.

"Maybe so, but I'm a good shot with it," Deputy Platt declared as he mounted his horse.

"Just about anybody *should be* a good shot with a shotgun," Yancy remarked.

Deputy Platt had no reply to that, and Flynn couldn't help but smile as he kicked up his horse, Laddie. Yancy and Deputy Platt fell in behind him, and they left town.

They followed the main road. Flynn rode in a brisk trot, and they made good time.

Several hours passed, and the terrain started to change. There were more trees scattered about, and several gentle hills. The Palo Pinto Mountains rose up in the distance, looking blue and lazy.

Flynn suddenly uttered a soft grunt.

"Up the hill," he gestured.

They squinted ahead, and they could see the stagecoach. It wasn't moving.

"Something's wrong," Platt declared, stating the obvious.

Flynn kicked Laddie up to a lope. They reached the bottom of the steep hill, and they had to slow to a trot as they climbed upwards.

They spotted the dead horses as they got closer, and they all felt a pinch of disgust in their stomachs. Then they saw a body, covered by a blanket, beside the stage.

The passengers were scattered about, and a few of them were resting underneath a shade tree. They all spun around when they heard them approaching.

The stage driver clutched his rifle. But then he recognized Flynn, and a relieved look crossed his face.

"It's all right," he calmed the passengers. "It's Sheriff Flynn."

The three horsemen pulled up, and everybody gathered around them.

"Everybody all right?" Flynn asked.

"Everyone but *him*." The stage driver gestured at the body.

"Jacob?"

The driver nodded somberly.

"Never had a chance," he said. "These are cold-blooded killers, I'll tell you that."

A hard look crossed Flynn's face, but he didn't say anything.

The stage driver told them what happened and Yancy narrowed his eyes when he mentioned how many outlaws there were.

"Four," Yancy repeated. "You sure?"

The stage driver nodded. "And one of them's wounded," he added.

"Good," Yancy grunted, and he looked at Flynn. "Sounds like the fellers I'm after."

"We'll know when we catch them," Flynn declared.

Yancy nodded, and it was silent as Flynn assessed the situation.

"That wounded man will probably slow 'em down some," Flynn finally said.

"Should," Yancy agreed.

"We hurry, and we might overtake them tonight."

"Only one way to find out," Yancy replied.

Flynn nodded and looked at Deputy Platt.

"We also have to look after these folks," he said. "Can you handle that, Platt?"

"How?"

"Hitch your horse to the stage, load up Jacob and the passengers, and make your way back to town," Flynn explained.

"With only one horse?" Deputy Platt objected.

"You'll make it. Just go slow."

Platt nodded slowly as he thought it over. "I can handle it."

"We'd stay and help, but ain't got the time," Flynn said.

"I understand, sir."

Flynn nodded and looked at the passengers.

"We'll catch them," he vowed.

Everyone nodded somberly, and Flynn turned back to Deputy Platt.

"Let me have that shotgun," he said. "Might come in handy."

"Sure." The deputy pulled it out and handed it over.

Flynn slid it in his extra scabbard. Then he turned his horse and rode out—Yancy followed.

The tracks were easy to follow, and they rode in a brisk road trot. They went down the ridge and headed south.

Flynn's face was hard and calloused. Yancy studied him a moment, and then cleared his throat. "You know Jacob?"

"I did," Flynn acknowledged. "Knew him well."

"I'm sorry."

"Not as sorry as *they're* goin' to be."

Yancy frowned at that. "Sounds personal," he commented, using Flynn's words.

Flynn grunted, and he turned in the saddle and looked at Yancy. Several seconds passed, and then he turned back around.

A few awkward minutes passed, and then Yancy coughed and changed the subject. "The stage driver said these men were cold-blooded killers," he remarked.

"Sounds accurate to me."

"I never understood that expression, myself."

"Understood what?"

"Cold-blooded killers," Yancy explained. "Every time I touch blood, it's warm."

Flynn thought on that, and then grunted. "Didn't realize you were such a philosopher."

"I have my moments," Yancy replied.

§§§

CHAPTER NINE

Jack walked forward a few steps. The sun was in his face, and he shaded his eyes with his hand as he squinted at the oncoming riders.

Karen motioned at Sam and Suzan. They hurried over, and they stood huddled together several feet behind Jack.

Jack began to feel uneasy. They were a filthy, mean looking bunch, and he didn't like the desperate, malicious looks on their faces.

"Karen," he said softly. "Where's the rifle?"

"In the wagon," she replied.

"Get it…Now."

"It's not loaded," Karen reminded.

Jack felt a sudden, desperate impulse, but there wasn't time to say or do anything else. He forced a grin and raised a hand in greeting.

"Hello!" he called out. "Welcome!"

There were no replies. They pulled up, spread out, and faced up to Jack.

Their faces were emotionless, but their eyes roamed all over camp. They studied the campfire, the wagon, and the mules. After that, they looked at Karen and the children, and then they looked back at Jack.

Jack noticed that one of them was hunched over some, and he spotted blood on the man's shoulder. He started to mention it, but decided against it.

"My name's Jack McKee," he said instead. "This is my wife, Karen, and my children, Sam and Suzan."

Nobody replied and Jack's skin started to crawl. It was painfully obvious that he was unarmed, and he felt small and alone as he stood there.

"I'm Lester," the apparent leader finally said. "This is Cad, Ned, and Hank."

"Pleased to meet you," Jack tried his best not to look worried.

"You folks traveling alone?"

"We're on our way to Jacksboro," Jack replied, purposely avoiding a direct answer.

"What's in the wagon?" Lester asked.

"Just our personal belongings," Jack said, a bit stiffly.

"We'll see about that," Lester grinned, but there was no humor in it.

Jack had no reply to that. Instead, he gestured at the campfire.

"My wife has prepared some coffee," he offered. "Get down and have some."

Lester grunted, and he leaned forward in the saddle and thrust out his jaw.

"I'm going to make myself real clear so there won't be any misunderstandings," he said. "You folks do as we say, *exactly* as we say, and maybe we won't kill you. Understand?"

Jack stumbled backwards, and his eyes grew wide.

"What is this," he said, his voice shaky.

Lester waved a hand at him as he dismounted.

"Call it whatever you want," he said. "But understand this...first sign of trouble, and that little girl of yours will be the first to die."

Jack swallowed hard. He glanced at his family and looked back at Lester.

"There'll be no trouble," he said softly.

"Good." Lester looked pleased. "Now, you..." he pointed at Sam. "Take care of our horses. Unsaddle them, and picket them beside those mules."

Sam looked at his father, and Jack nodded.

"Go ahead, son."

Sam nodded somberly and walked toward the horses. Meanwhile, Cad and Ned dismounted, and then Ned helped Hank down.

"Lady." Lester looked at Karen. "You go right ahead and cook us some supper."

Karen glared back, but she didn't say anything. She gestured at Suzan, and they went over to the fire.

Lester grinned wolfishly as he watched her, and then he looked at Jack.

"Hank is hurt," Lester told him. "He needs tending to."

"My wife was a nurse back east," Jack said without thinking, and he winced as soon as he said it.

"That so." Lester looked pleased. "Change of plans then. *You* cook supper while your wife looks after Hank."

A displeased look crossed Karen's face, and she uttered a disgruntled grunt. She stood beside the campfire with her hands on her hips and glared at Lester.

"Go on," Lester snarled.

She just stood there thinking it over, and Jack looked at her in desperation. A few seconds passed, and Jack was relieved when she finally nodded.

"I have a medicine bag," she said. "It's in the wagon."

"Go get it," Lester said.

Jack gave Karen an apologetic look, but she ignored him as she moved to the wagon and climbed inside.

The first thing she spotted was their rifle, and she wondered briefly if she should load it and jump out shooting. However, she knew she wouldn't stand a chance against four. So, she placed the rifle and their ammunition bag beneath their thick bedding, grabbed her medicine bag, and climbed back out.

Hank was sitting beside the wagon, and he was leaning against the wheel. He was pale and sweating.

Karen knelt beside him, and he moaned as she peeled back his shirt. She studied his wounds, and a concerned look crossed her face.

"I may not be able to save him," she announced. "I'm not a surgeon."

"You'd better," Lester grunted.

"What do you mean by that?" Jack asked from the campfire.

"Enough questions," Lester snapped. He glanced at Karen and said roughly, "Get to work."

Karen wasn't sure where to even start. However, she knew something bad would happen if he died, so she had to try. She took several deep breaths, gathered herself, and reached for her bag.

§§§

CHAPTER TEN

Flynn and Yancy traveled in silence. Their pace was brisk, and their faces were grim with determination.

Flynn finally pulled up. Their horses were soaked with sweat—Flynn removed his hat and wiped his brow with the back of his hand. "Hot," he commented.

"Is," Yancy agreed.

Flynn waited for Yancy to say something else. But he remained silent, and a faint smile crossed Flynn's lips.

"You really don't talk, do you."

"Not so much."

"Some folks feel uncomfortable with silence," Flynn stated.

Yancy thought on that and shrugged. "Silence is my natural element," he said.

"I can tell."

"I'll talk some, if you want."

"Wouldn't want to be a bother," Flynn said wryly, then asked, "Want to take the lead for a while?"

A hesitant look crossed Yancy's face.

"My brother and I have a routine," he said.

"I know," Flynn replied. "He does all the talking, and you don't."

"I meant when we're tracking someone."

"Oh."

"Cooper's a better tracker than I am," Yancy explained. "He always takes the lead, and I cover him."

"Sort of like the lookout?"

"More or less."

Flynn nodded at that, and then asked, "Are you suggesting I be Cooper?"

"It's a thought."

"Well, it makes no difference to me." Flynn shrugged.

Yancy nodded, and Flynn kicked up his horse and led out. Yancy followed, and he kept his eyes on the surrounding landscape, looking for anything suspicious.

They rode several miles in silence, and then Flynn pulled up abruptly. He studied the ground and grunted in surprise.

"What is it?" Yancy stopped beside him.

"Wagon tracks," Flynn gestured.

"Any idea who it might be?" Yancy asked as he squinted down.

"Nope," Flynn shook his head. "But, the fellers we're after decided to follow. Their tracks are right on top of the wagon's."

A concerned look crossed Yancy's face. "That could be trouble for whoever's in the wagon," he said.

"Sure might be," Flynn agreed.

"How fresh are the tracks?"

"About as fresh as you can get."

Yancy nodded and glanced at the sun.

"Do you think we'll catch 'em before dark?" he asked.

"Think so."

Yancy nodded again, and the conversation faded. Flynn kicked up Laddie, and Yancy followed, his watchful eyes on the horizon.

§§§

CHAPTER ELEVEN

The shoulder was a bloody mess by the time Karen finished. However, she was confident she had retracted all the buckshot.

Hank passed out from the pain, and she figured that was a good thing. She cleaned the wound and bandaged it as best as she could. Then, she stood and looked at Lester, who was eating supper over by the fire.

"All done?" Lester asked as he wiped his mouth with his shirtsleeve.

"Yes," she said plainly.

"Will he live?" Ned asked, his voice anxious.

"I don't know," Karen replied truthfully. "He needs a doctor."

"Aw, he'll be fine after a day or two," Lester replied.

Cad nodded in agreement, but Ned didn't look convinced.

"What happens now?" Jack spoke up.

He and the children were sitting on the ground across the campfire from them. Jack was trying his best to look confident, but his voice still shook when he talked.

"I'm in no hurry," Lester replied. "We'll probably just stay here and rest up a few days."

"We were on our way to Jacksboro," Jack reminded.

Lester grunted at that.

"Well, you ain't anymore."

"Now look here…" Jack tried to sound firm, "…you can't do this."

Lester looked at Jack, and his eyes turned dark and ugly.

"Maybe you need a little reminder who's in charge," he said softly.

"No," Karen spoke up, and shot Jack an urgent look. "We'll do as you say. Just leave us alone."

But Lester was already on his feet. He took a few steps toward them and pointed at Suzan.

"Come here, little girl," he said.

Her eyes grew wide, and she looked at her father.

"There's no need for that," Jack said, and his voice was suddenly steady. "We won't cause any trouble."

Lester studied him a moment. Then he grinned and started to turn back. However, something in the distance caught his eyes, and he squinted up the ridge.

He saw a flicker of movement. Seconds later, he spotted a lone horseman, and he was riding toward them.

A surprised grunt escaped Lester's lips.

"You expecting company?" he asked Jack.

"No, not us."

Lester frowned his suspicion.

"Well, *somebody's* coming," he said, and looked back at Jack. "You folks just sit there and keep your mouths shut. I'll do the talking…Understand?"

"I understand," Jack replied.

"You make *one* whimper, and it'll be the last sound you ever make," Lester warned, and he drew his hand like a knife across his throat.

"I said I understood," Jack said quietly.

Lester looked at Karen.

"You understand, too, lady?"

"Yes."

Lester grunted his satisfaction, and then he looked at Cad and Ned.

"You two spread out..." he said. "...and stay watchful."

They nodded, checked their firearms, and got in position. Meanwhile, Lester turned his attention to the oncoming rider.

§§§

CHAPTER TWELVE

"You smell campfire smoke?" Yancy asked, and they pulled up and sniffed the air.

"Do," Flynn said, and he gestured at a tall, steep ridge in front of them. "They must've made camp on the other side."

Yancy nodded his agreement and glanced at the sun.

"Still about an hour of daylight left," he commented.

"At least," Flynn agreed, and then he smiled and asked, "Silent partner, what do you think?"

"About what?"

"About how we should proceed."

"Oh," Yancy said. He scratched his jaw, and then said, "Well, I ain't one for walking, but I reckon we should climb that ridge and see what the layout is."

"Was thinking the same thing."

"Great minds must think alike," Yancy replied.

"Sometimes," Flynn agreed.

He squeezed his horse up, and Yancy followed.

They reached the base of the ridge, dismounted and tied their horses in amongst some trees. Yancy rummaged through his saddlebags, pulled out his spyglass and they trudged upwards.

It was a steep, difficult climb, and they were drenched with sweat by the time they reached the top. They took several deep breaths, and then squatted behind some bushes and looked below.

There, in plain sight beside a creek, was the camp. There were several horses and some mules picketed out a short distance from the wagon.

"Well, there they are," Yancy commented.

"Looks like," Flynn nodded.

Yancy looked through his spyglass, and it was silent while he studied their camp.

"I see eight folks," he finally said. "Two kids, and one woman."

Yancy lowered the eyeglass. He offered it to Flynn, and Flynn lifted the spyglass and squinted through it.

"Recognize anybody?" Yancy asked after a moment.

"Nope."

"Looks mighty peaceful down there."

"Does," Flynn agreed.

"Do you suppose the folks in the wagon are in trouble, or do you suppose they intended to meet up?"

Flynn lowered the eyeglass and pinched his face in thought as he pondered that.

"It's probably one or the other," he finally said.

Yancy smiled wryly, then asked, "Well, now what?"

"Be helpful if we knew what the situation was," Flynn commented.

"How do you suggest we do that?"

"Well, one of us should probably ride down there."

Yancy was startled.

"What if they start shooting?"

"They won't," Flynn replied. "Especially if we handle it right."

Yancy wasn't convinced.

"Only one?" he asked.

Flynn nodded.

"I think so. They might be more willing to visit."

"Or, they might decide to kill you and take your horse," Yancy pointed out.

"In that case…good luck."

"You stay here," Yancy offered. "I'll go."

"No, it was my idea," Flynn replied. "Besides, I talk more than you. Not much, but a little."

"Good point," Yancy replied. He thought it over, then added, "I'll just stay here then."

"You're a big help," Flynn said, his voice flat.

"I try," Yancy said, then asked, "If they don't shoot you, then what?"

"I'll ride back here, and we can contemplate things."

Yancy nodded, and he gestured at Flynn's sheriff badge.

"Unless you want to give them a target to shoot at, you might want to take that off," he suggested.

Flynn grunted in surprise.

"Yep, might ruin things." He smiled, and unpinned the badge and dropped it in his pocket. "Well, I'll mosey on down there."

"Good luck."

"Thanks."

"Remember," Yancy said with an emotionless face. "I've never been in these parts, and I could get lost by myself...So don't get yourself killed."

Flynn studied Yancy. His face remained blank, and he couldn't tell if he was joking or not.

"Try not to let you down," Flynn finally replied.

They nodded at each other, and Flynn made his way back down the ridge.

§§§

CHAPTER THIRTEEN

Flynn reached the horses, untied his blue roan Morgan, and stepped into the saddle.

There was a trail that led upwards, and Flynn allowed his horse to climb at his own pace. The trail weaved back and forth, and it took several minutes to reach the top.

He spotted Yancy, hunkered down behind some bushes a short distance away. He nodded at him, and then he started his descent.

They spotted him about halfway down the ridge, and there was a lot of movement in camp. The family huddled together back out of the way, and one of the men stepped forward while the others spread out. There was also another man leaning against the wagon wheel, but he never moved.

Flynn's face appeared calm, but he was watching them closely. His hand hung real easy-like over his gun handle, ready to draw if need be.

"Hello, the camp!" he called out in a pleasant voice.

"Come on in," the apparent leader said, and he was studying him with mingled distrust and interest.

Flynn trotted on up and stopped. His eyes went over their camp, and then he looked back at the closest one and grinned.

"Smelled your campfire from the ridge," he said in a Texas drawl. "Thought I'd ride over and say howdy. Name's Flynn."

"I'm Lester," the leader said, and then he introduced Cad and Ned. "You alone?"

"No, I'm with a cattle drive," Flynn came up with a story. "The herd is about a mile or so behind me. I came on up ahead to look the country over."

"Is the herd coming this way?" A concerned look crossed Lester's face.

"Pretty close," Flynn replied. "We're headed to Jacksboro."

Lester nodded, and Flynn took a peek at the family. They were listening intently, and their faces were strained and worried looking.

"Where you folks headed?" Flynn asked nonchalantly.

"North a ways," Lester replied.

Flynn nodded. He waited for him to explain, but he never did.

"Well, perhaps you'll see us tomorrow," Flynn kept the conversation going. "As big a herd as we've got, it'd be hard to miss us."

"Mayhaps."

Flynn looked over their camp once more, and then he nodded to himself. He had found out what he came for—it was time to leave.

"Well, reckon I'd best be on my way," Flynn said. "Don't want to miss supper."

"Best hurry along then," Lester said, a bit sarcastically.

"Nice meeting you folks," Flynn forced a grin.

He glanced at the family. They were staring desperately at him, and he could tell they wanted to say something. But they kept silent, and Flynn was glad.

He glanced back at Lester. He nodded goodbye, turned Laddie, and then nudged him forward. The horse broke into an easy trot, and he rode out.

§§§

CHAPTER FOURTEEN

Flynn met Yancy on the other side of the ridge. He dismounted, and his face was pinched with concern.

"Have a nice visit?" Yancy asked.

"No…don't talk much more'n you."

Yancy ignored the remark.

"Watched as you rode back. Nobody followed you."

"Didn't figure they would."

"Find out what we needed to know?" Yancy asked.

Flynn nodded, and his face turned grim.

"That's a fine looking family down there. They're being held hostage, no doubt about it."

"Afraid of that."

"The wounded feller don't look so good neither," Flynn continued. "But, the other three are mighty jumpy. I halfway expected a bullet in the back as I was leaving."

"It's a wonder they *didn't* shoot you," Yancy remarked.

Flynn smiled, and he told Yancy about the fake cattle drive.

"That was good thinking," Yancy said. "Made them think you weren't alone."

"I have my moments," Flynn said, using Yancy's words.

Yancy smiled faintly, then asked, "So now what?"

"I was hoping you'd have a suggestion," Flynn replied, then added, "…but, we've got to be careful. They seem mighty anxious to shoot somebody…First sign of trouble, and they'll start blasting."

"We need to separate 'em from that family," Yancy declared.

"Easier said than done."

"Mebbe not," Yancy said thoughtfully.

"You have an idea?"

"A thought, anyway."

"Well?" Flynn urged.

"After it gets dark, one of us should sneak down there and steal their horses."

Flynn was startled.

"Only one of us?"

"Less noise the better."

"What good would stealing their horses do?"

"They'll figure it was you, and that you lied about that cattle drive."

"I sorta did," Flynn admitted.

"They'll also come after us on the mules. They'll probably leave a man or two behind, but it would even our odds."

Flynn looked thoughtful, and after a moment he nodded slowly. "Might actually work."

"Glad you like it."

"We should probably wait a while though."

"Longer the better," Yancy agreed.

Flynn nodded, and he glanced around. "Might as well make camp," he suggested. "Long as we keep it small, we can even build a fire."

"Sounds good."

"You play cards?" Flynn asked.

"A little."

"Well, how 'bout I make some coffee, and we'll see how little."

"I can do that," Yancy smiled wryly.

§§§

CHAPTER FIFTEEN

"What do you think?" Cad asked Lester.

They were sitting around the campfire, drinking coffee. The children had gone to bed, and Jack and Karen sat close to them, away from the others.

Hank was asleep too, but he had awakened long enough to eat and drink some coffee. He was now snoring loudly, and everybody could hear him.

"Think about what?" Lester looked at Cad.

"The stranger that rode in."

"Him? He was just riding by."

"He sure seemed curious," Cad replied.

"Most folks are," Lester shrugged.

"Did you see that horse he was riding?" Ned spoke up. "Nice looking mount."

"Was," Cad agreed, then added, "I would have liked to have him."

"Don't be a fool," Lester snorted. "If we had killed him, his outfit would've come looking for him."

"If he even *has* an outfit," Cad replied. "He didn't look like a cowpuncher to me."

"Aw, you're getting too suspicious." Lester waved a hand at him.

Cad frowned, but didn't reply. Instead, he asked, "We gonna keep watch tonight?"

"Reckon we should," Lester replied.

48

"I ain't sleepy," Ned offered. "I'll go first."

"Works for me," Lester said. "Wake me up around midnight."

Nobody objected, and the conversation played out. They sat there a while longer, drinking coffee, and thinking their own thoughts.

§§§

CHAPTER SIXTEEN

"You ain't a very good poker player," Flynn commented.

"Never said I was," Yancy replied.

It was almost midnight. They were sitting around a small campfire, drinking coffee and playing poker on a saddle blanket.

It was a dark, clear night, and the stars shone brightly. There also wasn't much wind.

They played another hand, and Yancy snorted in disgust as Flynn won again.

"Good thing we ain't playing for money," Yancy commented, he yawned and stretched. "Well, I reckon now is as good a time as any."

"I'll cover you from the ridge," Flynn offered. "I'll be too far out to do much, but maybe I can confuse them some if there's trouble."

"Just don't shoot *me*."

"If I do, it'll be by accident."

"Thanks."

Yancy stood, walked over to his horse, and rummaged through his saddlebags. He pulled out a pair of moccasins, and Flynn watched curiously as he pulled his boots off and slipped them on.

"Got these from my brother," Yancy explained. "Makes it easier to travel quiet."

"Why Injuns wear them," Flynn said.

Yancy nodded and stood. The moccasins felt light compared to his boots, and they were also limber.

"I'll leave my rifle and hat here," he told Flynn. "If I don't come back, you can have them."

Again, Yancy's face didn't reveal if he was joking or not. But, Flynn chuckled and nodded anyhow.

"Appreciate that," he said.

Yancy returned the nod.

"Well, I'll be back," he said, then added, "I hope."

"Good luck," Flynn replied.

Yancy nodded again. He turned abruptly and disappeared into the darkness.

§§§

CHAPTER SEVENTEEN

Yancy barely made any sound at all as he made his descent. There wasn't much cover, and he kept up a relentless pace.

He was halfway down the ridge when he spotted the glow of a campfire. That meant someone was keeping watch, and he knew he'd have to be extra quiet as he approached the horses.

He was drenched with sweat by the time he reached the bottom. He could feel the drag of exhaustion in his legs, and they trembled slightly.

Yancy stayed in amongst some trees while he got his wind back, and then he looked around.

Traveling in a crouch, he crept forward from tree to tree and rock to rock. He was in no hurry, and he took his time.

Yancy crawled on his belly when he got closer. He held his knife, and he was as alert as he could be.

He edged over to a log. He peered over it and studied their camp.

Yancy counted seven lumps on the ground spread about, and they were all covered with blankets. He could also hear some snoring.

He spotted the lookout, sitting beside the campfire. His back was pointed towards him, and this pleased Yancy.

He left the log and crept towards the horses.

Their ears perked up, and they raised their heads when they saw him. But Yancy spoke softly to them, and he was relieved when none of them nickered.

Yancy continued to say soothing words as he came up beside them. He didn't take the time to untie them. Instead, he slashed the lead ropes with his knife.

Yancy was good with knots, and he tethered the horses together into a long line. He glanced back at the wagon, but he spotted no movement.

A grin split Yancy's lips. Moving in a crouch, he tugged on the lead horse's rope, and they followed him in a walk. They trailed along beside the creek, and the darkness slowly swallowed them up.

§§§

CHAPTER EIGHTEEN

"You made it!" Flynn grinned as Yancy led the horses into their camp.

"Sure." Yancy shrugged.

"Any trouble?"

"Naw. It was like taking candy from a baby."

"Only quieter," Flynn added.

"Yes, *much* quieter."

Flynn grinned as a thought occurred to him.

"They're going to be mad as wet hens in the morning," he said.

"Probably will be," Yancy agreed.

"It won't get daylight for several hours," Flynn reasoned. "You want to sleep awhile? I'll keep watch."

"I don't think I could *make* myself sleep."

Flynn smiled. "Me too."

"How 'bout some coffee instead?"

"Sounds like a plan," Flynn nodded.

They took care of the horses, and then they trudged over to the campfire. Flynn had already made another pot of coffee, and they filled their cups and leaned back.

"Should be a busy morning," Flynn reasoned.

"I imagine so."

"There's a good spot for an ambush about a mile back."

"I remember," Yancy replied, and he took a swig of coffee and looked at Flynn. "Could you handle the fellers that come after us?"

Flynn was startled.

"By myself?"

"Yes."

"Without getting killed?"

"Might as well."

Flynn mulled it over.

"Well, nothing's for sure, but I've faced worse odds."

"I could stay here," Yancy explained. "Soon as they ride out, I could sneak up to the wagon."

"Even in the daylight?"

"I like a good challenge."

"And you would take the fellers that stay behind?"

"That's the thought."

"*Before* they kill anybody?"

"I've faced worse odds."

Flynn smiled and scratched his jaw.

"Well, I'm willing," he finally said. "I just hope it works."

"Sounds simple in theory, but hard to accomplish," Yancy replied.

Flynn nodded in agreement, and they both took a swig of coffee.

§§§

CHAPTER NINETEEN

They didn't notice until after breakfast that the horses were gone.

Lester had a cussing fit. He threw his hat on the ground and stomped it, and everybody else just stood there and watched him.

He finally picked his hat up, and they spread out and looked around.

The tracks beside the creek were easy to find, and it didn't take them long to figure out what had happened.

"That stranger," Lester muttered. "He came back and stole our horses."

"Told you he wasn't a cowpuncher," Ned said.

Lester glared at him, and Ned knew not to say anything else.

Lester stood there and mulled things over. He was mad, but he also knew not to make hasty decisions.

A plan slowly came together, and he grunted in satisfaction. He looked at Jack and narrowed his eyes.

He couldn't explain it, but he just didn't like Jack. Maybe it was because he had a nice looking wife and family. One way or the other, he had already decided Jack's fate, and he now knew the method.

"You," Lester pointed at him.

"Yes?" Jack looked nervous.

"This is all your fault. Your boy picketed the horses too far out."

Jack wasn't sure how to reply, so he chose not to.

"You got a pistol?" Lester asked.

Jack's eyes grew wide.

"Yes," he said. "It's in the wagon."

"Go get it."

Jack swallowed. He glanced at Karen, and then he walked over to the wagon. He climbed in, and he dug his revolver out of their chest. He strapped it on, and it felt heavy and stiff.

He climbed back out and stood in front of Lester. He was trembling, and Lester grinned wolfishly as he watched him.

"Is it loaded?"

"Yes."

"Good," Lester said. "Now, go get our horses back. Don't bother coming back without 'em."

Jack's mouth fell open.

"You want *me* to go after them?"

"That is correct."

"But I've never...I mean...how am I supposed to do that?"

Lester pointed at the mules.

"Ride one of them. Just follow the tracks, and you'll find our horses sooner or later."

"What if he won't give them back?"

"Kill him then."

Jack looked uncertain, and he shuffled his feet as he stood there.

"Either you get our horses, or I'll kill you right now," Lester warned, and a smirk crossed his face. "Course, you're wearing a gun. Maybe you'll outdraw me."

Cad and Ned snickered, and Jack swallowed as he considered his options.

"I'll go," he said softly.

"Figured you would," Lester replied. "Now get going."

Jack looked at Karen.

"I'll be back," he tried to sound firm, but his voice still trembled.

"Be careful," Karen replied.

Jack nodded. They looked at each other a moment, and then he turned toward the mules.

§§§

CHAPTER TWENTY

It was still dark when Flynn and Yancy saddled their horses. Next, they tethered the other horses into a long line so Flynn could lead them easier.

By then the sky in the east was getting light. Yancy grabbed his eyeglass, and they trudged up to the top of the ridge.

They hid behind some bushes and got comfortable. Then, they took turns looking through the eyeglass as they kept a close lookout below.

Flynn was squinting through it when he suddenly leaned forward.

"Lots of movement down there," he said, and then he chuckled. "One of them just threw his hat on the ground and stomped it."

"Either there was a bee, or he's real upset," Yancy commented.

Flynn grinned, and neither one spoke for several minutes. But then, Flynn grunted in surprise.

"There's only one feller leaving camp," he announced, and he lowered the eyeglass and looked at Yancy. "It's the father!"

"You sure?" Yancy was startled.

"Yep. He's the only one with white hair."

"You must not have scared them much."

59

"What do we do now?" Flynn asked as he ignored the sarcasm.

Yancy shrugged, passing the decision back to Flynn, and it was silent while they pondered things.

"You *did* say you'd take care of the fellers that stayed in camp," Flynn finally reminded him.

"Did I say that?"

"Yep."

"That's what talking does. It gets you into trouble," Yancy declared.

Flynn smiled wryly. "Well, we might as well go back down and wait for him," he suggested. "We'll see what he has to say."

Yancy nodded. They slid backwards several feet, and then they stood and trudged back down the ridge.

§§§

CHAPTER TWENTY-ONE

Jack was troubled. He didn't like leaving his family behind, but there was no other way. He was no match for Lester, and he knew it.

He tried to think of a way to get the horses back without bloodshed, but no easy solution presented itself.

He was still deep in thought as he topped out on the ridge. There was a worn trail going down, and his mule followed it.

He was halfway down the ridge when the stranger stepped out in front of him. There was a smaller man with him, and Jack spotted a Texas Ranger badge pinned on his vest's pocket.

Jack was startled, and he almost fell off the mule. However, he managed to recover, and he stared wide-eyed at them.

"Take it easy now," the stranger said. "I'm Sheriff Mason Flynn, and this is Ranger Yancy Landon. We're here to help."

It took several seconds for it to sink in, and Jack stared numbly at them.

"I'm Jack," he finally mumbled. "You're really here to help?"

"That's right," Flynn replied.

"Why'd you steal the horses?"

"Actually, that was Yancy," Flynn corrected. "We were hoping to draw them out."

"No, they just sent me," Jack said flatly.

"Noticed that," Flynn replied.

"They've got my wife and children," Jack said, concerned. "We've got to do something."

A thought occurred to Yancy. He gestured at Flynn to come close, and they talked in hushed voices.

"Should work," Flynn finally said.

Before Jack could say anything, Flynn raised his rifle, aimed at the sky, and squeezed off a shot. It was loud and unexpected, and Jack jumped in the saddle.

Flynn waited a moment, and then he fired again.

"What are you doing?" Jack stared at him.

"You just died," Flynn explained. "At least that's what we're hoping *they* think."

"I don't understand."

"I'll explain later," Flynn replied. "Right now, we need to make tracks."

"Make tracks where?"

"That way," Flynn pointed to the south, and then he looked at Yancy. "Well, good luck. Be careful."

"I'll try," Yancy replied.

Jack frowned in confusion.

"You aren't coming with us?" He asked Yancy.

"Nope."

Jack waited for an explanation, but Yancy just stood there with an emotionless face.

Flynn grinned. He gestured at Jack to follow him, and then he nodded at Yancy and took off.

Yancy returned the nod, and he watched as Flynn and Jack went on down the ridge. Then, he turned and trudged upwards.

I'm sure getting tired of climbing this ridge, he thought.

§§§

CHAPTER TWENTY-TWO

Karen was changing Hank's bandages when they heard the rifle shots from afar.

She uttered a gasp of alarm, but Lester just grinned.

"Well, that was quick," he said.

"That stranger must have been waiting on the other side of the ridge!" Cad figured.

"Sounded like it," Ned added.

Lester grunted his satisfaction. He glanced at Karen, and she was staring up at the ridge. Her face was pale, and her lips trembled. Sam and Suzan stood behind her, and they tried not to cry.

Jack can't be dead, she thought. *He just can't!*

"Sounds like you need a new husband," Lester said sarcastically. "You might think on that while we're gone."

63

Karen had no reply for that. She glared at Lester, and his grin widened.

He turned to Cad.

"Let's go," he said, and then he glanced at Ned. "Stay here with your brother, and keep an eye on *her*. We'll be back."

Ned nodded, but Cad was worried.

"What if he's waiting for us too?" Cad asked.

"Then we'll kill him," Lester said plainly.

Cad didn't look so confident as he followed Lester to the mules.

§§§

CHAPTER TWENTY-THREE

Yancy lay on his stomach, hiding amongst several bushes. The only thing that moved were his eyes as he kept a close lookout below.

He finally saw some movement.

Two men were leaving camp, riding mules, and they were following the tracks beside the creek.

Unlike Jack, these two knew what they were doing. They took their time, and they were real watchful.

Yancy flattened himself against the ground as they climbed the ridge, and they topped out a few hundred feet from him. There was some brush between them, but Yancy could still hear them talking as they looked below.

"Don't see anything," one of them finally said.

"Rifle shots have a way of echoing," the other replied. "We probably need to ride further."

"I don't like it. Could be an ambush."

"Possible, but we have no choice. He has our horses."

"He does at that."

"Then let's go."

They nudged their mules forward, and Yancy breathed easier as he watched them disappear down below.

He waited a moment, and then he rose to a crouch and headed toward the wagon.

§§§

CHAPTER TWENTY-FOUR

Flynn and Jack rode back to the south, and they led the long string of horses behind them.

Jack was quiet, and his face was pale and drawn. Flynn studied him a moment, and then he cleared his throat.

"No need to worry," Flynn tried to sound reassuring. "Yancy'll take care of your family."

"Do you know him well?"

"Not so much."

"Then how do you know?"

"He has quite the reputation," Flynn replied. "And, seeing how he's still alive…it must be true."

"Oh."

Flynn nodded emphatically, and then he pulled up and looked around.

The trail had narrowed, and they were in the bottom of a long, slender valley. The walls were steep, and there was a lot of brush scattered about.

"This'll do," Flynn commented, and he looked at Jack. "You want to help?"

"Of course! Just tell me what to do."

"They'll be looking for a body," Flynn explained. "So, I want you to stretch out on the ground over there in that open spot. Now, I'll be hiding over there in those bushes, and I'll come up behind them when they stop to look you over."

"And you want me to just lie there?"

66

"No," Flynn replied, and he reached down and pulled out Deputy Platt's pump action shotgun. "I want you to lie on top of this. Soon as the shooting starts, roll over and start blasting...Just don't shoot me."

Jack nodded somberly, and he reached out and took the shotgun.

"I've never killed anybody," he admitted.

"Think you can?"

"I don't know," Jack replied truthfully. "But I'll try."

"They won't hesitate to kill us," Flynn reminded.

"I know that."

Flynn frowned. He watched him a moment more, and then he looked around again.

"Let's hide the horses up there..." he pointed at a cluster of trees at the end of the valley, "...and then we'd best get in position. They'll be here soon."

Jack nodded his agreement, and they nudged their horses forward.

§§§

CHAPTER TWENTY-FIVE

Hank was feeling better. His shoulder was still painful, but the bleeding had stopped.

Ned sat beside his brother, and they talked in hushed tones. Meanwhile, Karen and her two children sat across the campfire, and her face was pinched in thought.

Her husband was dead. It was a painful thing to accept, and she regretted the hateful things she had said to him the last few days.

They had lost everything back east, and they had no choice but to come west. Even though it wasn't his fault, she had blamed Jack.

She could see her mistakes now, and she wished she could go back and do things differently.

But she couldn't, and now she and her children were alone. If they were to get out of this mess, it would be up to her.

The time to act was now, before the others came back. The rifle was still in the wagon, and she nodded to herself as she came to a decision.

"Children," she said in a whisper. "When the shooting starts, I want you to run for it and don't look back."

They stared at her, and she looked sternly at them.

"Do you understand?"

"Yes, Ma," Sam said.

She squeezed their hands, and she stood and walked boldly toward the wagon.

Ned looked curiously at her.

"What are you doing?" He asked.

"My children are cold," she replied calmly. "I'm getting a blanket."

Ned considered this, and then shrugged.

"Go ahead," he sneered.

Karen nodded and climbed into the wagon.

She waited a moment, and then she pulled the rifle out from underneath their bedding. She loaded it, being careful not to make any noise, and then she worked the lever.

There was a small click, and she winced. But Hank and Ned were still talking and didn't hear it.

Suddenly, she couldn't move. Her hands trembled, and tears streamed down her face.

She said a silent prayer, and this calmed her some. Then, she stared out the front of the wagon as she gathered her thoughts.

Something caught her eye. She looked again, and she spotted some movement.

Seconds later, a small, spry man crawled out of the bushes and came towards the front of the wagon.

Karen was startled, but she managed to choke off a cry of alarm. She stared wide-eyed as he came closer.

He reached the front of the wagon, and then he stood upright. There was a Texas Ranger badge pinned on his vest's pocket, and Karen felt a glimmer of hope.

He dusted himself off, and then he checked to make sure his Colt was in place.

Satisfied, the small man nodded. He breathed deeply, and then he walked toward the front of the wagon. His gun hand hung over his Colt's handle, and he displayed a confidence that Karen had never seen before.

"Lord, help him," she prayed silently.

§§§

CHAPTER TWENTY-SIX

To wait can be the hardest part, especially when trouble was expected.

Flynn couldn't help but feel uneasy, and he could only imagine the emotions Jack felt. However, so far Jack hadn't moved, and Flynn was glad.

Jack was sprawled out on the ground. He was lying on his stomach, and his feet were spread apart. He really did look dead, and Flynn grunted softly in satisfaction.

Flynn was nestled down between two shrubs a short distance away, and he was nearly invisible.

A half hour passed, but it felt longer. But finally, Flynn heard noises.

He wanted to warn Jack, but there wasn't time. A few seconds passed and two riders appeared.

Flynn narrowed his eyes as he studied them. It was Lester and the one called Cad.

They spotted Jack, but they were wary. They rode slow as they looked all around them, and Cad held his rifle, ready for trouble.

Flynn held his breath. He avoided eye contact, and he didn't move a muscle as they rode by him.

"It's him, all right," Flynn heard Lester say.

They dismounted a short distance from Jack, and Cad squinted at the ground.

"All sorts of tracks scattered about," he commented. "Lots of horses."

"Yeah, *our* horses," Lester grunted.

Being as quiet as he could, Flynn rose to a knee, and then stood. Neither one heard him as they walked toward Jack.

Flynn stepped out into the open and cleared his throat.

"Hold it right there," he said sternly.

They were surprised, but neither one panicked. They glanced at each other, and then they turned around slowly, being careful not to make any sudden movements.

Flynn stood in front of them, and his gun hand hovered naturally over his Colt. He was calm and collected.

"It's you," Lester narrowed his eyes.

"Sure is," Flynn agreed.

"You stole our horses. We want 'em back."

"Sorry, but you're under arrest," Flynn announced. "Drop your rifles and unbuckle your gun belts."

Surprise showed in Lester's face.

"You're a *lawman*?"

"Sure am. Now do as I say."

Lester grunted at that, and several tense seconds passed.

There was no way Lester would surrender, and Flynn knew that. So, he didn't say anything else. Instead, he just waited.

Lester looked him over carefully, and then he grunted. In the same instant he dropped his hand, palmed his Colt and brought it up.

He thought he'd won, but before he could fire there was an explosion, and he felt a slug hit him below. He staggered backwards, but stayed on his feet.

Lester gasped as he lifted his Colt a second time. But, before he could shoot, Flynn fired again. The bullet struck him in the chest, and he dropped his Colt and fell over backwards. He tried to rise, but his strength had left him, and he collapsed in a heap and didn't move.

As soon as the shooting started, Jack yelled, rolled over, and swung the shotgun up. There was a round in the chamber and his finger was wrapped around the trigger.

Cad spotted him in the corner of his eye, and he turned towards him. He raised his rifle, but Jack aimed in his direction and pulled the trigger before he could shoot.

There was a loud blast from the 10 gauge, followed by a thumping sound. The buckshot took Cad in the face, and his body was flipped over backwards. He hit the ground, kicked out, and was still.

It was over. Flynn looked at Jack, and they nodded at each other.

Jack stood and walked over to Cad. Meanwhile, Flynn reloaded his Colt, holstered it, and turned to Jack.

Cad was missing most of his face, and Jack was silent as he stared down at him.

"You all right?" Flynn asked.

Jack nodded somberly.

"Well, looks like you killed him," Flynn said as he walked over.

"I did, didn't I."

"How does it feel?"

Jack thought a moment, then shrugged. "Necessary," he said.

"There you go," Flynn replied.

§§§

CHAPTER TWENTY-SEVEN

It took Yancy twice as long to reach their camp in the daylight. However, he kept at it, and he finally reached the front of the wagon.

By now, he figured that Flynn had already tangled with the other two. He was curious to know what had happened, but he didn't allow himself to think on it. All he could do was focus on the task before him.

He could hear talking at the back of the wagon. He stood, dusted himself off, and checked his Colt.

The two outlaws were startled when Yancy walked around the wagon. They grunted, and Hank forgot all about his shoulder as they jumped to their feet and faced him.

"Who are you?" Ned stared at him.

"Yancy Landon," he replied. "I'm here to arrest you."

Ned's eyes grew wide.

"Yancy Landon from Midway?"

"That's right," Yancy nodded. "Want to surrender?"

"You came a long ways," Ned replied.

"You killed a friend a mine."

Ned narrowed his eyes. He glanced at Hank, and then he looked back at Yancy.

"You can't take both of us."

"Only one way to find out," Yancy replied.

Several seconds passed as they thought on that. Then Ned snorted and made a grab for his Colt.

Yancy seemed to be in no hurry, yet he palmed his Colt with lightning speed. He fired from the hip, and Ned staggered backwards under the bullet's impact. Yancy fired again, and Ned fell on his back. He made several gurgling sounds as he died.

Meanwhile, Hank palmed his Colt and aimed at Yancy. But, before he could shoot, a rifle shot bellowed out from the wagon.

The slug hit Hank in the torso and propelled him backwards. He hit the ground, gasped a few times, and then was still.

Yancy spun toward the wagon, and he spotted Karen standing in the opening with her rifle in hand. Her face was pale, and her hands trembled.

"Take it easy, ma'am," Yancy said gently as he holstered his Colt.

She dropped the rifle and climbed out of the wagon. She glanced at her children, and they were staring wide-eyed at Yancy.

"Are they dead?" Karen asked.

"I'd say so, ma'am."

"They killed my husband," she sobbed.

"No, ma'am," Yancy shook his head. "That's what we *wanted* them to think."

The children jumped in surprise, and Karen's mouth fell open.

"Jack's alive?" she whispered.

"Yes, ma'am," Yancy reassured. He glanced up the ridge, and he grinned and pointed. "Look, here they come now."

Karen felt a flood of emotions. She turned and looked, and tears of happiness trickled down her face.

Without thinking, she ran towards Jack.

They were halfway down the ridge when Jack spotted Karen. A big grin spread across his face, and he jumped off his mule and ran toward her.

They met at the base of the ridge, embraced, and held each other tight.

"Now, now," Jack said gently as he patted her on the back. "I said I'd be back."

Karen was too choked up to reply. She said a silent prayer of thanks, and she looked up at her husband and smiled.

She felt like she had been given a second chance. And this time, she was going to make the most of it. She didn't care where they lived, just as long as they were together.

Hand in hand, they turned and walked back to the wagon.

§§§

EPILOGUE

It took them almost two days to reach Jacksboro. The mules were exhausted, and they had to go slow.

Yancy slept late the next morning. He drank some coffee, and then he saddled his horse, rode to the jail, and found Flynn.

"Headed home already?" Flynn asked, surprised.

Yancy nodded.

"Cooper's probably lost and confused without me," he explained. "It's time I got back."

Flynn grinned. They shook hands, and Yancy climbed back on his horse.

"Enjoyed working with you," Flynn said. "It's been, ah, *interesting*."

"Same here," Yancy replied.

Flynn waited for him to say something else. But he didn't, and Flynn chuckled.

"You still don't talk much."

"Nope, probably never will," Yancy admitted.

Flynn smiled wryly and said, "Well, if you're ever in these parts again, stop by and say howdy. I'll try not to talk too much."

"Will do."

"Well, take care."

"You too," Yancy nodded, and he kicked up his horse.

Flynn stood there and watched him go. Another grin started to split his lips, but instead he frowned as another thought occurred to him.

He pulled out his watch and looked at it. He grunted at the time, and he hurried down the street towards Sewell's Café.

§§§§

About the Author

Born in West Texas, Tell Cotten is a seventh generation Texan. He comes from a family with a ranching heritage and is a member of the Sons of the Republic of Texas. Besides writing, he is also in the cattle business, and he resides in West Texas with his wife, Andi, and their two children.

For announcements of new releases and all other information, please like The Landon Saga Page on Facebook
https://www.facebook.com/TheLandonSaga
Or, you can join The Landon Saga Fan Group
https://www.facebook.com/groups/784798154926122/
You can also visit Tell Cotten's website
http://tellcotten.wordpress.com/

Acknowledgements

I would like to thank my wife and my family for all their help and support. Without them this wouldn't be possible. I'd also like to thank God for the gift of writing.

Special thanks also goes out to Ken Farmer for including me in this project.

HELL'S HALF ACRE

BY

DUANE BOEHM

CHAPTER ONE

The diminutive Sneaky Ward arrived at Avery Young and Thad Hytree's cabin unannounced at suppertime. He'd earned the nickname from a reputation for items disappearing wherever he had paid a visit. Sneaky had turned thirty years old living life as a petty thief while doing occasional jail time, but managing to avoid prison.

"When did you get back and what do you want?" Thad asked in his gruff voice upon seeing Sneaky at the door.

Thad Hytree was the hard case of the trio and the oldest. He had done time in prison for beating a man to death in a saloon fight, and had a reputation for having a short temper and the brawn to back it up. Thad seemed to stay permanently mad at the world and made for a handy ally when trouble brewed. His icy stare alone was enough to make most men back away.

Sneaky grinned, exposing his buckteeth. "I have a plan for us to make some easy money," he said as he ran his fingers through his greasy hair.

"What is it?" Avery asked as he ambled over to Sneaky.

Avery was as tall as he was simple. He towered over the other two men and had a disposition as meek as a lamb. Sneaky and Thad liked to keep the younger Avery around because he would follow orders all day long and never complain.

"You know I was down in Fort Worth...I spent some time in Hell's Half-Acre and had me a fine time. I met the Chinaman there. He has...I don't know how many, whorehouses. He told me he'd pay two hundred dollars for every young white woman I delivered to him," Sneaky said, pausing to give the others time to think about the number.

Hell's Half-Acre was a section of Fort Worth that housed the largest collection of saloons, dance halls, and whorehouses south of Dodge City. Shooting, knifings, and muggings were commonplace. A man could find anything that he wanted to spend his hard-earned cash on, and if he was lucky, he just might live to tell about it.

"Are you going to tell us the rest or are we supposed to just guess?" Thad asked as he hitched up his pants.

"The McGregor family has three girls ripe for the picking and they're all blond and pretty...Seeing how it's Sunday, I figure we could go over there and kill off the mom, dad, and son. Nobody would know anything had happened until they're missin' from church next Sunday. They barely ever leave that little ranch. We'd have time to go to Fort Worth, collect our money, and be back before anybody was any the wiser.

"Since when did you get into the killin' bidiness?" Thad asked.

"Since I had the chance to make some easy money for a change. I'm tired of scroungin' around like a squirrel looking for a nut," Sneaky answered.

"How are we going to travel with three women and not raise suspicions?" Thad inquired.

"Since we won't have to worry about a posse, I figured we'd travel only at night and lay up during the day," Sneaky answered.

Avery dropped onto a chair and crossed his long legs as a woman would. "Don't know about this. We've never killed before."

"We've never made any real money before either an' we wouldn't have to go far to do it," Sneaky said.

"You going to help with the killin's or you goin' to leave that to me?" Thad asked.

"There's three people need killin' and there's three of us. I say each one of us kills one so as to have an equal stake in this," Sneaky said.

Thad pulled his gun from its holster and checked the loads. "I'm in...so are you, Avery. You can kill one of 'em just like the rest of us. Don't want to hear a word about it."

"Whatever you say, Thad," Avery responded.

§§§

CHAPTER TWO

Sheriff Mason Flynn strolled down the street of Jacksboro toward Sewell's Café. He enjoyed the fall weather where the afternoons weren't so all-fire blazing hot, and day and night just about shared equal time.

His belly was reminding him that it was time to eat. He'd had an uneventful Sunday—just the way he liked it. In fact, he'd read the *Dallas Morning News* from the first page to the last without so much as an interruption.

Out of a lawman's habit, Sheriff Flynn scanned up and down the street. He saw four riders approaching, two in the lead, and two following. A smile slowly came to Mason's face as he recognized the lead two riders. It wasn't every day that a painted mule carrying a tall raven-haired beauty graced the town of Jacksboro.

Coming down the street were Deputy US Marshal Fiona Miller and Deputy US Marshal Brushy Bill Roberts. Sheriff Flynn had worked with the officers before and enjoyed their company. And Fiona was easy on the eyes and sure made for more interesting conversation than most lawmen Mason had worked with in the past. The sheriff waited on the boardwalk until the riders arrived.

"What do I owe the pleasure of two Deputy US Marshals in my town?" Flynn asked.

"Hello, Mason," Fiona said with a smile as she flipped her hair off her shoulder. She locked her steel-gray eyes with the sheriff's sky blue ones. "Bill and I had to chase down these two horse thieves and we were close enough to Jacksboro that we thought we'd see if we could put them in your jail until morning and get a good night's rest at the Charter Hotel."

"Sure. Let's lock them up. I was just about ready for supper. Would you care to join me?" the sheriff asked.

Bill climbed down from his chocolate sorrel Morgan and offered his hand to the sheriff. "That's the best proposition I've had in quite some time. I could use some manly conversation," he said, smiling up at Fiona.

"You could use a few more manly things than just conversation," Fiona retorted.

§

After locking up the prisoners and taking the horses to Mom's Livery, the trio walked into café.

Molly, the waitress, remembered the two marshals and greeted them warmly. "Sweet tea for both of you, correct? Sunday night's special is meat loaf with carrots and potatoes. Apple pie for dessert."

"That sounds good, Molly," Fiona replied.

Mason and Bill ordered the same.

"So how has life been treating you, Mason?" Fiona asked with a smile that was known to turn men into hot butter.

"Better than I deserve. In fact, things have almost been too quiet and peaceful. Makes me paranoid that all hell is fixin' to break loose...Deputy Platt is about my only irritant," the sheriff answered with a chuckle.

'Can't same the same for us," Bill said. "Nothin' too terrible, but enough to keep us busy."

Molly brought the glasses of tea.

"I guess as long as there are people, us lawmen...and women will have a job," Mason said with a nod of his head and a grin. He leaned his large frame back into his chair and brushed his mustache with his fingers.

"It certainly is good to see you. Bill and I are together so much that we start to finish each other's sentences...We could use some fresh conversation," Fiona said.

Molly set the steaming hot plates of food onto the table. "Enjoy," she said.

Mason took a sip of tea. "Maybe we can go have us a drink afterward," he said.

"That sounds fine to me. I need to take two plates to the prisoners first. We can have a drink after Bill and I get checked into the hotel and I have a bath. I feel as if I'm double my weight in dust," Fiona said.

§§§

CHAPTER THREE

To call the McGregor place a ranch was to use the word in the most generous of terms. Cyrus McGregor and his nineteen-year-old son, Cooper, raised just enough cattle to keep the family clothed and provide for necessities.

The family grew a huge garden that Mrs. McGregor and her three daughters could be found tending to all summer. More than one man had noted that if Cyrus raised cattle half as fine as he did daughters that he'd be a wealthy man.

While Cyrus wasn't unfriendly, he was a loner by nature and preferred his own company. He also did his best to discourage any young men to come a courting his three teenage girls. The girls were the biggest source of contention between Cyrus and his wife. She warned him repeatedly that if he didn't let his daughters start courting, they would eventually up and elope, but Cyrus didn't want to hear of such things and preferred to ignore reality.

Becky was the oldest daughter at eighteen and the prettiest. Her presence was enough to turn all but the surest of young men speechless and cause them to fumble away in hopelessness.

Being the oldest, she had developed a protective nature and had defended her sisters more than once in school against other girls.

Rita, the middle daughter at seventeen, was the quiet one and a beauty in her own right. While more approachable than

Becky, her demeanor left her suitors struggling to carry on a conversation and most would give up in frustration.

At sixteen, Nancy was the youngest and most vivacious. She wasn't as attractive as her two older sisters were, but was still prettier than most of the girls that the local young bucks could ever hope to marry. Cyrus kept an eye on Nancy more than the other two girls. She was the one he feared would up and marry on a whim.

Sneaky, Avery, and Thad waited until nightfall to arrive at the McGregor place. They tied their horses a quarter of a mile from the home and started walking the rest of the way.

Sneaky had thought to carry strips of leather that he planned to use to tie the girls' hands. Avery was nervous and kept talking as they walked.

"Shut up before the whole county knows we're here," Thad whispered.

"Sorry, Thad."

"Are you sure that gun of yours will even fire?" Thad asked.

Avery carried an old Colt Navy revolver that had been converted to shoot centerfire cartridges. The cylinder had so much play in it that nobody liked to stand near him when he practiced shooting.

"It's never failed me yet," he said as he reached into his pocket and grabbed the grips to reassure himself.

As the three men walked into the yard, the family dog took a position in front of the door and sent out a warning with its barking and growling. Sneaky jogged up and stationed himself in front of the door just far enough away to keep the dog from leaving the porch. He pulled back the hammer to his revolver and waited.

Cyrus flung the door open. "Red, what it tarnation are you barkin' at?" he yelled.

Sneaky aimed his Colt Peacemaker and fired. The shot hit Cyrus in the chest and knocked him back into the house. A second shot dispatched the bothersome dog.

The men charged into the house as bedlam broke loose inside. The women were all screaming at the top of their lungs and running into each other as they scurried for cover.

Cooper made a dash for a shotgun hung over the door to the back rooms. Avery and Thad cut loose with their revolvers on the young man.

Cooper flinched, spun toward his attackers, and then dropped to the floor as a final shot found him.

Mrs. McGregor attacked Avery like a momma bear protecting her cubs. She dug her nails into his face and left a bloody trail of claw marks down his cheeks. Avery's scream added to the nerve-racking noise in the cabin. He sent a left jab into the woman's face, knocking her back, before gunning her down.

The three girls had found their way to a corner of the room and huddled together. They quit screaming and watched with apprehension as the three men surrounded them.

"If you want to live, you best listen up...first off, no more of that damn screamin'. Now stand up and let us bind your hands. Time's a wastin'...We're goin' for a ride," Thad announced.

Becky looked at her sisters and realized she needed to take charge over them if they were to have any chance at survival. The only option at the moment seemed to be to acquiesce to the killer's demands. She stood and held out her arms with her wrists crossed. Her two sisters followed suit.

Sneaky leered at the girls as he bound their hands, causing them to tremble with apprehension.

"What about Daddy and Momma and Cooper?" Becky asked as she looked at their bodies on the floor.

"Honey, they're beyond help now. Worry about your own survival," Thad warned.

"That woman ruined my looks," Avery lamented as he found a towel and mopped the blood from the gaping wounds on his face.

"You didn't have any to ruin," Thad said and laughed at his joke. "You'll get to explain for the rest of your life how you let a woman claw you up. I'd make up a better story than the truth...Now take a lamp out to the barn and saddle three of their horses."

By the time Avery led the horses out of the barn, Thad and Sneaky had the girls lined up on the porch and waiting. They quickly shoved them up onto the saddles. Thad tied the reins of the three horses together and ran a rope through them.

"Avery, you ride in the rear to keep an eye on 'em in case one tries to bolt...Just shoot her if she does. Don't want to spend all night trackin' one down," Thad ordered with the hope of instilling fear into the girls.

The group headed out into the night in a southeasterly direction. They rode hard toward the road to Fort Worth. A full moon was only a couple of days away from making an appearance and its light aided in the travel.

Rita had a death grip on the saddle horn. She wasn't a good rider and struggled to keep her balance in the saddle on a horse with a jarring trot.

As the horse descended into a gully, she nearly slid off the animal. Only the strength built up in her arms from countless days of hoeing the garden allowed her to pull her butt back into the saddle. She started wailing.

"What's your problem?" Thad asked as the group slowed.

"I'm going to fall off," Rita cried out.

"If you want to live, you better figure out how to ride real quick. Now quiet down."

The warning caused Rita to cry harder, irritating Thad to no end.

"We need to let the horses catch their wind anyway. Not in that much of a hurry an' I'd just as soon arrive with all three of 'em," Sneaky said in hopes of avoiding trouble.

"Yeah, you're right. You better quit that crying," Thad said as he nudged his gelding into a walk.

They continued at a walk for fifteen minutes before Thad got anxious to make time. He bumped his horse into a trot, pulling the three horses the girls were riding with him. Sneaky and Avery sped up to keep pace.

The wind kicked up as they traveled and blew in heavy cloud cover. The countryside suddenly became pitch black, forcing them to slow back to a walk.

"Well, if this don't beat all...Don't need this," Thad complained.

"Will you just relax? Nobody's goin' to be missing these gals," Sneaky said.

"Sheriff Flynn is nobody to reckon with. He won't take kindly to this happening in his county," Thad said.

"We'll be back drinking whiskey in the Coolwater Saloon by the time he knows what happened," Sneaky said.

They finally came to the road that led to Fort Worth and turned onto it. The cloud cover remained heavy and lightning flashed far off to the west. Thad set out in an easy single-foot trot. He wanted to go faster, but the darkness made even him fear taking a tumble.

The slower pace and the smoother road did much to help Rita stay in the saddle. Her fingers started to cramp from gripping the saddle horn, but she didn't dare lessen her hold or complain.

§

For the rest of the night into the wee hours of the morning they continued to ride. Thad refused to stop to take a break and would only allow the group to slow the horses to a walk to provide the animals some rest. Sneaky knew the area well and an hour before first light, he called out to stop when they reached Rock Hole Hollow Branch.

"Good spot to stop. We can go into the woods here a hundred yards or so and nobody'll see us…We've pushed hard enough for one night. The sun will be comin' up before much longer anyway," Sneaky said.

"I suppose you're right," Thad said.

The men dismounted and walked the horses into the woods along the stream until Sneaky was satisfied they were hidden from view from the road. Each man pulled a girl from the saddle.

"Awright ladies, listen up. If any of you have business you need to tend to, go behind one of those trees and do it one at a time. You won't get another chance for a while…Don't try anything or you'll be real sorry," Sneaky said as he untied their hands.

Each of the girls took a turn scampering off behind a tree.

Becky took her turn last, and when she returned, she marched over to the men. "Where are you taking us?" she demanded.

"Don't worry about it," Thad said.

"I demand to know this instant," she yelled.

In a haughty voice, Thad said, "We're sellin' you in Fort Worth to be whores…Don't you wish you didn't know now?"

Becky raised her hands above her head to club Thad. Sneaky, fearing what Thad might do to the girl, stepped between them and absorbed a blow to the shoulder. He grabbed Becky's arms before she could strike again and yanked her away toward the other girls.

"Sit down an' shut up," Sneaky warned.

The girls started crying in unison as Sneaky walked away.

Becky's outburst seemed to have excited Thad. He walked up to Sneaky and whispered, "You know there are three of us and three of them. We could have us a little entertainment before we sleep...break those girls in proper."

"The Chinaman wouldn't like that," Sneaky said.

"What do you mean? Why would he care?...They'll be whores anyway," Thad protested, his voice breaking just above a whisper.

"The Chinaman likes the new girls to be unsoiled. I think maybe he likes to break 'em in proper himself," Sneaky said.

"If this don't beat all. You made sure you kept that to yourself...I had my eye on that oldest one. That's a fine looking filly with lots of fire."

"You'll just have to use some of that money comin' your way on some other girl that catches your fancy," Sneaky warned.

Thad stomped off and retrieved his bedroll. He crawled into it and was asleep before Sneaky and Avery had finished securing the girls so that all of them could get some rest.

§§§

CHAPTER FOUR

Fiona and Bill walked to the jail to meet up with Mason. The trio had agreed to have breakfast at the café t together before the marshals departed with their prisoners. Once they were seated, Molly brought coffee without prompting.

"I know what you want," Molly said to Mason. "If our sheriff is anything, it is consistent. You could set your watch by him and he never varies his breakfast."

"Whatever Mason has is fine with me. There's not much that I don't like," Fiona said.

"Same goes for me, too," Bill added.

"Have your food in front of you before your cups need refilled," Molly said before darting away.

"You two look a sight more rested than you did yesterday evening," Mason noted.

"I slept like a baby on a full stomach…A bath, a little sour mash whiskey, and a soft bed will do that for me every time," Fiona said with a smile.

Bill blew on his coffee before taking a sip. "I barely remember crawling into bed. Did wake myself up snoring one time." He grinned.

"Your snoring could wake the dead," Fiona commented. "I'm surprised Indians never tracked you down in your younger days from all the racket you make."

Molly returned with plates heaped with scrambled eggs, bacon, biscuits, and a big chunk of ham. "Enjoy," she said.

Bill smiled down at his plate. "Now that's a meal that'll stick to your ribs for a while," he said before nabbing a piece of bacon.

"It's a pity you have to get your prisoners back to Gainesville so quickly. You could stick around here and keep me company," Mason said before scooping up a mouthful of eggs.

"I'm ready for my own bed at Faye's bording house," Bill said and grinned at Fiona. "This traveling all over Texas with a woman can grow tiresome."

"The man doth protest too much, methinks," Fiona said with a lilt in her voice.

"Ah, paraphrasing Shakespeare's Hamlet, I see," commented Bill.

"Since the actual quote is: 'The lady dost protest too much, methinks,' didn't think it quite fit," she retorted.

The three were laughing as Deputy Gomer Platt burst into the café. He rushed to the sheriff's table and spit his lemon drop into his hand. "Sheriff, you need to come quick."

Flynn was used to the young deputy's excited outbursts. They usually amounted to nothing. "What is it, Gomer?" he asked in a calm voice.

"Sheriff, you need to come see this for your ownself."

Mason eyed Platt with irritation and noticed how pale the deputy looked and that his hands were shaking. Deciding that the deputy must have a true emergency, he said, "Platt this better be worth my eggs getting cold."

97

The three officers of the law followed the deputy outside.

A plow horse with Cooper McGregor drooped over its neck stood in front of the jail. Blood from the young man had dripped down and covered the horse's shoulder. Bill and Mason ran to Cooper and eaased him down from the horse.

"Platt, go get Doc Mosier...an' hurry," Mason ordered.

Cooper opened his eyes at hearing the sheriff's voice. "Sheriff Flynn?"

"Cooper, can you tell me what happened?" Flynn asked as he scanned the young man's wounds. He had bullet holes in his upper chest and thigh. He also had a goose egg lump above his right eye.

"They kilt Momma and Daddy and the girls are gone. I think I hit my head when I fell...I tried to fight," Cooper said between grunts of pain.

"I know you did, son. How many were there? Did you know them?" Flynn interrogated.

"Sneaky, Avery, and Thad. They come last night after dark...We didn't have a chance," Cooper said before closing his eyes.

"You just hold on. The doc is coming and he'll fix you up. I'll find your sisters...I promise," the sheriff said.

Deputy Platt came running up with Doctor Curtis Mosier following as fast as his sixty-five year old skinny legs would carry him.

"Platt, you an' Slim'll have to be in charge of the town until I get back. I fear I'll be gone for a few days...You'll have to see to it that Mister and Miz McGregor get a proper burial. The preacher will help you, I'm sure," Mason said.

"Yes, sir."

"We need to carry Cooper to my office," Doctor Mosier said. "Be particular with him, now."

The sheriff looked up at the crowd gathering around them. "Some of you men carry Cooper to the doctor's office," Flynn said as he stood.

"Do you know those men that boy mentioned?" Fiona asked.

"Yeah, they're some ne'er-do-wells that hang around here. Thad Hytree did some prison time for killing a man, but even that was a bar fight that got out of hand...They've never stooped to something this low...Those girls are all in their teens," Mason said.

"We'll go with you. They're liable to be out of your jurisdiction by now anyway. They've had all night to get to where they're going. I would imagine they have a destination in mind that's not close by...Consider yourself deputized, again" Fiona said.

"Thanks...You okay with this, Bill?" Mason asked.

"Wouldn't have it any other way. We need to find those girls...God have mercy on those men's souls if they harm them," Bill said.

"Let me gather up some things and I'll meet you at Mom's Livery," Flynn said.

The horses and Fiona's mule, Spot, were saddled and ready to ride by the time Mason walked to the livery stable looking as if all the world were upon his back. His saddlebags were slung over his shoulder, and bulged with cartridges and food supplies. He carried his Winchester '76 in his hand.

Without a word being said, the law officers mounted up and followed Mason, riding west at a road trot.

§§§

CHAPTER FIVE

Doctor Curtis Mosier had treated more gunshot wounds in his time of practicing medicine than he could keep count. He'd saved a good many of those patients, but he'd also seen a fair share with too much organ damage to even begin to help rectify the injuries and others die from raging infections that he was powerless to combat.

"Deputy Platt, if you don't mind, I'd like you to wait up front until I determine what I need to do. I might need you to hold Cooper down if I have to put him to sleep. I'm not as stout as I once was," the doctor said.

"Sure, Doctor Mosier. Whatever you need. I'll be happy to help."

The doctor wasted no time as he cut away Cooper's clothing. As he examined the young man, he feared Cooper had lost so much blood that a chance for survival was slim to none. Cooper was as pale as a sheet—even his gums were white.

The bullet to the thigh had passed through cleanly and missed bone, but the injury had still not coagulated. The wound to the chest was above the lung and the bullet was lodged in the muscles.

Mosier gazed at the patient a moment as he pondered what to do. He didn't think Cooper was strong enough for surgery, but allowing the bleeding to continue unabated was sure death.

"Deputy Platt, please come here," he called out.

"What do I need to do?" Gomer asked.

"Just keep Cooper pinned to the table if he struggles."

The doctor searched the row of bottles on his shelf until he spied the chloroform. He pulled the bottle down, and retrieved a cloth. With the precision of years of practice, the doctor poured some chloroform onto the rag and quickly covered Cooper's mouth and nose with it. Cooper made a brief struggle as he fought for air, but in his weakened state, he quickly gave up fighting. Mosier held the cloth in place until satisfied that his patient would remain sufficiently sedated during the surgery.

"You can go now, Gomer," the doctor said.

"Is Cooper going to make it?" Platt asked.

"Well, I'm going to do my part to save him, but I think he made need a little help from above. You might want to say a little prayer for him."

"Sure thing. You know I will," Gomer said before hurrying out of the office.

Doctor Mosier moved to the thigh wound. With a pair of forceps, he fished around in the wound and produced a piece of material from Cooper's pants that the bullet had deposited.

Clothing left in a wound was one of the surest ways to gets an infection. Many a man had lost a limb or even their life from failure to retrieve the cloth. He then located a severed artery that was the source for the continued bleeding. With a scalpel in hand, he freed the end of the blood vessel and then tied it off with the dexterity to make a seamstress blush.

"I'd like to see some young buck fresh out of medical school match me on that," he said aloud to himself as he admired his handiwork.

The doctor checked Cooper's pulse and breathing. Satisfied, he began probing the chest wound. Using his scalpel, he widened the wound.

With room now to use his forceps, Mosier gripped the bullet and pulled the thirty-six caliber chunk of lead from the body.

He examined the wound and decided the best course of action was to do nothing further to it. The doctor finished the surgery by dousing both wounds with carbolic acid and applying bandages.

Doctor Mosier listened to Cooper's heart with his stethoscope. "Young man, if you are the fighter that I think you are, you just might live to tell your grandchildren about this ordeal." He patted Cooper's shoulder.

§§§

CHAPTER SIX

Mason, Fiona, and Bill reached the McGregor home in just under an hour. Fiona felt a shiver travel down her spine at the sight of the wide open door and the dead dog in front of it.

Mason let out a loud sigh as he steeled himself to go inside the home to see the carnage. He checked Earl and Edna McGregor and confirmed they were dead before looking the place over.

"This woman put up a fight. She has blood under her fingernails and I don't think it's hers," Fiona said before she covered the body in a blanket she had found. She then covered Mister McGregor.

"Not much to garner here...Better see if we can pick up the trail and be on our way," Mason said.

Finding the tracks for six horses going at a hard trot didn't take much work.

"I wonder where they're headed and what their plan is?" Bill questioned.

"Right now, have to admit that I'm a bit clueless and fear I don't want to know," Mason said as he adjusted his butt and shifted the saddle to the right to center it. "All the same, hope we find out sooner rather than later."

§

They found the job of trailing the kidnappers and their captives to be a mixed bag across the Texas landscape. The track was as plain as day across the grasslands, but in the hillier areas, the limestone and sandstone made finding signs hard to come by. Throughout it all though, it was apparent that they were staying in a southeasterly direction.

§

After a couple of hours of riding, they stopped to give their mounts a blow and to graze some. The aborted breakfast had left bellies growling.

As they dined on corn dodgers and beef jerky, Fiona voiced what all of them had been thinking.

"They're taking those girls somewhere to sell them. That's the only thing that makes sense."

"What I've been thinking," Mason said after washing a corn dodger down.

"I pity the life those girls will have if we can't track them down," Bill said.

"I wonder if they're headed to Hell's Half-Acre. There's nothing that men won't stoop to in that god-awful place," Fiona said.

"Fort Worth is mighty close to home...Only 'bout seventy moles. Think they'd want to put a little more daylight between those girls and Jacksboro," Mason said.

"They'd would never escape that place. Those men keep an eye on their girls like they're in a prison...And if somebody from Jacksboro ever came across them, I doubt they'd ever step forth and admit they were down there sampling the goods...That's one of those places you visit and never tell even your best friend," Fiona said.

"You make some good points. Guess we better get back in the saddle and make sure none of that happens," Mason said as he stood.

§

They reached the road to Fort Worth a short time later. Fiona and Mason exchanged glances at seeing that their quarry had taken the thoroughfare.

"Maybe we can make up some time now," Bill said. "Traveling at night with three captives had to slow them some."

"Hope you're right. Lost a fair amount of time ourselves tracking them this far," Mason said.

"We won't get any closer going this speed and jabbering," Fiona said as she heeled Spot into a into his smooth as silk fast single foot.

§

The trio held their pace until the animals had worked up a good lather. Mason was the first to slow his mount.

"You ever wonder why we keep doing this line of work?" Flynn asked.

"I think partly that some of us are just born for it, and the other is that we're driven to prevent happening to others what happened to us," Fiona said.

Mason's pregnant wife had been killed by Comancheros. He had tracked the outlaws down and killed them where they stood.

Fiona's husband was murdered by Cherokee renegade, Cal Mankiller. She had succeeded in her mission to bring the Indian to justice.

"Suppose so. We certainly paid a hell of a high price to find our calling," Flynn said.

Bill decided to try to bring some levity to the morose conversation. "Personally, I got into this business so I could ride with the likes of you two instead of looking over my shoulder at you coming for me. I cheated the hangman enough times to know when to quit."

"Do you ever miss those days?" Mason asked.

"About like a toothache," Bill said with a chuckle. Thank goodness for Sheriff Pat Garrett's help.

§§§

CHAPTER SEVEN

Avery was the first to rise a little after noontime. The scratches on his face were burning as if they were on fire. He touched his cheeks and realized they were swollen and oozing. In a panic, he shook Sneaky awake.

"What is it? Is it the girls?" Sneaky asked as he tried to get his wits about him.

"Look at my face. What does it look like?" Avery whined.

Sneaky cursed as he crawled out of his bedroll. "You look like hell. Those scratches are inflamed," he said.

"What am I going to do?"

"How do I know? We can't just go stop and visit a doctor now, can we? Go wash up in the branch. That's all I know," Sneaky said.

The conversation awakened Thad and the girls. Thad arose in his usual ornery mood and stomped off into the woods while Sneaky freed the girls.

When Thad returned, he said, "Let's get everybody fed. It feels like a month of Sundays since I had something to eat."

Sneaky passed out hardtack and jerky as Avery walked back to the camp.

"Well, ain't you a sight for sore eyes. You're liable to ruin these little girls' appetites," Thad taunted.

"You best shut up if you know what's good for you. I'm in no mood for you," Avery warned.

Thad glared at Avery as he tried to decide whether to ride his partner some more. Avery had never back talked him before now and he wasn't sure how far to push. He decided to hold his tongue rather than chance a licking in front of the girls. Thad grabbed a hardtack biscuit and began chewing as he took a seat.

The girls were starving and began devouring what little food that Sneaky allotted them. Becky watched her sisters eat and worried about them. Both of them looked as if they had already given up in defeat. Seeing Rita struggle didn't really shock her. She had always been the softest of the kids.

Nancy's behavior surprised her though. If anything, Becky felt as if Nancy was the strongest of all of them – even stronger than Cooper. She quickly banished her brother from her mind. Now was not the time to mourn the dead, but rather try to save the living.

Becky washed down the last of her biscuit and got to her feet. With determination to show her sisters that now was not the time to lose hope, she took a couple of steps and stood over Thad.

"You're never going to get away with this. Sheriff Flynn will hang the three of you as sure as my name is Becky McGregor...You can only hope that your neck snaps and you die a quick death," Becky said.

"Little lady, you best take a seat and keep your mouth shut," Thad warned.

"What are you going to do if I won't? I don't imagine they pay top dollar for a beat up girl, now do they?"

Thad stood and tried to stare down the girl.

Sneaky nervously got to his feet. "Thad, watch yourself. She's right," he said.

"You're a little spitfire. I like that. What I'd give to be your first. Too bad it'll be some Chinaman. Your Momma and Daddy will be ripe by the time anybody finds them," Thad said.

"Tom Wendt was coming over this morning to buy a couple of heifers from Daddy. We were going to go to town today and get new shoes for winter with the money," Becky lied. "I would bet that the sheriff has a posse on your trail by now…Sheriff Flynn will probably never give you the opportunity to hang."

Thad and Sneaky exchanged glances and Avery stood up and started pacing. Becky's intention of riling up the gang had exceeded beyond what she could have hoped for, but had the unintended consequence of causing Thad to consider riding out before nightfall. Thad grabbed Becky by the arm and shoved her down into her sisters.

"Come here," Thad said to Sneaky as he walked toward the water.

"What is it?" Sneaky asked.

"Maybe we should head on out," Thad said.

"Are you crazy? People will see us on the road and might even be somebody we know from Jacksboro. That girl could be lyin' for all we know," Sneaky said.

"I don't think she is."

"Even if she's tellin' the truth, Flynn has to be several hours behind us. Let's just wait 'til dark and stick to our plan. We can't push the horses too hard," Sneaky warned.

"We can wait a couple of more hours, but we need to move. I don't want to tangle with Flynn," Thad said.

"I don't trust that girl to keep her mouth shut if we see anybody," Sneaky said.

"Oh, she'll keep her mouth shut. Just watch what I do before we ride. She'll understand real good how to keep quiet," Thad said and grinned sadistically.

Thad and Sneaky walked back to the camp.

"Avery, keep an eye on them. I'm goin' back to sleep," Thad ordered before crawling into his bedroll.

He and Sneaky were soon snoring, leaving Avery with guard duty.

A couple of hours later, Thad awoke again. Sneaky was still sleeping and Thad kicked him. "Wake up."

The girls were sitting in a row biding their time. Thad walked up to Nancy and yanked her up by the hair of her head. She screamed as her feet left the ground. Thad wrapped his arm around the girl's neck in a choke hold and pulled out his knife. He poked the point into Nancy's cheekbone until a single drop of blood bubbled to the service.

"Now, listen up. We're going to start ridin'. You girls won't be bound, and if we meet anybody on the road, you just smile and keep ridin'...If any of you tries anything, I'm goin' to carve up the face of your little sister so that she looks a lot worse than Avery does…Do you understand?" Thad yelled.

Becky and Rita nodded their heads rapidly and got to their feet.

"Awright then. Let's saddle up," Thad said as he slung Nancy onto the ground.

§§§

CHAPTER EIGHT

Sheriff Flynn was the first to spot the tracks leaving the road. He climbed off his horse and studied the hoof prints. That's when he noticed fresher tracks a few feet away coming back onto the road.

"I think we missed them. Looks like they might have rested and got back to traveling," Flynn said.

"We'd best go find their camp to be sure and maybe at least learn something," Fiona said.

"Suppose it wouldn't hurt except for wasting some time," Mason concurred.

They walked the horses into the woods a few yards and tied them to saplings. Flynn led the way through the timber and drew his Colt just to be on the safe side. He reached the obvious campsite where bedrolls had flattened the grass and leaves.

"Cold camp. Being cautious," Bill said as he looked over the sight.

Flynn holstered his revolver. "Bet we didn't miss them by more than a couple of hours. I sure would have liked to have ended this before they make Fort Worth."

"We can ride until dark, but then we're going to have to let the horses and Spot rest," Fiona commented.

"Yeah...Kind of what I was thinking. We've pushed pretty hard today. Hope we don't lose all the ground we made up on 'em," Mason said and started walking back toward the road.

At about the time that the law officers were investigating the campsite, the kidnappers and the girls were making an arc around Springtown, Texas, to avoid riding through the town.

The group had encountered a few travelers on the road, but nobody they knew, and Thad had put such a fear into the girls that none of them dared try to signal for help.

Avery began whining that he didn't feel well and nobody doubted that he was telling the truth. His cheeks were clearly infected from riding in the dirt kicked up on the trail. Both sides of his face were swollen and he had to use a kerchief to mop up the oozing from the wounds. His shirt and forehead were covered in sweat and he looked feverish.

"Fellers, I don't know how much farther I can ride," he said.

Thad looked over at his partner and actually felt some compassion for him. "You're going to have to toughen it out for a while. We have to get close enough to Fort Worth that we can make it to town tomorrow. After we get rid of the girls, we'll find you a doctor…I promise," Thad said.

"Okay, Thad. If you say so."

"Be glad when nightfall gets here. This travelin' by daylight is liable to get us hanged…Still think that oldest one just made up a story to make you nervous," Sneaky said, giving Becky a hard look.

"You're going to hang all right. Bet Sheriff Flynn slips the noose over your neck himself," Becky said.

"You best just shut up and ride. Thad could still carve up your sister…if you're not careful," Sneaky responded.

§§§

CHAPTER NINE

Deputy Platt came ambling into the doctor's office carrying a heaping plate of scrambled eggs. Doctor Mosier was sitting at his desk reading a newspaper and looked up in confusion at seeing the food.

"Had supper at the café and Miz Sewell sent these eggs for Cooper. She thought he might need somethin' to eat," the deputy said.

"Well, bless your and Ruth Ann's heart," Mosier said. "I was thinking about getting him some food and I didn't want to leave because he hasn't awakened yet and I was afraid he'd be confused if he did and nobody was here."

"How is Cooper doing?" Gomer asked.

"He's rested peacefully all afternoon…That boy is strong, and is doing better than he has a right to, considering how much blood he lost."

"Cooper and me are the same age…We went to school together and had some fun times."

"Cooper and I," Mosier corrected.

"Yes, sir."

"Let's go see if we can get those eggs down him before they get cold. I'm sure he'd appreciate a friendly face." The doctor stood.

Doctor Mosier led Deputy Platt into the next room and gently shook Cooper until the young man opened his eyes.

"Cooper, how are you feeling?' he asked.

Cooper looked at the doctor and then at Deputy Platt as he slowly recalled all that had happened.

"Did the sheriff find my sisters?" he asked.

"He's out looking for them right now and he has two of the finest Deputy US Marshals in Texas helping him. Don't you worry about your sisters. Mason will bring them home safe and sound...Now how do you feel?"

"Kind of rough...Am I going to die?"

"Not if I can help it. You've made it through the worst part of things. You need to eat now to get strong. You've lost a lot of blood." Doctor Mosier started shoving pillows behind him to get him in a reclining position.

Deputy Platt deposited the plate of eggs on Cooper's stomach. He tried to move his right arm toward the plate and let out a groan of pain.

"Here, let me feed you," the deputy said and grabbed the fork. With the care normally reserved for a mother toward her child, Platt fed Cooper.

After eating a few bites, Cooper said, "They shot Daddy as soon as he opened the door. Took me a moment to realize what had happened...I froze. If I hadn't, might have got to the shotgun in time to defend my family. I did try, but it was too late."

Doctor Mosier patted Cooper's leg. "Don't go blaming yourself for what others have done. Anybody, Sheriff Flynn included, would have done the same thing. When something so out of the ordinary happens like that, it's only human nature to take a moment to process what has occurred...You showed your bravery just by trying to get to the gun. Now try to eat some more."

Cooper ate a few more bites before feeling full. He looked at the doctor. "What will the girls and I do now that Daddy and Momma are gone? How am I going to take care of them?"

"Your daddy was a fine man, Cooper, but he was also a man that didn't want to see his children grow up and become adults. There are a lot of girls even Nancy's age that are married. All four of you are old enough to be out on your own. You'll all be fine running the ranch together...There is nothing on that place that you don't' know how to do."

"Suppose you have a point," Cooper said before his eyes started drifting shut.

"You get some rest."

Cooper's eyes shot open. "Where are Daddy and Momma's bodies?"

Deputy Platt moved the plate out of the way. "They're out at your place. The preacher and some neighbors are taking care of things...Your folks will be buried tomorrow."

"Guess I won't get to go," Cooper said.

"No...no you won't. Now get some rest." Doctor Mosier motioned with his head for Deputy Platt to leave the room also.

§§§

CHAPTER TEN

The trio of law officers rode until dusk before begrudgingly making camp. They climbed out of the saddle weary from a long day of riding.

Flynn and Bill walked stiffly into the woods to gather firewood while Fiona staked the animals so that they could get to the creek and graze on the grass along the banks.

Once the fire was burning well, Fiona cooked some salt pork and warmed a can of beans for supper. A day in the saddle with little to eat had left the group so hungry that any shortcomings of the meager meal went unnoticed and made the food seem like a feast.

"Believe I'll live for another day now," Bill said.

"Me and you both," Mason said. "Fiona is liable to take up workin' at Sewell's Café and leave behind this line of work."

"I'll make you think twice about thinking I'm best suited for cooking. You're liable to find pebbles amongst your beans next meal…You can chew on that," Fiona said.

The two men laughed and exchanged winks.

"Didn't mean to rile you. Just giving you a compliment," Mason replied.

"Uh-huh, I bet that's what you were aiming to do."

"You'd think after once being married, I'd know how to praise a lady…proper like," Flynn said.

"Don't blame yourself, Mason." Bill winked again. "They're all she-devils at heart."

119

"You two are fixing to feel the end of my pitchfork if you keep talking like that," Fiona said.

Turning serious, Mason said, "I wonder how Cooper made out. Sure hope the doctor was able to save him."

"I bet he's a fighter. He showed a lot of grit by making it to town," Fiona said.

"He did. It would sure make things easier for his sisters if they at least have him to come home to," Flynn commented.

Bill stood and stretched his legs. "Been doing some thinking. I'm guessing we travel a couple a miles an hour faster than they do considering their situation…If we were to go ahead and get us some rest and then head out at about three in the morning, maybe we'd be able to catch them before they get to where they're going. That'd give our mounts time to recover…Otherwise, I fear we'll be tryin' to find them in Hell's Half-Acre."

Mason and Fiona exchanged glances to get a read on what the other thought.

Fiona picked up the coffee pot with her folded black deerskin glove and refilled her cup. "Sounds good to me. I suppose there's a chance we lose them in the dark, but I think it's worth the risk…What do you think, Mason?"

"I'm up for it if ya'll are. The sooner we find 'em, the sooner we can head back…And I don't mind going to sleep right now. Fiona's threats have plumb tired me out," the sheriff said, grinning at his female companion.

§

Avery couldn't sit upright in the saddle any longer. He draped himself over his horse's neck and occasionally let out a moan.

The girls were exhausted and would doze off in the saddle from time to time.

"We're going to have to stop. Everybody is worn out from traveling all night," Sneaky said as he struck a match with his thumbnail and checked his watch to see that it was ten o'clock. "Tried to tell you to wait 'til dark. We didn't accomplish a dang thing by leaving early. We should have rested longer."

"For all you know, Sheriff Flynn might have already found where we camped," Thad said.

"I never knew you were so scared of the sheriff. Figured you thought you could take him any old time you wanted," Sneaky commented.

"You've never been in prison. It's nothing like spendin' a few days in jail...changes a man. You'd be cautious, too," Thad said.

"Maybe so. No matter what though, we need to stop at the next woods we see. Maybe Avery will improve with some rest. The horses are as tired as the rest of us, too," Sneaky said.

A few minutes later, they came to a creek with woods on either side of the road.

Thad stopped without any further prompting. "Let's make camp," he said with resignation in his voice.

After finding a suitable spot to set up camp out of sight of the road, Sneaky passed out jerky and hardtack biscuits to everyone.

Rita took her portions and divided them between her sisters before curling up into a ball on the ground.

"Rita, you have to eat," Becky chided.

"I'm ready to die. Momma, Daddy, and Cooper are all gone and I'd just as soon join them as be a prostitute…Nobody is going to save us," Rita said.

"Momma and Daddy didn't raise us to be quitters. You can't give up hope," Nancy added.

Rita covered her head with her arms and didn't respond.

"You girls need to shut up. You don't want me to come over there," Thad warned from his seat.

Becky shot up like a fired cannon ball and charged Thad. She knocked him onto his back and managed to deliver a couple of blows before Sneaky yanked her off his partner.

He shoved Becky to the ground over by her sisters and kept himself between her and Thad to serve as a barrier in case he planned retaliation.

Thad got to his feet with a smirk on his face. "You are a feisty thing. I just might stick around Fort Worth so I can be your first customer…Wouldn't that be fun?" he asked.

"How are you feelin', Avery?" Sneaky asked to divert attention away from the girls.

Avery had only eaten a few bites of food before crawling into his bedroll. "I'm so tired. I just want to sleep."

"We all need some sleep. I'll tie the girls up so we can get some rest," Sneaky said.

He retrieved the leather pigging strings from his saddlebag and tied each of the girl's hands. After making them get into their bedrolls, he tied rope around each of their bedding so that they were cocooned inside. Sneaky and Thad wasted little time in spreading their soogans and going to bed.

Nancy planned to stay awake until everyone else had gone to sleep. Seeing Rita in such a desperate condition had convinced her to escape or die trying. She had kept her wrists spread just far enough apart that Sneaky hadn't noticed as he tied her in the dark, leaving some play in the bindings.

While she waited on the others to fall asleep, her weariness got the best of her as she fought to keep her eyes open. She was soon slumbering.

§

"Wake up, my sleeping beauties," Fiona said as she fished in her saddlebag for some jerky and corn dodgers. "You both thought this was a good idea, so no complaining."

Bill let out a groan that could have made a wolf answer with a howl. "My God, seems as if we just went to sleep. I'll lose my good looks if we keep this up much longer."

"You'd have to doze about as long as Rip Van Winkle to make you pretty," Fiona teased.

Mason crawled out of his bedroll. "This will teach you to do some thinkin'…as you say. It really doesn't become you."

123

"Well, listen to you two. I'd say you both got up on the wrong side of the bed, providing we actual had beds," Bill said.

"To show you that I'm a good sport...promise to buy the first meal we get to eat when this is all said and done," Mason offered.

"Now that sounds a little more hospitable," Bill replied.

They made quick work of eating the food, not bothering to make coffee. By the time they saddled the horses, the fog was lifting from their brains and they mounted up ready to find the girls.

The bright moon cast plenty of light as they took off. They rode the horses at a walk until the animals' muscles warmed and then sped to an easy trot.

§

Nancy woke with a start. She had no idea what time it was, but morning still seemed likely to be a long time in coming. As she listened, she heard the snoring and rhythmic breathing of the others. She pulled her right hand against the leather binding for all she was worth. The leather felt as if it was pealing the hide from her hand as she freed herself.

Nancy was so skinny that her brother and sisters sometimes teased her by calling her Bones, and she managed to shimmy her way out of the bedroll without much effort.

Once she was on her feet, she contemplated whether to free her sisters or go try to find help. She reluctantly decided that the chance of making noise was too great to untie her siblings.

After successfully tiptoeing out of the camp, she made her way back to the road. She tried to remember the last house she had seen with a light burning, but they had traveled well past the time most people stayed up and she had no idea where to go. Hoping to find a house, she started running back in the direction she had come. She ran until she had to slow to catch her breath.

"Hello. Can anyone hear me? I need help," she yelled.

Not even a dog answered her call. Refusing to quit or get discouraged, Nancy trudged on. She would walk until she felt rested, calling for help occasionally, and then take off in a jog. After a while, she could have sworn she had traveled far enough that she should be back in Jacksboro let alone the last town they had ridden past.

The law officers had been traveling at an easy pace for close to three hours, only slowing twice to give their mounts a blow.

Fiona was the first to spot something moving on the road. She couldn't see well enough to identify what she saw and drew one of her Peacemakers.

"Something is coming," she warned the others.

"It's a girl," Mason called out as he peered into the dark.

"Help me, please," Nancy yelled at the sound of voices.

"Nancy, that you?" Flynn hollered as he jumped down from his horse and ran to the girl.

"Sheriff Flynn. Oh, Sheriff Flynn, you have to help my sisters," Nancy cried out as she ran into his arms.

She burst into tears and couldn't speak for sobbing and trying to catch her breath.

Flynn patted Nancy's back as he embraced her. "That's why I'm here. We came to bring all of you home...I promise," he said.

After gaining some composure, Nancy said, "I didn't want to leave Becky and Rita, but I had to try to get some help."

"You did the right thing. How far have you run?" the sheriff asked.

"I don't know...It felt like forever. I had to take off my shoes and I think my feet are raw. We made camp at a creek. There's not another one between here and there," Nancy said.

"We have less than an hour until dawn," Fiona announced.

"Let's go get your sisters. You can ride behind me," Flynn said.

"Put her up here with me," Fiona said. "Your horse already has enough of a load on it and Nancy can get her arms wrapped around me better than you."

The sheriff helped Nancy up behind Fiona.

"Let's go see what we find," Fiona said as she nudged Spot into moving.

§

A nature call woke Thad up before first light and he scurried behind a tree to relieve himself. As he walked back toward his sleeping spot, he noticed how flat Nancy's bedroll appeared.

With swift steps, he moved toward it, picking up the bedroll and slinging it when he realized it was empty. "Sneaky, Avery, wake up. The young one is gone," he bellowed.

Sneaky jumped up in a panic and started looking around as if Nancy were playing hide-and-seek. Avery barely stirred.

As Sneaky walked past Avery, he reared his leg back and gave him a swift kick. The kick got Avery's attention and he crawled out of his bedroll.

"We got to find her. That girl could get us hung," Sneaky said.

Becky and Rita were still secured in their bedding. Thad walked up to Becky and grabbed her by the hair, causing her to shriek.

"Which way did you send your sister?" Thad yelled with his face so close to the girl that she could smell his foul breath.

"I didn't know she was gone, I swear," Becky cried out.

Thad released Becky and turned toward Sneaky.

"This is your fault. If you'd have bound her right, she couldn't have escaped."

"You could have tied them up just as easily as me. You think you're above doing the dirty work...Just shut up. I don't want to hear it. Avery can watch these two and we'll go find her," Sneaky said.

Avery was sitting up and holding his head in his hands.

"Are you feelin' any better?" Thad asked.

"Don't know. I can watch those two…Go find that girl," Avery answered.

Thad and Sneaky quickly saddled their horses and rode away.

Becky waited to speak until the first hints of morning made its appearance to the east. "Avery, I need to take care of business," she said.

"Me, too," Rita chimed in.

Avery lifted his head out of his hands and looked over to where the girls were bound in their bedrolls. "You can just wait," he said.

"I can't. I'm going to wet myself. Please," Becky pleaded.

Reluctantly, Avery walked over and untied the rope around the bedding. Becky freed herself from the bedroll and held out her tied hands toward Avery.

"I'm not untyin' your hands. Either manage that way or not," he said.

Becky, deciding not to push things any further, took off behind a tree while Avery knelt down and freed Rita.

The sisters exchanged glances as Becky returned and Rita disappeared.

"Sit down," Avery ordered.

Doing as she was told, Becky sat on the ground. Rita came walking back, and with a nod of her head, she charged Avery as Becky shot off the ground and did likewise. Rita flung her legs around one of Avery's legs while Becky launched herself into his chest. They took him down like they had their brother countless times.

Today wasn't a game though, and they attacked with the belief that their lives depended on succeeding. Becky crawled to a straddle position on Avery's chest and rained blows onto his infected face. Avery yelped and reached for his revolver.

Rita managed to get her bound hands over his arm. As she clutched Avery's arm to her breast, she chomped down on his hand until she could taste his blood. Avery let out a bloodcurdling scream as he worked to free his arm.

When he snatched his arm from Rita's grasp, she swiped the gun from the holster. She darted away, and awkwardly pulled the hammer back with her bound hand.

"Run, Becky," Rita screamed.

Becky delivered one final blow and scrambled away.

Avery lay stunned on the ground for a moment until he rolled onto his stomach and pushed himself up to standing position.

"Give me that gun. You don't want killin' on your hands. And besides, that gun is tricky. It's liable to blow up in your face," Avery said as he took a step toward Rita.

"You killed Momma with it just fine," she said.

"Girl, give me that gun if you know what's good for you." Avery took another step.

"Never," Rita yelled as she squeezed the trigger.

The shot drove into Avery's chest and knocked him back a step. His facial expression revealed more shock that she had shot him than it did pain. Rita cocked the gun and fired again, taking him down.

Becky, fearing that Avery might still recover, ran to the body and snatched his knife. She cut her sister's binding. Rita took the knife and did likewise.

With Rita holding the gun ready to shoot again, Becky crept up to Avery and checked his pulse. Avery had died from his own gun.

§

The sound of the two shots carried to Mason, Fiona, and Bill. They simultaneously spurred their mounts into gallops. In the gray light, they saw two riders ahead of them.

Spotting the charging riders, Thad and Sneaky wheeled their horses around and hightailed it. The kidnappers had fresh horses and were gaining a little ground on the law officers.

Thad and Sneaky made the mistake of firing their revolvers wildly at their pursuers. Fourteen years of serving in the US Second Cavalry had left Flynn an expert shot from the back of a horse.

He pulled his Winchester from the scabbard and chambered a cartridge. In the dim morning light, he tried to get a bead on the bigger of the two men. Flynn fired his rifle, cocked it, fired again, and repeated the sequence one more time before Thad flopped over onto the horse's neck.

The kidnapper bounced in the saddle a couple of times before falling headfirst off the horse. Sneaky made it to the creek and jumped from his horse before the animal came to a stop.

He stumbled to his knees and jumped right up, firing two shots as he ran for the cover of the trees.

Fiona drew both her Colts and Bill had his Colt Thunderer cocked. The two unloaded a barrage of shots at the fleeing outlaw in what sounded like a war. Sneaky took five hits in the hail of bullets and died before he hit the ground.

"He won't be doing anymore kidnapping," Bill said as he pulled his horse to a stop.

"No, he won't," Fiona responded.

Mason had stopped at Thad's body. He climbed from his horse and checked for a pulse. "This one's dead!"

"So is the other one," Fiona yelled.

Fiona and Bill dismounted and Nancy slid to the ground.

"The other one killed my sisters, I heard the two shots," Nancy said and started crying.

"Now you don't know that. You need to stay right here and let us go see what happened," Fiona said as Flynn rode up and joined them.

The three officers spread out as they worked their way through the woods.

Mason yelled, "Avery, this is Sheriff Flynn. Thad and Sneaky are dead. Give yourself up."

"Sheriff Flynn, this is Becky. We killed him."

Flynn took off in a run. He found her sitting on the ground with her arms around Rita.

"Are you hurt?" Flynn asked.

"No, but we don't know where Nancy is." Becky started to cry.

"We have her. She's fine."

Fiona returned for Nancy upon hearing that Avery was dead.

§

A few moments later, she walked into the camp with the youngest sister.

Nancy ran to Becky and Rita, and wrapped her arms around them.

"I went for help. I wouldn't abandon you," Nancy said between sobs.

"We can see what you did. You saved all of us," Becky replied.

Mason, Fiona, and Bill stood around the campsite and waited for the girls to cry themselves out. The ordeal and its sudden end had overwhelmed the sisters. They stayed huddled together until they finally grew quiet. Becky stood and walked to the sheriff.

"How did you know to look for us?" Becky asked.

Flynn looked down at his feet a moment as he chose his words. He didn't want to give false hope to the girl. "Don't want you to get your expectations up, but Cooper was alive and made it town…He was hurt badly and I don't know if he lived. Doc Mosier is as good a doctor as there is…but I don't know if he could save your brother."

Becky covered her mouth in shock. Rita and Nancy joined her. The girls had been so sure that the rest of their family had died that night that the news dumbfounded them.

"Why don't you girls sit down and rest. You look exhausted," Fiona said as she chaperoned them to the bedrolls.

"What are we going to do now?" Bill asked as Fiona rejoined him and the sheriff.

Mason let out a sigh. "As much as I'd like to take a nap right about now, I was thinkin' that Bill and I could take the bodies on in to Fort Worth. I know the sheriff there a little...think he'd take them off our hands. We could get some supplies, then come back here and have a decent meal. Fiona could stay with the girls...The girls and horses need some rest. Hell, all of us could use some rest. We could head home tomorrow mornin'."

"That sounds fine to me," Fiona said.

"Let's get them loaded up," Bill added.

§§§

CHAPTER ELEVEN

The return trip to Jacksboro proved uneventful. As they traveled, Mason had a bad feeling about Cooper. He and Fiona did their best to dampen down expectations in the sisters about their brother's survival.

Some good food and rest had gone a long way in restoring the girls. They were responding to the tragedy as well as could be expected though the sheriff feared a lot of their outlook was based on the assumption that Cooper was still alive.

After Flynn offered to take credit for killing Avery to save the girls from being questioned about the death, Rita had perked up considerably. She acted as if one burden had been lifted from her shoulders.

As they rode in front of the sheriff's office, they found Deputy Platt sitting outside.

"You found them," the deputy said excitedly, jumping to his feet.

"We did. You look hard at it," Sheriff Flynn said.

"I can keep an eye on things from right here. Cooper is sure going to be relieved. Doc Mosier said the only thing holding Cooper back is all the worrying he's doin' over his sisters."

In unison, the girls made an audible gasp.

"He's alive then?" Flynn said in astonishment.

"Sure, he's alive. Dr. Mosier did a heck of a job in saving him. Cooper's as strong as an ox...That's what the doctor said saved him," said Platt.

"Girls, let's go see your brother," Flynn said as he stepped down from Laddie.

The girls followed the sheriff like ducklings in a row to the doctor's office.

Doctor Mosier looked up from his desk as Flynn and the girls entered his office.

"It's about time you got back with those girls. It's a good thing I'm not as slow at saving my patients as you are finding their relatives," the doctor bragged, and then grinned.

Flynn shook his head. "Are you going to take us to him or would you rather sit there and complain all day?"

"Come on ladies. I'm sure you've had your fill of our sheriff," Mosier said as he arose from his seat. He led the girls to the room with their brother.

Cooper was left speechless at the sight of his sisters. The toll the last few days had taken the better of him and he started to cry.

The girls also burst into tears as they surrounded their brother and delicately hugged him.

"Don't fret, girls. I promise to take care of all you," Cooper managed to say.

Freed from the worry over her brother, Becky giggled at the irrational statement. "Looks like we'll be taking care of you for quite some time."

"I guess you have a point there," Cooper said.

"Just as long as you get well," Rita added.

"I'm told that Momma and Daddy got a proper burial," Cooper said.

The girls grew silent at mention of their parents. Flynn and the doctor decided to take their leave and walked back to the front of the building.

"Looks like you did some fine work in saving that boy, Doc," said Flynn.

"And you also in saving those girls. You must have had your hands full."

"Let's just say I hope I don't have to ride for a few days…talk to you later," Flynn said before departing.

§

Flynn walked to the jail where he found Fiona and Bill. Platt had taken the stock to Mom's.

"How are your prisoners?" Mason asked.

"Looks to me as if they're getting fat on jail food. Your deputy must have taken good care of them," Fiona said.

"Speaking of food, believe I promised you both a meal when we got the chance. Let's head to the café…Listen, think I hear a steak calling my name," the sheriff said, cupping his hand to his ear.

"Wondered if you'd remember," Bill said.

"My belly wouldn't let me forget. Want to thank ya'll for all you did. Don't know what I would've done without the both of you," Flynn said.

Deputy Platt walked into the jail. "Mom's taking care of the horses...and mule."

"Come on, Gomer, I'm buying everybody steaks. We've all earned a big juicy one," the sheriff said as he led the way toward the door.

§§§§

About the author

Duane Boehm grew up on a farm outside of Petersburg, Illinois. The two passions he developed early in life were the love of playing guitar and reading books. He eventually moved to a mini-farm outside of Murfreesboro, Tennessee with his wife and replaced planting corn with trees and raising dogs. For a number of years he worked as an IT consultant and eventually became inspired to begin his journey as a novelist.

To date, Duane has written eight Bestselling novels, including all the books in the *Gideon Johann Western Series* and *Where The Wild Horses Roam.*

You can find Duane's books on Amazon:

http://www.amazon.com/Duane-Boehm/e/B00GV0HDQ2/re f=dp_byline_cont_pop_ebooks_1

To learn of future novels by Duane Boehm, like his FaceBook page:
https://www.facebook.com/DuaneBoehmAuthor/
or join his mailing list: http://eepurl.com/Jg0yD

THE BRAZOS

BY

KEN FARMER

CHAPTER ONE

JACK COUNTY, TEXAS

A puff of white smoke appeared from near the top of a limestone ridge on the west side of Rock Creek. The man on a blue roan Morgan gelding fell to the rocky ground as his gray Stetson flew from his head in a cloud of red. A little under a second later, the boom of a long gun echoed up and down the valley from a little over three hundred yards away.

He caught the ball of smoke across the white water creek that tumbled its way into the rugged Brazos River canyon area of Palo Pinto County in the corner of his eye.

THE BRAZOS

His effort to duck was only partially successful as the bullet plowed a deep furrow across the side of his head, just above his ear, instead of in the center of his forehead.

Fourteen years in the United States Army Cavalry and five years as the Sheriff of Jack County had honed Mason Flynn's instinctive reactions to danger to a fine edge. He moved just far enough to save his life.

His limp, unconscious body slid and rolled down the steep slope of the bank, into the boiling, churning water of the creek and was swept downstream. Rock Creek was up due to a recent heavy thunderstorm last night.

The cool water revived him to a degree and he tried to slow his bobbing trip toward the Brazos by grabbing boulders, tree limbs and roots. The current took him to the gravel bottom, and then back to the top like a piece of flotsam.

Most of his blue bib-front shirt was torn away, carrying with it his badge. Not that it mattered much as he was now in Palo Pinto County.

Luckily, his stag-handled .45 Colt Peacemaker was still in his holster, held there by a leather hammer thong.

His gelding whinnied and trotted along the bank, following his master, shaking his head and avoiding stepping on his loose reins.

The man grabbed a limb sticking out of a ten-inch diameter cottonwood tree floating down the creek and pulled himself partially on top of the trunk. The tree had sloughed off into the raging waterway several miles upstream during last night's storm.

The turbulence slackened as the creek neared the high canyon walls on both sides of the wide Brazos. The early Spanish explorers called it the *Rio de los Brazos de Dios* or The River of the Arms of God. It is the 11th-longest river in the United States of America. The Brazos began at Blackwater Draw in New Mexico and emptied into the Gulf of Mexico some 1,280 miles later.

The rugged canyons of the Brazos in Palo Pinto County were typified by hardwood tree-choked bottoms and tall limestone cliffs with numerous caves. The vicinity was popular as a protected hiding area with the early plains Indians and later by outlaws and lawbreakers on the run.

Sheriff Flynn had been tracking a vicious gang of the latter from Wizard Wells where they had robbed the local bank and murdered the bank president, two tellers and a woman customer.

The cottonwood tree trunk ground itself on a sandbar a little over one hundred yards north of the confluence of Rock Creek and the Brazos.

Laddie, his blue roan Morgan gelding, intently watched his master still holding on to the tree from his vantage point on a cliff almost one hundred and fifty feet above the water. He stamped his front left foot on the ground several times and snorted to show his displeasure. He turned and headed along the top of the cliff, downstream.

A barefoot sixteen year old girl, with stringy, dirty blond hair, in a very worn blue calico flour sack dress, waded across the five foot cutoff of the creek between the sand bar and the bank. She squatted beside Flynn and shook his shoulder.

"Mister...You all right?"

Mason didn't move.

Laddie trotted along the top of the cliff until he found a game trail that led down to the river. He worked his way down the steep narrow trail as it zigzagged its way to the bottom, sliding much of the way on his hocks.

"Mister! Wake up." She shook his shoulder harder.

Flynn groaned and raised his head slightly to look at the greenest eyes he'd ever seen. "Huh?...Who...who are you?"

"I'm Lisanne. What's yer name?"

"Uh, give me a second..."

He placed his hand to the side of his head, and then looked at the sticky, clotted blood on his fingers when he pulled it away. "Ow."

Lisanne grabbed his right arm and attempted to pull him further up on the sandbar, but, his muscular two hundred and ten pounds were too heavy for her. "You have to help me git you outta the water."

"Don't know if I can…dizzy." He slumped down back on the log as he passed out again.

Lisanne turned and saw the blue roan pounding along the sandy bank directly at her. He was slinging his head from side to side and snorting. He reached the pair, stopped, reared and squealed as he pawed the air with his front feet only six inches from her face.

She held up one hand and said in a soothing, melodious voice, "Oh, now, stop that. I'm tryin' to help him."

Laddie stopped and extended his nose toward the girl as she held out her right hand, palm down and her fingers curled slightly. The horse sniffed of the back of her fingers, and then snuffled as she made kissing sounds.

"Thank you."

She saw the braided rawhide riata attached by a leather saddle string to the right side, took it loose and slipped the loop over Flynn's head and under his arms.

THE BRAZOS

After taking a dally around the saddle horn, she held on to the end with her left hand and put her right fingertips on Laddie's shoulder. "Back, back up, boy."

The gelding obediently tucked his muzzle to his chest and backed away from the log, pulling Flynn out to the middle of the sand bar. "Whoa, boy. That's good."

Lisanne pulled some slack in the loop and slipped the lasso back over Flynn's head as his eyes fluttered, and then opened again. He looked at her, at Laddie, then at her again.

"How'd you do that?

"What?"

"You got my hors…Ahhh." He put his hand to his head again. "You got my horse, Laddie, to pull me outta the water…He don't let nobody, but me touch him…God, my head hurts."

"He likes me…Who are you?"

He squinted and looked up at her again. "I'm…I'm…Dang…I don't know." He rubbed his forehead with his fingertips.

ROCK CREEK

"You sure you got him, Bittercreek?" asked Jubal as he poured some of the stout trail brew he had made into a tin cup. He set the pot back on a flat rock next to the medium-sized fire just inside the entrance to a shallow cave less than a hundred yards from Rock Creek.

"Shore, Jubal. Seen a cloud of red come from his head 'bout a half second after I squeezed the trigger on this here Sharps. "No man alive kin take a head shot from my buffler gun and tell the tale...Plus, blowed him plumb outta the saddle an' he slid down the bank an' into the Rock...His body'll wind up in the gulf, I'd say...What's left after the snappin' turtles an' alligator gar git 'im."

"Yeah, damn lawdog's been close enough on our tail to sprinkle salt on it since we passed Jacksboro."

"Think we oughta git a bit deeper into the Brazos canyon, jest in case 'nbody else comes a trackin' us...like say a ranger or a Deputy U.S. Marshal. Hear tell that sheriff is tight with a few," said Bittercreek.

BRAZOS CANYON

"You mean you don't know your own name?" asked Lisanne.

He started to shake his head, then thought better of it. "I know my horse's name an'..." Flynn looked around their location. "...an' I make this to be the entrance to the Brazos canyon…But, I couldn't tell you my name if'n you held a gun on me." He furrowed his forehead again. "An' 'sides, what's a young girl like you doin' in this wilderness?"

Lisanne looked at her bare feet for a moment before she finally replied, "It's kind of a long story…Say, we better get you off this sandbar. Whoever shot you might come alookin' for your body."

"Might have a point there, missy. Where do we go?"

"How do you feel? Up to a short walk?"

"Depends on how short. I got dizziness comin' an' goin', 'long with a little dyspepsia."

"Does that mean sick to your stomach?"

He nodded.

"You lead your horse…"

"No need. Just wrap his reins around the saddlehorn an' he'll follow wherever we go…Be right behind you."

"That's good…The worst part will be climbin' the game trail up that steep bank…Gotta get to the top. Probably how he got down here." She looked at Laddie.

"Wonderful…Tell you what do. You show the way, I'll hold on to Laddie's tail an' let him pull me up…If I pass out, just stop till I wake back up."

"Try not to do that."

"Do my best."

When they reached the top, she looked back to check on him. "Gonna make it?"

"How much further?" he asked as he leaned over with his hands on his knees and threw up.

"Not far.

He moaned and rubbed his forehead. "That's a good thing. Bein' shot in the head can give you a whale of a headache."

She led on down the narrow game trail that paralleled the ridge top, and then turned in toward a mixed copse of cedar and persimmon trees that grew up against the cliff facing.

Weaving their way through the trees, Lisanne disappeared into an irregular shaped dark opening over six feet across and eight feet high. She picked up a coal oil chimney lamp with the wick barely glowing, turned it up, and held it high.

"Come on in."

"What about Laddie?"

"There's plenty of room for him too, plus a small pool fed by a spring toward the back."

Flynn stepped in, followed by the Morgan. He looked around and up at the ceiling that arched up to almost twenty feet. There were stalactites and soda straws hanging down. Fifteen feet from the entrance was the pool at the base of a bacon flow of travertine.

In the back, at the edge of the light from the lamp, she had two racks made of willow limbs with meat strips on one and fish on the other hanging above a slow smoking fire of hickory and pecan deadfall and blowdown. The meat smoking for jerky was mostly rabbit and squirrel with a couple of long strips hanging down that appeared to be snake.

A cooking fire pit was closer to the front with a rolled up bundle of blankets over against the side.

"All the comforts of home...Ahhh." Flynn sunk to his knees and held his head.

"Let's get you laid down so I can clean that bullet graze."

Lisanne helped him to his feet and over to her bedroll, undid it and got him to lay down. She grabbed a piece of cloth from a sack, wet it at the pool, wiped the clotted blood out of his hair and rubbed some lard-based salve on the wound.

"Ow, ow, ow."

"There, it's clean now and that salve will protect it...You're a lucky feller. Just a mite deeper and you wouldn't be here...How're you feelin'?"

"Still a bit dizzy an' keep seein' two of you."

"Might have cracked your skull a little."

"Meby…I'm purty hardheaded, though…Say, you never told me what you're doin' out here…You an orphan or a runaway?" Flynn looked her in her green eyes.

She turned away, stared out the opening for a moment, and then replied, "I had to run off from my step-daddy."

"He beatin' you?"

Lisanne returned his hard gaze with her own and set her jaw. "No."

"Oh…I see."

§§§

CHAPTER TWO

BRAZOS CANYON

A middle-aged man in filthy blue denim bib overalls and wearing a battered brown fedora, worked his way along a game trail on the east side of the Brazos. He was riding bareback on a red mule, with a single-shot 10 gauge across his thighs.

He spat a stream of amber tobacco juice at a persimmon tree growing along the side of the trail. The heavily stained sleeve of his once-white boiled shirt was handy to wipe the spittle from the five day stubble on his chin.

"Damn worthless little split-tail...Ol' Anse'll find ye. Count on it." He spat again. "I'll not be deprived my due."

Anse stopped, slid off the mule, knelt down and examined the packed earth of the trail. He pulled the filthy hat from his sweaty, balding head and grinned, showing his gapped tobacco-stained teeth. "Uh-huh, been along this here trail since the rain, ain't cha?"

There was just a trace of five little toes showing of a partial footprint.

"Runnin' from or to somethin'," the odoriferous former mountain man and army scout mumbled as he looked from the track on down the trail. "Where, oh where, has my little girl gone? Oh, where oh, where can she be?" he grinned and sang softly out of tune, as he moved along the narrow trail, searching for additional sign. "Gonna find you."

CAVE ON THE BRAZOS

Lisanne built a small hat-sized cooking fire of dry wood about ten feet inside the mouth of the cave. The smoke collected at the ceiling and worked its way to the outside through a narrow crack in the limestone overhead.

She put a battered old tin pot on a flat rock next to the fire beside an equally battered coffee pot.

"Have some coffee in a bit, plus some rabbit broth," said Lisanne.

"Coffee sounds good. Maybe it'll help this headache of mine," commented Flynn. "An' don't believe I ever had rabbit broth...'course in my present state, cain't guarantee that."

"Do you remember what you were doin' up on that ridge above Rock Creek?"

"Nope, don't remember that either...Seems like I was trackin' two men horsebackin', but cain't for the life of me tell you why."

"Well, think you'd best stay inside here. Don't believe it would be too smart takin' on a couple of fellers who done tried to kill you."

"Point."

"Already pulled your tack from Laddie an' gave him a bait of grain outta that bag you had tied to your saddle...That all right?"

"Shore. Try to always take good care of him. He's my best friend."

"I gotta go out an' check my traps an' trotline. Don't have no gun, so big game like deer is kinda out of the question...Also gotta cover any sign we left."

He nodded. "Reckon that coffee's ready?"

She grabbed a rag and lifted the pot away from the fire for a moment, and then set it back down. "Needs to come to a boil one more time, then it'll be ready…Won't take long. Got a cup in your saddlebags?"

"Should." He moved to get up, groaned, sat back down and put his hands to the sides of his head. "Mistake."

Lisanne opened his saddlebags and came up with a blue speckled graniteware cup. "Looky here…Oh, and here's a spare shirt you musta packed." She handed him the cup and the clean, faded red bib-front shirt.

"Just what the doctor ordered…both of 'em." He took the shirt, slipped it over his head and slightly dragged it across the wound. "Ow, ow…Dang. "

Flynn buttoned the flap three-quarters of the way up and tucked it into his pants. "Well, almost feel human."

She checked the pot again. "All right, that should do it…Hold out your cup." After she filled it, she set the pot back down a little further from the fire to keep it from boiling again, but still keep it hot. "Enjoy your coffee and I'll be back in a bit."

He smelled the stout trail brew, licked the rim of his cup, blew across the surface, and then took a sip. "Mmm, nectar of the gods."

THE BRAZOS

Anse reined his mule to a stop and lifted his nose a little higher in the air. "Smoke, Ol' Ted...I smell smoke."

He looked around the woods trying to spot a telltale tendril above the trees—nothing. Holding up his finger after wetting it with saliva, he tested the wind. *From the southwest.* He went that direction hoping the smell would get stronger.

After a few hundred yards, he sniffed again. "Damnation! Wind shifted...Fergot it does that here in the canyons. Be a puredee accident I was to find where's it's a comin' from down here."

He rode a little further along the narrow trail and stopped the mule again. "Coffee! Got coffee with the smoke this time...Believe it's thataway, ol' son."

He nudged Ted forward fifty yards when two rough-looking men stepped out of the brush from each side of the trail. Each held a Winchester at his hip, pointed in the general vicinity of his chest.

"Who the hell are you an' what 'er you adoin' down here?" asked Bittercreek Rudabaugh.

Anse held up both hands leaving his shotgun balanced across his legs and spat a stream of tobacco juice into some whoa vines at the side of the trail. "Hey, hey, fellers. Jest doin' a little huntin's all."

"He asked who you wuz, Pilgrim…an' he's been knowed to git a mite testy when folks don't do as he says," said Jubal Atz.

"It be Anse…Anse Hulbert, an' like I said…jest huntin'."

"Huntin' what?" asked Jubal.

"Well, see, that's the thing. I'm ahuntin' my daughter. She be sixteen an' done run off on me."

"You tryin' to git a little poke in, were ye?" commented Bittercreek. "Yer own daughter?"

"Looky here, it ain't like she's really my own flesh an' blood. She wuz my wife's 'fore we hooked up…Makes her my stepdaughter…I reckon. Her mama died of the consumption, God rest her pore soul…The girl wadn't but nine year old at the time. Had to raise her my own self…Figure I be due…'Sides she stole some of my traps an' all my coffee."

"So you was gonna break 'er in proper, wuz ye?" said Jubal. He glanced over at his partner. "Man after my own heart, Bittercreek."

Rudabaugh grinned. "I'd say…Why don't you git down from that plow mule an' foller us to our camp. Woods is too thick to ride through…We gots some coffee on."

"Thought I smelt Arbuckle back yonder. Made my mouth water."

"Come on, then," said Jubal.

THE BRAZOS

Anse slid off Ted. "Damn razorbacked, jugheaded mule is rough as a cob anyhoo...Say, you fellers on the scout, air ye?"

"I'd be a mite careful askin' questions, Pilgrim. Might git you in a world of hurt...bein' nosey, like that," responded Jubal.

"Naw, naw, now looky here, wadn't bein' nosey. Hell, on the dodge my own self."

"Oh, yeah? Fer what?" asked Bittercreek.

"Well, let's jest say I got real tired of a particular cavalry officer a bossin' me 'round."

"So, you're a deserter, then?" said Jubal.

"In a manner of speakin'...Wanted me to scout out a band of renegade Comanch to see if'n they had guards posted 'round their camp...Hell, one thang you don't do is sneak up on a Comanch at night...an' live to tell 'bout it." He spat off into some bushes. "Jest never went back that night...Headed fer the Brazos...Been here ever since...Goin' on seven year."

They broke into a small clearing in the thick brush with a stream running through it.

"Picket yer mule down yonder near that branch with our horses. They's plenty graze and water fer 'em," said Bittercreek. "Bring yer cup."

Lisanne stepped into the cave carrying a dead cottontail by its back feet, three blue catfish on a willow stringer and a gray Stetson.

"Looks like we got fish for supper," commented Flynn, as he looked up from his pallet. "Hey, you found my hat."

"Nice ones, ain't they? 'Bout three pounds each, I mind," she replied as she handed him his hat. "This was up creek a ways from that sandbar…Musta been 'bout where you got shot."

In the hand with the rabbit, was the tattered remains of a blue bib-front shirt. She laid the rabbit down, held the torn garment up and turned it over to show the five-pointed, silver star pinned to it. "This yours? Found it downstream a ways, hung on a partially sunk log near my trotline."

"Huh…I 'spect so…It's like this'un, 'cept a different color."

Lisanne handed it to him.

He turned it over, and then looked closely at the badge. "Well, what do you know? Sheriff's badge…Jack County. Reckon I was right 'bout tailin' two men…Wonder what they done?"

"You mean besides shootin' you?"

"I 'spect that's why they shot me…on account I was trailin' 'em."

"Makes sense."

"Now if I can just remember why."

"Maybe it'll come to you soon."

"Probably not till this headache goes away."

"Next time I go out I'll bring back some white willow bark an' brew you up some tea…It'll help the pain."

She added a couple of pieces of dry driftwood to the fire. "Seen my step-daddy when I was runnin' my trapline…He's lookin' for me again."

"He see you?"

Lisanne shook her head. "I'm real careful, plus he always rides his mule down here…Can hear him comin' a mile away. He's lookin' for tracks."

Flynn nodded. "Noticed you brushin' our tracks away…even Laddie's."

"Uh, huh, I been doin' better at coverin' my sign than he has findin' it…There was a scent of coffee brewin' in the air, wasn't ours, that he went off followin'."

"Musta been those two what shot me."

"I followed him a ways. He crossed to the west side of Rock Creek at a rock-bottomed ford, near where it flows into the Brazos…The wrong side for us…Sometimes I leave a false trail to confuse him. Figure he'll eventually quit tryin'."

"Then what?"

"Then I reckon I'll go to Fort Worth or maybe Waco and try to find work."

"Well, I have to say I'm impressed with your resourcefulness…What would you do?"

"Not sure. Just know I don't want to work in no saloon."

"Good thinkin'…Have you had much education?"

"My step-daddy made me quit goin' in the seventh grade. Said I had to stay home and work the garden, if we was goin' to eat…but, I've read everythin' I could get my hands on…The Bible three times."

"I mind you might get work as a housekeeper or a nanny…or considerin' how you handled Laddie, you could get a job on a ranch, breakin' horses…Injun style."

"Horses an' me get along for some reason…What's a nanny?"

"Someone who takes care of children for wealthy folk."

"I could do that. Took care of my little brother till he was six…" Lisanne stared at the fire for a moment as a black cloud seemed to pass over her face. "…died of the pox."

"Oh, I'm really sorry, Lisanne." Flynn paused for a moment as he too stared at the fire. "What does your step-daddy do?"

"Traps, mostly. Sells the skins down to Brad or over to Graford. Both are 'bout seven or eight miles from the farm…It become his when Mama died."

"So, they had a marriage ceremony?"

She shook her head. "Well, not that I know of. Just lived together...an' he said that they was married."

"Well, if that's the case, he doesn't own it...You do."

"I do?"

Flynn nodded. "Yep, that's the law. In the absence of a legal wedding or a will, any property goes to the closest next of kin...That'd be you, I'd say...What happened to your real daddy?"

Lisanne shook her head. "Mama said he was killed tryin' to stop some bank robbers in Graford when I was about seven...She took up with my step-papa when I was eight."

"Sounds like your daddy was a good man...Do you know the size of your place?"

She nodded. "Mama said it started out as a 160 acre homestead an' then my real daddy planted forty acres of pine trees a couple times. Then he planted forty acres of pecan an' the government give him another 480 acres all told."

"Yeah, called the Timber Culture Act...My, my, you own 640 acres. That's a full section of land You're a wealthy young woman...You own a square mile of Texas."

She frowned and looked down at her bare feet. "Don't make any difference. My step-daddy won't never leave."

"Might not have any choice...Where 'bouts is it located?"

"Near 'bouts five mile west of Perrin...Makes it twelve mile or so from here."

"Perrin, Perrin...That's in Jack County. Well, well...now, if I'm the sheriff, I can see to it that he leaves."

"How is it you know all this stuff...Your horse's name, where Perrin is located, facts 'bout the law an' such, an' you can't remember your own name?"

Flynn chuckled. "I 'spect if'n I could tell you that, I'd know my name...What's your step-daddy go by?"

"Anse...Anse Hulbert. He's 'bout your age or maybe a shade older."

"Anse Hulbert...Huh?" He furrowed his brow and rubbed his temples. "Dang, sounds familiar. Meby I seen a wanted dodger on him or somethin'. Could be it'll come to me when my own name does...*If* it does."

§§§

CHAPTER THREE

BRAZOS CANYON

"What else you done?" asked Bittercreek after he took a sip of his coffee.

"Oh, not too much. Jest enough to keep body an' soul together," replied Anse.

"Like, say rustlin' an' such?" asked Jubal.

"Like I said, jest enough to keep body an' soul together, plus a little extry food on the table...Why?

"Oh, mind we could use a feller with yer skills who knows the country an' all," said Jubal.

Anse sat down cross-legged on the ground and took a sip of the stout trail brew. "Know this country all the way to the cap rock like the back of my own hand."

"Uh, huh...that's what we mean," commented Bittercreek.

"I jest make it a practice of not crappin' too close to the house...like my old daddy used to say." He spat a stream of tobacco juice into the fire where it sizzled on a burning limb. "What you fellers got in mind?"

Jubal glanced at Bittercreek. "Well, since we done taken care of that war hoss of a sheriff outta Jacksboro, figure it might be a good time to make hay...so to speak...'fore they kin git 'round to holdin' a 'lection fer a new one."

CAVE ON THE BRAZOS

Flynn raised up on his elbow and looked around the cave. "I've been unconscious, haven't I?"

"More like just asleep, I'd call it...You slept the night through and most of the day."

He glanced at the opening. "You mean I've been out for almost twenty-four hours?"

"Uh, huh...You laid down after I fixed you that willow tea an' slept like a baby...Figured you needed it."

She handed him a bowl of rabbit stew. "Here, this should give you some strength... 'Member your name yet?"

He took the bowl and sipped a bit of it. "Nope... Say this ain't too bad, Lisanne... By the way do you use your step-daddy's last name or your real daddy's?"

"Mama always wanted me to use my real daddy's name, Gifford. His name was Hank Gifford."

"I heard tell of him when he stopped that bank robbery you mentioned in Graford. Killed two of the robbers 'fore they got him. Kept a bunch of folk from gettin' hurt at the bank... He was a real hero. The robbers lit a shuck when he started shootin' at 'em... One of the miscreants got in a lucky shot while they were ridin' outta town."

"Now see, there you go again."

He furrowed his brow. "Go again, what?"

"Rememberin' some things an' not rememberin' your own name... Makes no sense at all to me."

"Me neither. They say nobody really understands what goes on inside our heads... You know, intuition, dreams an' such?"

"Suppose so. Just wish I had somethin' to call you besides Mister."

"Well, how's 'bout you call me... Dixon?" He took another spoonful of the stew.

"Dixon? Where'd that come from?"

"Beats me. Just kinda popped in my head while we were talkin'."

She added some more blowdown wood to the fire, sending up a shower of sparks toward the ceiling. "All right, you say so…But, that's kinda scary if you ask me."

SHERIFF'S OFFICE
JACKSBORO, TEXAS

"This ain't like the sheriff," said Deputy Gomer Platt.

"What's that?" replied Chickasaw Freedman, Deputy Slim Parker.

"He don't never take over a day to track down yahoos like what robbed the bank over to Wizard Wells…Ain't like him, ain't like him atall." Platt pulled his feet from the top of the desk and rocked his bow chair back to the floor.

"Reckon we ought to call Marshal Miller over to Gainesville?"

"I do…Yer closer to the box, you call her. 'Spect she's at Sheriff Durbin's office or he can git 'er."

Deputy Parker got to his feet, stepped over to the square oak box with a cone-like black metal mouthpiece on the front and two metal clapper bells at the top. A black bakelite earpiece hung on a hook at the side and there was a hand-crank on the other.

He picked up the earpiece and turned the crank three times.

"Whatcha need, Slim?"

"How'd you know it was me, Miz Mabel?"

"On account of I know that Gomer is still afraid to use the telephone...scared he'll break it. Now, who do you need?"

"Ring Sheriff Durbin's office over to Gainesville, if you would, Ma'am."

"Just a second." She moved some plugs on her board. "Alright, he's on the line."

"Sheriff Durbin," Slim shouted into the mouthpiece. "...is Marshal Miller about?"

"She just happens to be sittin' right here, Slim."

"Kin I talk to her?"

"Why didn't you say so in the first place?"

"Uh..."

"Never mind, here she is." Durbin handed the receiver to Fiona. "Deputy Parker over to Jacksboro."

"I figured that out, Walt." She grinned. "Deputy Parker, how may I help you?"

"Marshal, we're kindly concerned 'bout Sheriff Flynn. He's a mite bit overdue gittin' back to town. He took out two days ago trailin' a couple nabobs what robbed the bank an' shot some folks over to Wizard Wells…fetched 'em dead, they did," Slim shouted into the mouthpiece.

Fiona held the receiver away from her ear. "I'll head over that way this afternoon, Deputy…and you don't have to shout."

"Yessum, it's jest that Gainesville's a purty good ways from Jacksboro," he shouted.

She shook her head and grinned again. "I'll be there tomorrow. Which way did they go?"

"Southwest…t'wards the Brazos."

"I understand. Good bye."

She quickly hung the receiver back on its hook and rubbed her ear before Slim could respond and grinned at Walt.

"How you gonna git to Jacksboro by tomorrow?" asked Walt.

"Take the train to Ringgold this afternoon, and then head south to Jacksboro on Spot. Camp out around Puddin Valley and I should get there by noon or so, I expect."

Sheriff Durbin nodded. "That'll work."

CAVE ON THE BRAZOS

"How are you feelin'?…Still gettin' dizzy?"

Flynn looked up at Lisanne from staring at the fire. "Headache's not near as bad…reckon that willow tea of yours is helpin'. Only get dizzy when I try to stand too quick…But, still cain't remember my name."

"Think that maybe we ought to get you to Jacksboro an' have Doc Mosier have a look at you."

"You know the doc?"

She nodded. "He tried to help mama when she had the consumption."

"He's good. But, there's not much anybody can do once someone gets that stuff."

"Nope…nor the pox neither."

"Yeah, he told me one time that ten percent of doctor's patients die…They cure ten percent…an' eighty percent get well in spite of them."

Lisanne cocked her eyebrow at him. "Not really?"

"What he said an' I 'spect he's fair close to bein' right…He's patched me up a time or two. Probably a good idea for him to check my melon…Maybe he won't find anything." He winked at her.

She paused for a moment. "Oh, that's funny. Have you ever thought about goin' on the Chautauqua circuit?"

"No, but I was asked to do a minstrel show once, but the black-face makeup was too hard to get off...When do you want to go?"

She shook her head and grinned. "Most anytime, I reckon...Think Laddie will carry both of us?"

"Oh, I think so. He's taken a bit of a shine to you...'sides you won't weigh a hunderd pounds soakin' wet an' with rocks in your pockets."

"Well, I expect we'll have to keep him at a walk...Shakin' about at a canter or especially a trot won't do you much good."

"Think I'll probably have to agree with you on that...It will take us a couple of days then, I would wager," said Flynn.

SANTA FE DEPOT
RINGGOLD, TEXAS

Fiona stood at the bottom of the cleated ramp as the station hostler led her red and white Tobiano mule down.

She rubbed the faithful animal's forehead. "See, that short trip wasn't too bad, was it, Spot?"

He nuzzled the side of her face.

She handed the hostler a silver dollar, moved to the mule's left side, snugged his girth, and then stepped up easily into the Texas style double-skirted saddle.

"Thank you for taking good care of Spot," she said to the hostler.

He looked at the silver coin in his hand and nodded. "Yessum...an' thank you."

Fiona turned the mule to the south and nudged him into his smooth-as-silk single foot. She glanced to the west, where the sun was casting long shadows as it neared the horizon. "I expect we can get eight or nine miles in before we need to make camp for the evening, don't you, Spot?"

The big smooth-moving mule flicked his long ears back at her as she spoke, and then forward again.

Three rough-looking, itinerant cowboys were loitering under a large red oak. Two smoking a quirly and one with a large chaw in his cheek, watched her trot away from the station to the south.

"Well now, that looks interestin'," said the tall one of the bunch. "Ya'll a thinkin' what I am?"

"You beat me to it, Rankin. Looks like that split-tail is a goin' to do some horsebackin', or in her case, mulebackin', all by her lonesome to git where she's a goin'," said

Stubby—his name fit his countenance. He pitched what was left of his smoke to the ground and crushed it with his heel.

"Ya'll awaitin' on me, yer abackin' up...since we been pissin' up a rope tryin' to git on at some of these ranches 'round here an' most of 'em 're keep guards on the herds, anyway," said skinny-as-a-rail, Dollar, the third of the bunch, as he spat a long stream of amber tobacco juice at the base of the tree.

The three cowboys moved to their horses, mounted, and followed Fiona at a safe distance out of the small north Texas agrarian community.

SOUTHERN JACK COUNTY

The sun was setting as they pulled rein at the edge of Salt Creek. Lisanne looked around.

"This is the western edge of the property you said I own." She slid off Laddie's rump to the ground.

"You reckon your step-daddy is to home? The house 'bout a mile thataway?" Flynn pointed east.

"No an' yes...'Peared he was gonna spend the night at them two feller's camp when I snuck a peek. Couldn't hear what they were talkin' 'bout, but looked like they was gonna make a night of it...They had some whiskey."

172

"Well, that's a good thing...for us," said Flynn. "Don't think I'm ready for a dustup just yet."

"You feel like gatherin' up some deadfall?"

He grinned and headed toward some trees. "Won't know till I try."

After sundown and some beans and fatback from Flynn's saddlebags, they sat around the small fire having coffee.

Flynn looked upstream northwest and saw the glow of a campfire. "Looks like we got some neighbors campin' up the creek a couple of miles."

"Probably some cowboys. They run a right smart of cattle on that place to the west."

"Judging from what I've seen here, you could run at least a cow an' calf to three acres. Got plenty graze an' year 'round water."

"Goodness! That would be right at...two hundred head of mama cows."

"'Nuff to make a good livin'. Now that the railroad is close, cattle are goin' for 'round thirty dollars a head...Should be able to send at least eighty steers an' heifers to private markets or the feed yard an' keep twenty or so replacements per year...if you set up a good breedin' program."

"What about raisin' horses instead of mama cows?"

"Well, if you get some blooded stock, a good saddle horse will bring seventy-five dollars to a hundred or more…Would't have to run near as many head."

SALT CREEK

"'Pears as though we got some neighbors," said Jubal as he looked to the southeast at the glow of a small campfire.

"That looks to be on my property…Meby oughta go take a gander at 'em," said Anse as he got to his feet.

Bittercreek pulled a bottle of bonded rye from his saddlebags. "Go right on ahead. Me an' Jubal 'er agonna test this high-dollar whiskey whilst yer gone…I mind it's jest some punchers lookin' fer stragglers, anyhoo."

Hulbert glanced off to the southeast at the tiny flickering pale glow, and then back at the full bottle of whiskey Bittercreek was pulling the cork from. "'Spect you got a point there," he said as he pitched the remains of his coffee off to the side and held his cup out…

§§§

CHAPTER FOUR

NORTHERN JACK COUNTY

"Something tells me we're not alone, Spot." Fiona turned in the saddle an studied her back trail. "Too many mesquite, scrub oak and persimmon trees…No dust."

Her Tobiano mule flicked his ears again, never breaking his smooth as silk natural singlefoot.

She rounded a bend in the trail and quickly reined to her left, up a hill. Once at the top, Fiona scanned behind her for a much further distance than she could down on the trail.

Nothing...But my instincts and the hairs on the back of my neck tell me different.

She looked to the west as the sun disappeared behind the low-lying scattered trees casting long red streaks through the high cirrus clouds and creating silver linings. "Guess we'll camp up ahead at Puddin Valley Creek...should merge with Lodge Creek further south...You keep those big ears tuned, son...There's somebody back there."

Dollar raised up in his saddle, spat a stream of tobacco juice in the dirt of the trail and studied the narrow ranch road headed south toward Jacksboro. Then he scanned the little-used trail at their feet.

"See 'nythin'?" asked Rankin.

He shook his head. "Too many turns in the road 'tween here an' the creek..." He pointed down. "But, see them tracks there? They's mule tracks...Lots more narrow than a horse. We still on her trail."

"Betcha she camps down to the creek. Gittin' close to evenin'," said Stubby.

The sun had set and the gloaming had given way to moonless darkness. Fiona leaned back against her saddle and sipped on her after-supper coffee.

THE BRAZOS

She had trained Spot to roam free around the campsite at night, taking advantage of the best grazing. Fiona knew he wouldn't go far and was as good as any dog at being aware of potential danger around the camp—four or two legged.

After pitching the remains of her coffee in the fire, where it sizzled on a burning piece of deadfall, she rolled up in her soogan and looked at the myriad stars overhead that resembled millions of tiny campfires. A soft smile crept across her face in the darkness as she listened to Spot crop the lush grass along the creek bank before she drifted off to sleep.

Her eyes snapped open when she heard the mule stop grazing and snort. She kept still, but wrapped her hand around the grip of one of her .38-40 Peacemakers.

The dying camp fire was casting eerie flickering shadows against the nearby edge of the woods.

Abruptly, Spot charged into the brush at the edge of the camp with his ears laid back. Fiona sat up as she watched him disappear into the darkness.

Terrified, almost woman-like, screams and screeches pierced the stillness of the night. They were accompanied by the sound of panicked men running through the thick woods, followed by Spot's pounding hooves.

Fiona got to her feet, stirred the fire and added a couple of pieces of driftwood left over from the last high water on Puddin Creek. "Well, guess that'll break them from trying to sneak into the hen house…for awhile, anyway."

She chuckled as she looked up when Spot trotted back into the light being cast by the renewed campfire. "Good job, son…Believe I'll warm up the coffee. That was too funny for me to go back to sleep for a while."

"Ow, ow, ow, Jesus H. Christ," Stubby exclaimed as Rankin poured a little of their whiskey on a large wound on the back of his left shoulder.

"That mule took a hellova plug outta you, Stub, yessir, a hellova plug," commented Dollar.

"Weren't no mule, jughead, it was a puredee demon from the fires of hades itself…Ow, dammit," Stubby glared up at Rankin.

"Well, either I sew it up now, er you kin wait till t'morrow when it's all swole up an' even more sore an' have the doc in Jacksboro do it…Yer choice," said Rankin as he held up a large leather needle threaded with deer sinew.

"Leastwise he won't be a usin' a railroad spike an' lariat rope," answered Stubby.

Dollar looked at him an' took a pull from the bottle. "How do you know? Ol' Doc Mosier jest might. Hear tell he's salty as the underside of a saddle blanket."

Stubby nodded and reached for the bottle. "Probably right...Jest let me have a touch of that who-hit-John to dull the pain."

"Want it on the inside er the outside?" asked Dollar.

"Think I'd jest as soon have it on the inside...all the same to you."

"I git some more, too. That damn painted devil kicked me in the side whilst he was a bitin' you...'Spect they's a couple broke ribs," said Rankin.

"What about that split-tail?" asked Dollar.

"Looks like she's headin' to Jacksboro...There'll be a time when she ain't 'round that devil mule of hers," said Rankin, with a sneer.

SOUTHERN JACK COUNTY

Flynn rolled over in his blanket at the smell of fresh brewed coffee and sizzling fatback in a skillet. "Mmm, smells good."

He looked off to the east at the red clouds that preceded the sun breaking the horizon. "'Like a red morn that ever yet betokened, Wreck to the seaman, tempest to the field,

Sorrow to the shepherds, woe unto the birds, Gusts and foul flaws to herdmen and to herds.'...That english feller, Shakespeare wrote that in a..."

"A poem called *Venus and Adonis*. Means there's goin' to be a storm before nightfall."

"Thought you said yer step-daddy made you quit school in the seventh grade?"

"Did, but I also said I read everything I can get my hands on. One of the books my real daddy had was the complete works of Shakespeare." Lisanne paused and stared at the fire a moment. "My step-daddy burned it. Said I spent too much time reading."

"Dang! Burnin' a book...any book, oughta be a crime in itself."

"Uh, huh, I agree...but, there you go again, you can quote Shakespeare word for word, an' can't remember your own name...Just makes no sense."

"I know. Seems like it's almost on the tip of my tongue an' then it's gone."

"Yeah...How're you feelin' this mornin?"

"Got a bit of a headache again. Too bad you don't have any of that willow tea."

"Look down to the creek bank. What do you see?"

Flynn looked over his shoulder at the waterway. "Huh?...Willows."

"I'll go down an' peel off some of the bark from the smaller branches...You can chew on it after we break camp an' head north."

"Reckon that'll work...Now, how 'bout a cup of that coffee? Might do as much good as anythin'."

She filled his graniteware cup and handed it to him after he'd sat up on his soogan. "It's a good thing you don't want any sugar in it, 'cause neither one of us had any."

"Wouldn't want to ruin it, anyhow." He blew across the surface and licked the edge of the cup before he took a sip. "Mmm, good."

A movement at the edge of camp caught his eye. He turned to see a large yellow dog watching him with his head cocked. "Well, who are you?"

Lisanne followed his glance. "Barney!"

"You know him?"

"He's my dog. Raised him from a pup...How did you find me, boy?"

Barney walked directly to her, every part of his body was wagging along with his bushy tail. He raised up almost five feet from Lisanne and walked the rest of the way erect on his hind legs, and then pressed the top of his head against her chest.

She hugged her faithful dog. "Oh, I missed you, too."

There was a piece of cotton clothesline rope hanging from his neck. "The bastard tied you up, didn't he?" She held up the loose end. "Chewed his way free."

"I'd say," commented Flynn. "What kind of dog is he?"

"The housewares drummer that gave him to me said he was what they call a Labrador Retriever. His female had nine pups. He was lookin' for good homes for 'em."

"Let me guess, your step-daddy didn't care much for the idea."

She shook her head. "Uh, uh, said he'd eat too much. That's when I started trappin' rabbits an' such."

JACKSBORO, TEXAS
MOM TUCKER'S LIVERY

"Marshal Miller…" said Mom as she pulled her corncob pipe from her mouth. "…good to see you. What brings you to our fair city?"

Fiona dismounted as Mom got up from her slat-back rocker beside the open double-wide alleyway of her livery barn.

"Got a call from Deputy Parker that Mason was overdue from chasing a couple of bank robbers and murderers from over at Wizard Wells…Said it wasn't like him to take this much time."

Mom pulled on her pipe and noticed it had gone out. She tapped the bowl on the heel of her boot, knocking the ashes out, and then stuck it back in the front bib of her overalls.

"Slim's right as rain on that. If anything, the sheriff is efficient at trackin' down ne'er-do-wells…as you well know…He didn't take 'nythin' more that what was in his saddlebags, in the way of supplies when he picked up Laddie."

"That tells me he wasn't figurin' on being gone long."

"My thoughts exactly…Want me to feed, water an' brush down Spot 'fore you hit the trail lookin' fer 'im?"

"Be a good idea, Mom. Give him an extra bait of grain…He earned it last night."

"Oh? What'd he do? Run some varmints off, did he?"

Fiona grinned. "Could say that."

"Haircut, git out here," Mom Tucker yelled at her son.

"What do you need, Mom?" asked the straw-headed teenager as he poked his head out of the alleyway.

"Take care of Marshal Miller's mule here. He knows you."

"Yessum." He took the reins from Fiona and led Spot inside.

"Thank you, Haircut." She turned back to Mom. "Do you think Deputies Platt and Parker are at the office?"

Mom pulled out her pocket watch from her overalls and popped the lid. "Nope, purtnear noon...They'll be down to Sewel's Cafe havin' the blue-plate special. Hell would freeze over before them two would miss a meal...'specially one fixed by Ruth Ann Sewel an' served by her sister, Molly."

"Oh, I remember...Outstanding victuals."

SEWEL'S CAFE

Fiona opened the nine-foot tall front door, ringing a two-inch brass bell attached to the header.

"Come right in...Oh, Marshal Miller. Guess you're looking for the deputies. They're right over yonder against the far wall...Can I bring you something?"

"What's the blue-plate today, Molly?"

"Meat loaf, corn on the cob, fried okra, smashed taters and fresh yeast rolls."

"Sounds good...Bring me a glass of iced tea, also, if you would."

"Sweet with a sprig of mint, right?"

Fiona smiled. "Excellent memory, Molly."

"It's my job, Marshal," she said over her shoulder with a smile as she headed for the kitchen.

Fiona pulled out a chair at the deputy's table, startling both men. They jumped to their feet. Gomer knocked his chair over in the process.

"Marshal!" Platt said as he set it back up. "Didn't expect you quite so soon."

"You exhibited concern over the sheriff...I took the train to Ringgold."

"Wow, I'd a never thought of that," said Gomer.

Fiona tried to hide a smile. "I know...So, no word from Mason?"

Slim shook his head. "Uh, uh...Nary a word. Somethin's wrong, bad wrong. I jest know it."

"Well, like Bass would say, 'Don't go to borrowin' trouble you ain't got yet, son'."

"Here you go, Marshal," Molly said as she set down the special in front of Fiona along with a covered basket of rolls and a dish of butter.

"Be back in a sec with your tea...You boys ready for desert?"

"What is it today, Molly," asked Gomer.

"Well, not that it makes a difference, but it's buttermilk pie."

Slim rolled his eyes. "Oh, oh, twist my arm, Molly."

She touched his elbow lightly. "Ow, calf rope, calf rope…I give…I'll take a double slice."

Molly shook her head. "Thought you would."

"You and Ranger Hickman would make quite a pair, Slim," commented Fiona.

"Don't like buttermilk pie neither?"

"Hates it with a passion."

Slim downed his third slice of buttermilk pie while Fiona and Gomer were on their first.

"I'm gonna check the Coolwater Saloon while ya'll are finishin' up…see if'n they's 'ny strangers in town," said the Chickasaw Freedman as he wiped the crumbs from his mouth and big black mustache.

"We'll join you in a couple of minutes, Slim," said Fiona. "Looks like I get to pay the ticket."

She glanced over at Deputy Platt fumbling through his pockets and looking up at her with a sheepish grin.

COOLWATER SALOON

"Well, looky here, looky here, this one horse town is scrapin' the bottom of the barrel."

"How's that, Rankin?" asked Stubby as he picked up his shot glass with his good right hand. His left was held against his body with a sling made from a wild rag.

"Got a nigger totin' a badge whilst their sheriff has gone missin'..." He glanced at the bar. "Didn't you say he was a mite overdue, barkeep?"

"Why don't you boys just have your drinks and keep your comments to yourselves?" said Truman, the bartender and owner of the Coolwater.

"You got a big mouth there, barkeep. Meby I oughta close it for you."

"Awright, that's enough. There'll be none of that," said Deputy Parker as he placed his hand on the butt of his Remington.

"Ohhh, would you listen to that? Damn nigger's talkin' uppity," said Dollar. "Meby we should teach him some manners, too."

"You cowboys want to teach someone some manners, I suggest you start with yourselves," said Fiona as she eased through the batwing doors followed by Deputy Platt...

§§§

CHAPTER FIVE

SOUTHERN JACK COUNTY

"God, this stuff is bitter," said Flynn as he made a face while chewing the willow bark.

"Which would you prefer, the headache or the taste?" Lisanne slid off Laddie's croup to the ground.

"Got a point. Laddie is some kinda smooth, but still felt like I was bouncin' down a stairwell…You gonna walk a spell?"

"Uh, huh. Thought I'd give him a little break an' walk along with Barney." She looked up as the Lab paused in the road to smell some coon scat.

"Maybe I'll walk a bit, too. Bitter as this stuff is, my headache is not near as bad when I chew it…Where'd you find out about it?"

"My real daddy hired a Chickasaw Freedman one time, I was about eight, I guess. He showed me how to work with horses the Injun way an' told me 'bout willow bark takin' the edge off pain."

"Don't say?"

"Just did."

Barney barked and tore off into the brush.

"Oops, gonna be one less rabbit in the world in just a minute," said Lisanne as she watched the big dog disappear.

JACKSBORO, TEXAS
COOLWATER SALOON

"It's her," exclaimed Stubby as they all turned toward the voice at the door.

Fiona took notice of the sling on the short man and the body posture of the taller one protecting his ribs. "Well, looks like you're the boys that picked a fight with my mule last night…and lost."

"Damn you…" Dollar said as he moved to slick his Colt from the holster.

He had not even cleared leather when one of Fiona's Peacemakers roared. The itinerant cowboy dropped his pistol to the sawdust covered floor, grabbed his right ear, and then pulled back a bloody hand.

A full second later, Deputy Platt drew his Colt.

"My ear! You done shot it off," Dollar screamed.

"Could just as well put that bullet between your eyes, Slick," she responded.

"Who the hell are you?" asked Rankin.

"Deputy United States Marshal F. M. Miller and you boys are under arrest."

"Fer what?" spoke up Stubby.

"Let's call it disturbing the peace for now. Not any laws against being stupid that I know…"

Fiona grunted and fell to the floor as Bittercreek Rudabaugh laid the barrel of his Navy Colt across the back of her head from behind.

Jubal followed his partner through the batwing doors and quickly backhanded Deputy Platt with his gun before he could react to Marshal Miller going down.

"Jest drop the shooter, nigger," said Bittercreek. He glanced over at the cowboys. "Damn, Rankin, cain't believe you let a woman an' a darkie git the best of you."

"Hidy, Bittercreek…Jubal. We didn't know she was a marshal." He turned to Deputy Parker. "What the hell was she doin' here, smoke?"

Slim glanced nervously around, first at the bartender, the three men at the doorway, at Fiona on the floor, and then finally at Rankin. "I sent for her when the sheriff didn't show back up."

Jubal cackled. "He ain't likely too, neither, African. I put a .50 caliber ball in his melon down at the Brazos. 'Spect his body…what's left of it…is down to Waco by now."

Slim ground his teeth and looked at Marshal Miller again as she began to stir.

"Anse, git her shooters…Hell, never seen a woman carry two an' damn few men."

Hulbert bent over, picked up the pistol she dropped, and then removed the left one still in its holster. "Whoa, looky here…Kindly fancy ain't they?" He said as he held up the nickel-plated, ivory-gripped matched set.

Deputy Platt sat up, rubbing the side of his head and looked over at Fiona. "You all right, Marshal?"

She glared at him. "No…Do I look all right?"

"Anse, take these three *intrepid* lawdogs down   to   the sheriff's office an' lock 'em in their own jail. Keep that ten gauge on 'em, too," said Bittercreek as he stepped over to the bar. "Whiskey, barkeep...The good stuff for me an' my friends. Don't be a givin' us none of that baptized crap."

Slim stepped over and helped Platt and Fiona to their feet, as the three cowboys and Jubal joined Bittercreek at the bar.

"We'll have you a drink when you git back from lockin' them badge toters up, Anse." He turned back to the bar and picked up his shot glass.

"Don't reckon you boys are gonna pay for those?" said Truman.

"Damnation, barkeep, you didn't fall off'n the hide wagon, did ya?"

"Oh, I think it would be a good idea if you paid for those drinks, Rudabaugh," came a voice from just inside the batwing doors. The figure was silhouetted against the bright sunshine from outside.

He stepped forward out of the glare.

"Flynn," Fiona exclaimed.

"One in the same, Marshal,"

"The devil an' Tom Bell! I seen you fall in the creek after I put a hole in yer head," said Bittercreek.

"Just a word of advice, nabob...Gotta quit trustin' your lyin' eyes," said Flynn.

Lisanne came in behind him. "You remember who you are!"

192

Without taking his eyes from the men at the bar, Flynn replied, "Yep, come to me the second I laid eyes on Marshal Miller there over the top of the batwings...We've ridden the river together...mor'n once." He turned to Fiona. "Lisanne's been wonderin' who I was since she pulled me out of the river...an' me too."

"Damn you, that's my daughter." Anse reached out and grabbed Lisanne by the hair and jerked her toward him.

He had no more than touched her when Barney launched himself through the air and clamped his teeth on Hulbert's wrist. There was the sickening sound of bones crunching under the big dog's jaws as the man fell to the floor, screaming.

"Git 'im off! Git 'im off," he whined.

"That's enough, Barney...but watch him," said Lisanne.

The dog slowly released his hold, stepped back less than a foot, sat down and kept his lips up in a snarl. He never took his eyes off the man.

"I think that's stepdaughter," said Flynn. "Say, I know you...Cavalry Scout Anse Hulbert...Deserter."

"You still got a problem, there Sheriff," said Jubal, with a grin.

Flynn cut his eyes over at the outlaws. "Oh?...And that would be?"

"I'd say we got you outgunned…five to one, even with that dirt farmer there outta commission. This jest ain't gonna be yer day."

The sheriff chuckled. "Yep, you boys don't realize just how much trouble you're in, do you?…Now, you can go to jail…or hell…Your choice."

Bittercreek and the others shared a round of laughter and slapped each other on the back. Flynn took the momentary distraction to draw his .45 and drop Rudabaugh with two fanned shots to the center of his chest—one on top of the other.

Fiona had palmed her hideaway gun, a .455 Webley Bulldog from inside her right boot while Slim was helping her up. She squeezed off three quick rounds from the double-action revolver—two nailed Jubal in the chest, less than an inch apart, with audible thumps.

The third shot went through Rankin's throat just above his collar and blew the back of his neck out. Both men dropped to the floor like rotten apples falling from the tree—their still unfired pistols in their hands.

The noxious white cloud of black powder smoke from the five rounds hung in the air of the saloon like a pall.

"Dang, Truman, why don't you open the back door and see if some of this smoke can find its way out."

"Right away, Sheriff," he said as he headed toward the back.

Flynn turned to Lisanne's stepfather still laying on the floor, holding his mangled wrist, moaning in pain. "Well, Hulbert, always said I'd find you one day. You deserted in time of war with the Comanche…Caused some of my men to get killed.

"But consider yourself lucky, I'd just as soon put a couple of holes in your worthless hide right here an' right now for making Lisanne run off and hide from your lecherous ass—the Army will probably give you a hemp necktie."

Slim pulled his hat off, held it in both hands in front of him and spoke to Lisanne, "Howdo, Missy…'Member me?"

"Oh, my goodness…Slim Parker." She hugged the skinny black man's neck, and then turned to Flynn. "Dixon, or I guess I should call you Sheriff Flynn, this is the Chickasaw Freedman I told you about. Mama had to let him go when papa got killed."

He grinned. "Reckon it's a small world then."

"Did you also figure out where the name Dixon came from?" asked Lisanne.

Flynn pursed his lips, looked at the floor, nodded and softly said, "Dixon was my twin brother…He's not with us anymore."

"Oh, I'm so sorry for your loss. What happened?" asked Lisanne.

"Kind of a long story. Tell you about it sometime…" He quickly changed the subject. "Looks like you have someone to help you set up your horse business." Flynn glanced at Slim.

"You gonna raise hosses, Missy?" asked Parker.

She looked at Flynn, and then nodded back to Slim. "Found out I inherited my papa's place…a full section of land down south of here, in Jack County."

"Wooee!…Natural hoss country." He glanced at Flynn. "This little gal has a way with hosses, yessir, a real way…Hey, I seen a wild mustang down near the Brazos…Steeldust, black mane an' tail, with a stripe down the middle of his back. Best lookin' stallion I ever seen. Looks to me like he's got a lot of that Andalusian type hoss in him the Spaniards brung over here…Shonuff make a herd sire, yessir, a Jim Dandy herd sire…gotta be sixteen hands. Might give the great Dan Patch a run for his money…We jest gotta go ketch 'im…The Comanch calls him a spirit hoss."

"Sounds like an adventure," said Fiona. She paused in thought for a moment. "You know, Sheriff, your friend, Texas Ranger Yancy Landon, brought some dodgers by my office in Gainesville last week."

She glanced over at Lisanne and smiled. "Couple of them showed that there's two thousand dollars in reward on Bittercreek Rudabaugh and Jubal Atz...Think that will give you some start up money for your horse operation."

Flynn grinned and nodded his approval.

Lisanne put her hand to her mouth. "Oh my goodness, I don't know what to say."

"Beats us looking all over this country for Flynn." She smiled back at the Sheriff. "It's a good thing they hit you in the head...Anywhere else might have hurt you."

He put his hands on his hips after cocking them to one side. "Wait a minute...I come home to this type of abuse after being in some kind of perdition for the last few days?"

"You might consider yourself lucky to come home at all. If it weren't for Lisanne here, you might still be in the river."

"'For in that sleep of death what dreams may come, When we have shuffled off this mortal coil, must give us pause'," said Lisanne.

Fiona looked at her in surprise. "You know Shakespeare?"

She beamed. "Yes, Ma'am...that's from Hamlet."

Flynn lightly nudged Lisanne's shoulder with his elbow and whispered in her ear, "Don't call her Ma'am."

§§§§

THE AUTHOR

Ken Farmer didn't write his first full novel until he was sixty-nine years of age. He often wonders what the hell took him so long. At age seventy-five. Ken's currently working on novel number twenty…*COLDIRON.*

Ken spent thirty years raising cattle and quarter horses in Texas and forty-five years as a professional actor (after a stint in the Marine Corps). Those years gave him a background for storytelling… as he has been known to say, "" always been a bit of a bull---t artist, so writing novels kind of came naturally once it occurred to me I could put my stories down on paper."

Ken's writing style has been likened to a combination of Louis L'Amour and Terry C. Johnston with an occasional Hitchcockian twist…that's a mouthful.

In addition to his love for writing fiction, he likes to teach acting, voice-over and writing workshops. His favorite expression is: "Just tell the damn story."

Writing has become Ken's second life: he has been a Marine, played collegiate football, been a Texas wildcatter, cattle and horse rancher, professional film and TV actor and now…a novelist. Who knew?

Thanks for reading *THE BRAZOS*. If you enjoyed it and this western anthology, *FLYNN the SERIES*, we would really appreciate a review on Amazon.
My Author Page is:
www.amazon.com/Ken-Farmer/e/B0057OT3YI
Email - pagact@yahoo.com
Personally autographed books available at my web site: www.KenFarmer-Author.net
or: www.timbercreekpress.net

THE COMANCHEROS

BY

BUCK STIENKE

CHAPTER ONE

JACK COUNTY, TEXAS OCTOBER, 1892

Dawn broke blood red that fateful day over the two bedroom
white washed frame ranch house in the rolling prairie land of
northern Texas. Crimson streaks of Indian summer sunlight
cut though the narrow gap in the blue gingham bedroom
curtains, causing tiny particles of dust to dance in their
beams.

THE COMANCHEROS

The baby boy—just entering his sixth month of life—kicked hard enough to cause his mother to gasp as she awoke with a start. "Oh," she said softly as she placed her left hand on her belly and inhaled deeply.

"You all right, there, darlin'?" Mason placed his hand on top of hers.

"Sure, honey bunch. The baby is getting a mite restless, is all." Betty smiled over at her husband. Strands of her long raven locks fell across her face as she turned towards him, coming to rest just beneath her slightly upturned nose.

Mason chuckled aloud as he reached over and brushed them back. "For a minute there, I thought you were tryin' to look jest like me. You know I never would have married a gal who had a mustache."

"Mason Flynn, you stop that teasing right now. You told me I was the prettiest woman you ever saw!" Her blue eyes sparkled in the growing light of day as her smile widened.

"That's a pure dee fact, Ma'am. When you came marching down those schoolhouse steps, my eyes couldn't believe what they were seeing. And to think that was only…let me see…fifteen months ago."

"Sixteen. We got married fifteen months ago…right after you left the Army."

The muscular thirty-five year old propped himself up on one elbow. He made a halfhearted attempt at a frown, causing his bushy brown mustache to form an inverted U. "Now is that why a man gets hisself hitched...to have young whippersnapper of a woman correct him every single time he opens his mouth?"

"Only when you are wrong dear...only when you are wrong. Now, if you will be so kind as to fetch us some more eggs from the hen house, I will be more than happy to rustle up some breakfast...for the three of us."

"Three? What do you..." He caught himself and rubbed her tummy as he face broke into a broad smile. "You think it is a boy? Always wanted a son..."

"Quite likely. Missus Johnson in town told that I am carrying high and that always means a boy."

"Reckon she would know. She has had six kids of her own." Mason leaned in and gave Elizabeth Ann a soft kiss on the lips and then winked. He tossed back the light bedding and slipped out of bed.

Outside, a large brown Leghorn rooster flew to the top of the whitewashed chicken coop. He strutted up and down the length of the ridge line before flapping his wings and puffing up the orange feathers of his hackle. He tilted his head back and let fly a tremendous crow to greet the breaking dawn. Satisfied with his effort, the dominant bird spread his dark brown wings leapt off the end of the ridge and glided down to the mostly barren soil inside the fenced in enclosure.

Mason chuckled. "Ol' Jake outdid hisself this mornin'. You would think he was still a courtin' those laying hens."

"And what is so wrong about that?" Betty sat up in bed and crossed her arms.

"Nothin', I suppose." He pulled on a khaki-colored pair of canvas pants, leaving the suspenders hanging as he reached for a light blue bib front shirt—one of only four shirts he had to his name. He pulled it over his head and fastened the top button near the collar and left the side of the bib unbuttoned one-third of the way down. After tucking the shirttail into his pant waistline, Mason thumbed the elastic suspenders into place.

His square-toed black boots were leftover from his days in the US Cavalry. They came nearly to his knees—made from two pieces of quality leather, one in the front and another in the back—but were not nearly as shiny as back when he stood inspections. An unadorned set of silver-colored spurs adorned the working man's footwear, and each had a small brass rowel with nine teeth. Simple black latigo straps held them in place and were fastened with plain brass buckles.

Mason turned the boots upside down, slapped the them together, and shook them with some determination. Many times out on the trail, an unwelcome visitor would tumble out—usually a scorpion or spider. Only a few stray seeds from the local prairie grasses came out that morning.

He slipped them on over his bare feet, not quite ready to go to the trouble to tug on his woolen socks before breakfast. A funny thought raced across his mind. "I wonder what it would be like to live like a rooster, uh, you know…having ten wives to keep satisfied?"

The look on her face spoke volumes. "Mister Flynn, do not even concern yourself with such an absurd happenstance. If you do not get a move on, and I do mean right smartly, you will not even keep *one* woman satisfied."

Mason flashed his best smile and then ducked the feather pillow that sailed past his head. "Just a thought dear…just a thought."

In a bend in deep creek bed some three miles north of the small ranch house, the first of eight men camped out began to stir when one of their horses whinnied. He blinked the sleep from his dark eyes as they slowly began to focus in the early morning light. The dark skinned Mexican ran his fingers through his dirty, shaggy hair and tried to get some of the Indian gramma grass stems dislodged. He was only partially successful. Tossing the top half of his bed roll back, he sat up and stretched.

THE COMANCHEROS

Gomez was still fully dressed as were the other members of the motley gang of cutthroats, horse thieves and deserters. He stood up and nudged the closest man with his boot. "Hey, gringo. Get up. Make us something to eat."

The twenty four year old white man gave him a side look. "I got a name, you know. Why don't you use it?"

Another one of the men sat up, and leaned on his saddle with his elbow. "White eyes, when you have ridden with us for a full year, maybe we call you by your name."

Billy Satterwhite, the US Army deserter who was originally from Kansas City, scowled at the Comanche. "Nobody died and made you chief, Yellow Bird. This ain't even your gang."

The pocked-face renegade sprang to his feet. In a flash, he drew a six-inch blade from beaded sheath on the left side of his gun belt.

The distinctive sound of a Colt Single Action Army being racked back to full cock froze him like a statue.

"Damn you, Bird! You kill our new cook and I'll drop you where you stand. *Sabe*? You know you cain't cook for spit."

Billy looked back over his shoulder at the leader of the scruffy band. Gomez was grinning, showing off the gold trimmed tooth he had had repaired in San Antonio—not that it improved his looks by any means. A long curved scar on his left cheek—earned in a knife fight with a married man trying to defend his wife—reminded all that knew him of his violent temper as well as his insatiable lust for female companionship. He holstered his shooter.

The young Kansas native took in a deep breath. He relaxed his grip on his own Colt, still ensconced in its Slim Jim holster. He got to his feet, and then yawned. "Well, boys, what'll it be this morning, y'all? Beans and bacon or bacon and beans?"

Mason brushed the last crumbs of a buttermilk biscuit from the corner of his mouth, using a plain white cotton napkin. A dark brown smudge appeared on the cloth. *Tarnation! Did it again.* He snaked his tongue out and captured the last remains of the sorghum molasses that had dribbled onto his lower lip. Instantly, he felt a pair of eyes upon him.

Betty tried to look stern, but the effort didn't really have the effect she had hoped. Both broke out laughing.

"I can dress you up but you are not quite ready to be taken out in polite society, I suppose." She turned her head away slightly to try to regain her composure.

"In my defense, Ma'am, them biscuits are larapin' good. 'Specially with that sweet butter and black strap. Apologize for making a mess on your napkin."

"Those biscuits, not them biscuits, dear. Were you raised by wolves?"

"Not exactly. My dear old Daddy got killed by a Yankee over in Louisiana 'fore I turned seven." His eyes turned a little darker at the memory and instantly lost their sparkle.

Betty sighed. "I am so sorry, Mason. Please forgive me. It was just a figure of speech." Her eyes teared up.

He forced a smile. "Stop right there, Missus Elizabeth Ann Flynn. All that was a long time ago...over thirty years, I reckon. We had us some hard times, we did. My brother Dixon getting captured and hauled off by Injuns. It was tough sleddin' after daddy died, but my ma...well, she did the best she could."

The memories were etched upon his face as he swallowed. "Was not much help, me being so dang little and my sister only three years old when the Battle of Mansfield took place."

Betty reached across the painted pine table and placed her hands on his. "I know, sweetheart. You told me all that before...but we have each other now and that is what really matters."

"Yep. That was then, and this is now." He stroked the young woman's soft white hands, marveling at the contrast in color and texture between his tanned calloused ones and her smooth alabaster skin. "This is now...and I like it just the way it is."

Mason stepped up onto the platform of the tall-sided Studebaker freight wagon and unwrapped the reins from the hand brake. He sat down on the unpainted wooden seat, picked up the Spencer carbine that had been leaning against the footrest and laid it across his lap. Taking the ribbons in his gloved left hand, he waved good-bye to Betty. "Should be back before five o'clock…assumin' we can get loaded up and headed back this way in a right smart manner."

She stood on the front porch of the whitewashed ranch house, leaning against one of the peeled pine supports. Dressed in a store-bought blue gingham dress with a starched white apron, she stood tall and looked a picture of perfection, as she smiled and waved back. "Take care of yourself, dear. I'll be just fine. Got a bit of washing to do while the weather holds out."

Flynn took a glance to the east. A line of cumulous clouds had begun building on the horizon. He looked back at his wife and gave her a characteristic wink and a nod, but said nothing. Taking the reins in each hand, he spread them a few inches apart and popped them lightly over the dappled rumps of his steel gray Morgans. "Come on up, Smokey. Git up there Charlie boy. Got us a barn to build."

The well-muscled horses leaned into the harness and then took a few steps. With a creak of old leather and the squeak from a slightly dry and seldom used front axle bearing, the

210

green painted wagon with faded yellow wheels began the fifteen mile trek into Jacksboro.

The eight long riders crested a ridge covered in deep grass—a dense native prairie mix that came up almost to the horses' bellies. A few longhorn steers, a half dozen cows and a rangy, but well-muscled, herd bull grazed on the open pasture lands west and north of the whitewashed ranch house that was sited near a ridge top. The bull's burnt umber hide bore the marks of battle scars earned in fending off attacks from coyotes and the earlier tests of dominance before Flynn purchased the 2,000 pound sire from a breeder south of Decatur, Texas.

Its coat was striped with some darker, almost black vertical streaks through the dewlap and shoulder, giving rise to the name Flynn had picked out for him—Tiger.

The bull stopped grazing as the riders approached. It turned to face them, raising his head so that there was no way the potential threat could miss seeing his massive curved horns. A beam of sunlight broke through the distant cumulus clouds that were beginning to dominate the eastern sky as they rose higher. The light glinted off the polished nine foot horns, where they dipped slightly and then rose parallel to the horizon. Tiger shook his head and bellowed out a warning. A thin stream of mostly clear mucous dripped from his right nostril as he panted.

"*Jefe*. That bull…he no like you." The thirty year old native of Jalisco, Mexico reined up his paint horse. The gelding stamped his front feet as he eyed the bovine.

"Hell, Ramon. You think I do not know it when I see a bull full of himself?" Gomez spat a stream of dark brown tobacco juice in the general direction of the belligerent critter. He wiped the dribble of his chin onto the sleeve of his already dirty white cotton shirt. He casually reached down to his right waistband and thumbed the well-worn holster retention tab off the hammer of his Colt. His eyes narrowed into a near squint as his jaw muscled tightened visibly. "If that bad hombre wants to see another sunrise, he will not challenge the Raoul Gomez gang."

Pedro Rojas, the youngest of the bunch at age nineteen, laughed nervously. "If he was not so stringy and tough, we would make us some steaks…Is that not so, Boss?"

Gomez grinned. "*Es verdad*. I think that I have had my fill of bacon and beans this week."

He let his gaze drift away from the bull as he focused on the buildings in the distance. He placed his hand just under the brim of his brown Mexican sombrero and blocked the sun for a moment.

THE COMANCHEROS

"*Mira*, Burt. You got better *ojos, mi amigo*. Does that look like a smokehouse to you?" He pointed at the ranch house and outbuildings some three hundred yards distant.

Burt Wilson, a twenty-six year old murderer on the run from the Indian Territories, squinted under his flat-brimmed Boss of the Plains hat. "Yep. You be right as rain. They's got a chicken coop, a little corral and a smokehouse, too...best I can tell."

A wry grin came to his sun burnished face. "Fried chicken...Eggs and ham. Damnation, that there is makin' my mouth water already. Purty sure I can see smoke comin' from the chimney."

Gomez took little time in assessing the situation. *Eight of us against some lone Anglo sodbuster. I will take those odds any day.* He turned in the saddle and pointed back at the twenty-year old firebrand. "Three Fingers. You and Bird circle around the south and come in behind the chicken coop. Get in close to back us up if need be." He made a half circle motion with his gloved right hand.

The renegade Kiowa brave nodded once and reined his pony south. Yellow Bird, a Comanche by birth, followed close behind, keeping one eye on the belligerent longhorn.

§§§

CHAPTER TWO

FLYNN RANCH

Tiger followed the two renegades with his eyes, turning his head as they moved abeam him and continued to circle south, and then turned east.

Gomez took the opportunity to ride a loop south as well, making certain not to come between the bull and his harem. Tiger lost interest in the six mounted men and resumed grazing, as they departed his personal security zone.

Raoul reined to a halt about one hundred and fifty yards southwest of the isolated ranch house. He crossed his hands, resting them on the leather-wrapped saddle horn and let the horse's head drop free to graze. His face showed no emotion, as the two Indians ground tied their mounts outside of the small corral east of the chicken coop.

Three Fingers—aptly named after a wild mustang threw him and then stomped on his left hand, crushing the ring and pinkie fingers—led the way around the corral fence, and then past wire enclosure surrounding the coop.

A copper-colored sorrel mare watched nervously as the stranger men circled her enclosure. Without making a sound, he and Yellow Bird crept low up to the corner of the house. He waved a signal to the other that they were in place.

Betty stood near the stove inside watching the large cast iron kettle filled with water from the hand-dug well out front. She brushed a strand of long black hair from her forehead as tiny beads of perspiration began to form. "I swan…If we ever get rich enough to send our laundry out, I will praise the Lord…This is most assuredly not my favorite day of the week." She picked up a small kitchen towel and dabbed at the small droplets on her face and neck.

Sticking her hands in a pair of store-bought oven mittens, she lifted the bail of the blackened kettle and struggled to get it off the wood-burning stove. *If Mason was here, he could lift this big old pot as if was a feather*.

She made her way to the front door, unlatched the wooden keeper with her left elbow and eased the custom made portal open with her toe. Keeping a sharp eye on the hot water sloshing around the kettle, she carefully stepped out and turned toward the galvanized wash tub she had pre-positioned on the porch.

Betty carefully tipped the pot, and began pouring the nearly boiling water over the washboard and into the cavernous tub.

The whinny of an approaching horse broke her rapt attention. She looked up, instantly startled at the sight of six mounted strangers with bad intentions written across their faces.

Her mouth flew open. The kettle fell from her hands making an awful racket as it banged into the washboard and flipped over. Betty spun around to run for the safety of her home. She gasped at the sight of Yellow Bird holding a knife in his hand, a sardonic grin on his face, standing only inches away from her.

Three Fingers held a well-worn revolver in his good hand and slipped into the open front door. A blood curdling scream came from her lips, "Mason!"

THE COMANCHEROS

JACKSBORO, TEXAS

Flynn drove his team into position near the stacks of freshly sawn cypress at the newly built lumber yard. The sleepy little town was not exactly the hub of metropolitan commerce, but did offer the amenities of a hotel, a couple of restaurants and some purveyors of dry goods.

An enterprising middle aged man from Tennessee had moved his family from Murfreesboro and set up a saw mill near the West Fork of the Trinity River bottom. There were plenty of mature cypress trees that would provide lumber for years to come. It held up much longer than pine or fir to the oft times harsh Texas climate.

Mason set the brake and climbed down from the wagon. He rubbed his backside vigorously, leaned left and then to the right, trying to shake of the rigors of the jaunty ride. "Never let anyone tell you that them muleskinners don't earn their keep." He doffed his cavalry hat and beat the dust off onto his pants.

Moving to the rear of the Studebaker, he dropped the tail gate, giving easier access to the stout wooden floor.

Two younger men exited the back of the office building and approached him. "Mister, we can get this loaded up for you if you want to head on over to Sewell's Cafe and have a bite."

Flynn thought it over for a second. *Hell's bells. I ain't got nobody out on my place to help me unload all this mess of lumber, so might as well take advantage of the offer. These young bucks can make do, just fine. I'll even throw in a tip.* "Sounds like a deal to me, boys. I'll hang feed bags on my team while I'm at it. They'll have their work cut out this afternoon."

"Our pleasure, Mister...Sorry, sir. Didn't catch your name," the lanky teenager said. "Mine's Ronny...My daddy owns this place."

"Flynn...Mason Flynn's the name. Please to meet you, son."

He removed his gloves, tucked them under his gunbelt and extended his hand. The young man shook it firmly. *Good sign. He'll go far.*

Mason gathered the two feed bags and a small cloth bag of oats he had stashed under the wagon seat. He split the grain evenly between them and slipped them over the muzzles of the Morgans, looping the straps behind their ears to hold them in place. He patted the neck of Smokey, his admitted favorite of the two. "Eat up, big boy. You're gonna earn these this afternoon."

218

The steel-colored stallion nodded as if he understood. Flynn turned and headed for the restaurant. He passed a lady on the boardwalk, tipped his hat and simply said, "Ma'am."

"Good day to you, sir," she replied as he opened the door to the cafe.

"'Nother glass of sweet tea, Mister Flynn?" Ruth Ann Sewell asked.

"No, Ma'am. I'd bust wide open if I did...Y'all sure know your way 'round the kitchen."

"Always happy to see a man that knows good cooking from bad."

"My Betty learned a thing or two. She can cook purty darn well herself."

"How is our Elizabeth Ann doin'? We sure miss her around these parts."

Flynn nodded. "Figured as much. She sure is something special, all right." His face broke into a wide grin. "Betty is in her sixth month, now...Missus Johnson thinks we're havin' a boy."

The waitress and owner of the small cafe beamed. "Oh I'm so very happy for you two! You tell her Ruth Ann said hello, won't you?"

Flynn made an X across his chest. "Cross my heart and hope to die...Promise I will."

She turned away to wait on other customers. Flynn dug out a shiny fifty-cent piece from his pant pocket to cover the cost of the meal and a tip. He laid it on the red and white checkered table cloth, dabbed his mustache with the napkin and pushed away from the table.

Mason got to his feet and adjusted his gun belt a little lower to make room for the fried streak, mashed potatoes and gravy that had left him feeling full as a tick. He looked around. No one had paid much attention to him, and that suited him just fine.

FLYNN RANCH HOUSE

Elisabeth Ann awoke with a throbbing pain in her jaw. Her left eye was swollen shut and a dribble of blood had run from the corner of her mouth and dried on her alabaster cheek. She tried to sit up but found her hands tied to the peeled pine head board with latigo strips. Her heart began to race wildly. She raised her head and discovered that she was naked. Both legs were also tied to the foot board of the bed,

Pedro Rojas stepped into the doorway of the small bedroom as he peeled off his badly stained and stinking union suit. He already had a wide, evil grin. "My turn, *mamacita*."

THE COMANCHEROS

Betty screamed as the brutal reality of her hopeless situation hit her like runaway freight train. Pedro winced at the piercing scream. He ripped off a section of the top sheet, rolled and twisted it up into a long, ragged rope-like gag and forced it into the struggling woman's mouth.

"*Aye, caramba*! I don't desire to listen to that caterwauling." He lifted her head in a rough jerking motion, tucked one end under it and then tied the gag off on the right side by her ear.

She gagged slightly as the cotton cloth pressed down forcefully on her tongue almost cutting off her air. Tears rolled down both cheeks as he straddled her.

"*Mucho mas mejor, no*?" Pedro placed his hands on her ample breasts. "*El Jefe*, he wants to take you to Mexico. Raoul say you bring a thousand dollars in Monterey." He leaned in closer until she could smell his fetid breath. "But Pedro..." The Comanchero laughed heartily. "...he have you for free!"

Twenty minutes passed. All the gang members had had their turn at raping the beautiful housewife—all save Jim Bob Jones. He twenty-three year old from Wichita Falls couldn't bring himself to rape a pregnant woman.

Betty bore a passable resemblance to his own sister, and the visual was not an erotic one, especially after the beating she had suffered as she fought off the initial contact with Yellow Bird.

The Comanche sported a string of bloody scratches the left side of his face, but had not used his knife. He knew that Gomez would have been less than pleased had the woman been killed outright.

One thing that none of the gang members wished was to get on the wrong side of their sociopathic leader.

Gomez rifled though the chifferobe and found five other dresses. He picked one and turned to the naked, dazed woman staring blankly at the bedroom ceiling. He tossed the dress across her swollen belly.

"Get dressed. Make us some food."

She reacted extremely slowly, as if in a deep trance.

"*Chica*! I am talking to you!" He was agitated by her slow response and drew out his belt knife.

She panicked as he kneeled on the side of the bed. Her one open eye grew wide with fear. Betty tried to roll away from him, but was still tightly bound.

The smarmy Mexican grinned. "How stupid of me…you cannot get dressed until I release you." He reached across and cut the upper latigo thongs with a slight pressure of his razor sharp blade. "Do not get any crazy ideas, now. One wrong move and…". He drew the blade in a slicing motion an inch off his throat.

Betty suddenly snapped out of her state of shock. Her hands flew first to the dress, as she attempted to cover herself up as best she could. She could feel her face flush, but it was no longer an all consuming fear, but rage that began to build inside her like a wild prairie fire driven by a summer wind. Her hands went to the gag and she ripped it in two with her newfound burst of adrenaline. "Release my feet. I cannot reach those knots," she demanded coldly.

Gomez grinned, but mocked her as he cut the lower pair of restraints. "Oh, yes, your majesty." He chuckled. "I like my gringo women with a bit of fire in them."

"My husband will kill you all when gets home." She pulled the latigo strips on her wrists up to her mouth and began to bite and tug at the knots until she could loosen them and slip her hands free.

The Comachero leader laughed heartily. He shook his head. "We will be long gone by that time. What makes you think one lone sod buster could stand a chance against the eight of us?"

"He fought Indians in the United States Cavalry." She glanced at the tintype on the bedroom wall.

Raoul followed her line of sight, stepped over to the framed picture of Flynn in his military uniform and pulled it off its nail. He stared at it for a moment and then grinned broadly. "This old man? I should shake in my boots for him?" He laughed again. "I thought maybe that this was a picture of your father…How old is this husband of yours? This cradle robber?"

Elizabeth Ann's jaw grew tight as she stared at the despicable man with her right eye that wasn't swollen shut. "He is thirty-five…and ten times the man you will ever be."

"Thirty-five? He is almost ready for a rocking chair. A soft man like him is no match for a young hard man like me. You will see…Now get dressed and make us something good to eat." He turned to go back into the one large room that had the kitchen on one end and a fireplace on the other.

Betty's mind raced as she tried to figure out what the man had meant by 'You will see.' *Will they really take me with them like that one boy said? I cannot let that happen…Mason will surely follow us and they might kill him after all. What will happen to our baby? Oh my Lord, what should I do?*

§§§

CHAPTER THREE

JACKSBORO, TEXAS

Flynn tipped the two teenagers who had loaded the cypress planks and covered the load with a khaki-colored canvas tarp that he just purchased from the general store.

He glanced skyward at the buildups that were already turning dark and menacing overhead. *Dangnation. What is that old sayin'?...Red sky at morning, sailor take warning.*

Red sky at night, sailor delight. Glad I brought along my slicker, just in case.

He clamored up into the front and took his seat. *Damn bench is already harder than it was when I started out this morning.* Flynn took the ribbons in his hands and spilt them wide enough to touch each horse. "All righty, boys...fun is over. Now you get to earn your keep." He pulled up the slack and popped the reins lightly on each horse's rump. "Hiyah! Get on up!"

The two Morgans reacted as trained and leaned into their traces. Slower than before, the heavily laden wagon started rolling across the level back lot of the lumber yard.

Three hours later, the first of the scattered rain showers crossed over Flynn. He donned the slicker and pulled the collar up to keep the rain that was dripping off the back side of his hat brim from running down his neck.

He scanned the horizon for other down bursts. *Oh hell...One way to keep the dust down, I reckon. Hope this road don't get too muddy for these two oat burners. If I bury this rig axle deep, it will be a month of Sundays 'fore I can dig it out.*

He calculated the distance remaining to be three miles. *Bet my sweet Betty has a fire goin' in the fireplace. Getting kinda cold with that northeast wind startin' to blow. Wonder if she made us a special pie for supper?* The thought of another apple pie made his mouth start to water. He remembered the smell of cinnamon, cloves, and sugar when the last one came out of the oven. *Love the way she likes to surprise me sometimes.*

Flynn let out a small sigh of relief when the rain stopped at the same time he caught sight of the remote ranch house in the distance. *Boy howdy...my poor ol' butt is gonna be flatter that a fritter by the time I get myself off this plank. Probably have a blister or two, to boot.* He leaned to the left to try to restore some semblance of the circulation on his right cheek. It didn't help much, but he tried the same remedy on the left one.

As the rode closer to his home, a strange sense of unease began to build inside him. *Funny. Can't make out any smoke from the chimney.* The corral came into view and he could see the individual peeled pine poles he had used when he built it. *Where the hell is Penny?*

The sorrel mare—a wedding gift to his young bride—was nowhere to be seen. He blinked, stared intently at the enclosure and noted that the gate was wide open. *That's not right. She wouldn't be out for a pleasure ride in this kind of weather. I would've met her if she had headed to town.*

"Hiyah!" He popped the reins over the two tired horses, but they responded by picking up the pace as they broke into a trot. The road for the last hundred yards to the house was on a slight incline and the hardworking Morgans began to breath heavier with the effort.

Mason tried unsuccessfully to swallow the lump that was forming in his throat, but it wasn't just the trail dust. His heart pounded faster and faster as he drew nearer. *What the hell is going on?* His mind raced as his eyes picked up on scattered patches of white strung out over a large area.

Seemingly hundreds of chicken feathers littered the ground in front of the homestead. The front door of the house gaped open. Forty yards out, he reined the team back. The wagon creaked to a stop, with both horses breathing deeply.

Flynn yanked the wagon brake aft and threw a single loop with the four reins around it. He grabbed the Spencer carbine and leapt off the Studebaker's driving platform, hitting the ground running. *What's happened here?*

The sight of several chicken heads and strings of entrails mixed with scattered patches of feathers was totally out of place. *Coyotes and foxes carry off their prey.*

The front yard was covered with tracks from numerous horses and human footprints. His mind raced with more questions than answers, as he sprinted to the house.

"Betty!" He leapt across the porch in a single bound and charged into the main room as he screamed out her name again. "Betty! Where are you?...Betty! Betty!"

Silence awaited him. Adrenaline coursed through his veins as his heart beat a tattoo inside his broad chest. He panted as if he just finished a foot race and then turned as he tried to process the filthy condition of the disheveled house.

Remains of fried chicken bones littered the small table as well as the wooden floor surrounding it and into the kitchen area. Dirty plates were left on the dining table and on the work area in the kitchen. His mind raced as it tallied eight of them.

Doors to the kitchen cabinets were left ajar. *Coffee and sugar sacks are missing.* With great trepidation, he moved to the doorway to the bedroom.

He thumbed the hammer back to full cock and held the Spencer at the ready, using the muzzle of the .55 caliber rimfire carbine to push the door open.

Flynn half expected to find his wife's body lying on their bed. He didn't even realize that he was holding his breath until the door swung wide banged against the wall. The noise startled him as his eyes adjusted to the dim conditions inside the unlit room. He stepped inside as he gasped slightly for air. *She's not here!*

Mixed emotions crashed down upon him like breakers in a hurricane. Thankful she was not dead—at least not yet—he struggled to piece together what had transpired in his absence.

He started to leave the room when a dark strip of something lying on the corner of the bed caught his eye. He reached down, took hold of it and tried to pick it up but it was attached to the foot of the bed. *"What the hell is this?"*

He threw the carbine down on the bedspread, tore off his working gloves and examined the foreign piece of material. *Latigo strap? What is it doing...*

His mind froze, unable to process the evil possibility for a moment. His eyes darted to the other corners of the bed. More half inch wide strips of leather confirmed his worst fears. *Oh, God.*

He stumbled out of the room and over to the dining table. Taking a strike-anywhere match out of the cylindrical copper canister, he scratched it on the table top and lifted the glass on the coal oil lamp in the center of the tabletop.

The smell of the sulfur somehow always reminded him of the fire and brimstone sermons the Baptist preachers often referred to back in Henrietta, Texas as a child.

He touched the flame to the flaxen wick. A tendril of black smoke drifted up and out the graceful glass chimney, but dissipated as the flame pattern grew. Flynn lowed the chimney, shook the match twice, and then dropped the still smoking lucifer to the floor.

Flynn managed to swallow the lump in his throat as he picked up the lamp by its brass base and carried it back into the bedroom.

He noted the dresser had been ransacked—several of Betty's dresses were missing. All of his spare shirts were gone as well. The lamplight shown down on a pile of fabric beside the bed.

Mason stooped down and picked it up. Instantly he recognized the apron and gingham dress she had worn that morning. He lifted them to his face and breathed in her scent.

Tears formed in his eyes and rolled down his suntanned cheeks. He laid the clothing on the bed and noticed that the dress was torn from the neck down through the middle of the bodice. Dried blood stains dotted the collar.

Mason's jaw clenched involuntarily as the fingers of his fist curled tightly into the palm of his hand. Brown dots of dried blood were smeared across the pillow and on a bit of rolled up cloth that he quickly determined had been used as a makeshift gag. His blood began to boil as the yellow lamp light showed dried stains in the middle of the bed. *Damn it to hell! Son of a bitch!*

The mental image of his wife's savage attack flashed across his mind. For a moment, he felt sick and fought the almost irresistible to vomit. Mason gagged, gasped and closed his eyes tightly, unable to gaze upon the site of his beloved wife's apparent violation.

He gathered himself together after a few anxious seconds. *You bastards! I'll hunt you down to the ends of the earth for hurting my Betty.*

He knelt back down and reached under the bed frame. It took a few seconds, but he found the hidden release for the storage box he had custom built into the bed frame. Once it was unlatched he lowered the six foot by five foot by six inch deep open topped hideaway.

He had felt so clever when he came up with the design, complete with counterbalanced coil springs that were only visible if the mattress and box springs were removed.

The huge drawer slid out once it reached the lowest position, revealing his stashed arsenal, extra ammunition and related specialty items he had collected while serving with the cavalry.

He pulled out the Sharps 1884 rifle in .45-90 and laid it on the bed. The pair of army issue binoculars he had used, came out next, followed by a nickle plated brass compass.

Flynn's mind had reverted into military mode, taking stock of his need for ammunition, food supplies and the like. He set out a full box of .56-56 rimfire ammo for the Spencer carbine. Suddenly, he remembered the numerous set of tracks and footprints outside and eight dinner plates. Grabbing another box for the Spencer, two for the Sharps and two more boxes of .45 Colt for his six-shooter.

He recalled his issue Colt pistol was wrapped up in a woolen cloth lightly impregnated with gun oil and quickly unwrapped the 1873 Cavalry model with the 7 ½" barrel. It showed some holster wear on the cylinder and sides of the barrel. For some reason, he had purchased a Single Action Army with a 4 5/8" one and stag grips after he mustered out.

Now that he was going after some unknown force that had kidnapped his wife, he wanted all the firepower he could get his hands on.

Almost as an after thought, he lifted up the dark blue woolen bib-front cavalry shirt and pants he had worn a little over a year previously. They smelled of mothballs, but would have to do as spares. He had nothing else to wear, save the clothes on his back. *Thievin' bastards.*

He got to his feet. A sense of resolute power came over him as he spoke aloud, "Elizabeth Ann Flynn…I swear by all that's holy that I'll do my dead level best to bring you home, safe and sound…May God have mercy on their mortal souls, because I shall have none."

Flynn stepped back into the main room and set the lamp on the table. Quickly, he made his way back to the waiting team. "Sorry, boys, but we ain't done today…not by a long shot."

Leaving the loaded wagon where it had come to a stop, he rapidly unhitched the team and led them one by one to the hitching post out in front of the house. He went back inside, picked up the lamp and walked to the second smaller room—the one that he and Betty had planned to eventually make into a bedroom for their children.

In the interim, it served well as a tack room until the new barn was raised. Mason stared at the empty rack where Betty's side saddle had been stored.

Another pang of overwhelming guilt and loss struck him instantly and nearly brought him to his knees. *Steady, boy. Get hold of yourself*. He mentally steeled himself to the task at hand, a skill he had learned in the army.

He set the lamp on the floor and yanked his McClellan saddle off its rack. It was a lightweight utilitarian rig designed more for the horse's comfort than the rider's. It featured a split tree and plenty of D and O rings to attach saddlebags, sougans, canteens, rifles, ropes and other combat gear. In his other hand, he grabbed a headstall and saddle blanket and headed for the door.

After loosely cinching up the rig on Smokey, he strode back inside and retrieved the pack saddle tree, halter, panniers and blanket that Charlie would tote.

THE COMANCHEROS

He then checked the smokehouse and found, to no surprise, than the invaders had taken almost everything. Two sugar-cured pork bellies, some beef jerky and a lone ham shoulder were all that was left. *Reckon the sorry bastards were plum sick of bacon.*

He carried the remaining smoked goods to the panniers he had strapped onto Charlie.

It had taken almost forty minutes to gather all the needed supplies, clothing, tack, pack the panniers and saddlebags.

Flynn closed the front door of the house, walked out and grabbed the lead rope attached to Charlie, he stepped into the stirrup and swung easily into the saddle on Smokey.

He took one last look at the house that he had built for his bride. The image of her standing on the front porch earlier that day seemed like another lifetime. Then it hit him. *Christ Almighty. I never even said good bye.*

The sun was setting low behind the clouds. He followed the trail of tracks leading due south into the tall prairie grass. *They're bunched up and riding single file. Makes for easy tracking if the rain doesn't get too heavy. Who could do such a vile thing? The Indians are mostly all rounded up on reservations now...Mostly.*

He contemplated his own question for a couple of minutes and absolutely hated the conclusion he came to.

235

Comancheros. They'll sell her south of the border...My dear, beautiful Betty. A slave.

He shivered at the thought, but tried to blame it on the cold wind at his back. He rode on but the light began to fade and he looked for a protected place to camp while he could still see...

§§§

CHAPTER FOUR

PALO PINTO COUNTY

Betty finally fell asleep about three in the morning, tossing and turning on the cold ground with only a tarp for a bedroll. She woke up to the not-so-gentle nudging of a boot to her ribs, only to find that her nightmare was not imaginary.

"Get up, *gringa*. Build a fire and make us some food... *Pronto*."

She opened her eyes and tried to focus. The swelling in her left eye had subsided considerably, but she had a significant black shiner under it. She blinked and the image of Ramon Diaz looming over her came in sharp and clear in light of the dusky dawn.

Betty attempted to toss the tarp back and found both hands bound together, as were her high-top, button-up shoes. She held her hands out from under the cold canvas. "Can you untie me?"

Ramon sneered, his pencil-thin mustache curling up slightly at the ends. "Say pretty please."

Her backbone stiffened at the suggestion. She shook her head slowly. "Do you want to eat or not?" Fire dripped from her words.

"You stupid *puta*! I will teach you a lesson you will never forget!" He drew back his pointed toe boot to administer a bone-breaking blow.

A shot rang out and the bullet ripped through the brim of the twenty-year olds sombrero. Ramon ducked and wheeled to see Raoul holding a smoking shooter pointed at his belly.

"Damn you, Ramon. I warned you about damaging the merchandise. Next time, *amigo*, will be your last time…*Sabe usted?*"

Diaz hung his head and raised his hand in surrender. "*Si, patron. Lo siento.*"

THE COMANCHEROS

Gomez accepted the apology in an almost offhand manner. He pointed the pistol at the woman. "Untie her! I'm beginning to get as hungry as a panther."

"*Si, jefe.*" The properly chastised young thug tore at the bindings as Betty's eyes bored intently into him. He could not even bring himself to make direct eye contact with hers.

JACK COUNTY

The gusty wind whistled through the tree tops in the copse of oaks lining the ravine. Flynn awoke to the sound, his head nestled against the folded saddle blanket laid across the McClellan. After a fitful night of sporadic sleep, he sat up in the gray dawn and stretched his shoulders. *It's been a while since I slept on the ground. Didn't miss it a bit.*

He made a small hat-sized fire with some relatively dry deadfall oak sticks and limbs, knowing that they wouldn't smoke much.

He filled a coffee pot with mostly clean water from the small creek below and added a handful of old ground coffee beans from his saddle bags.

Flynn opened a drawstring pouch from the pannier and removed a stock of his homemade beef jerky, crafted from a longhorn steer. The spicy black pepper and cayenne offset the sweetness of the brown sugar and molasses marinade he had whipped up for that occasion. Plenty of salt helped preserve the meat once it was dehydrated in the mesquite smoke.

Flynn tore off a mouthful with his strong white teeth, and chewed it slowly as the coffee boiled. He ate another bite and figured the coffee would be as stout as it was going to get. He used his glove to lift the hot pot off the flat rock surrounded by coals.

He poured the ebony stream into the blue-speckled stoneware coffee cup. Steam drifted up and he savored the aroma of the admittedly old coffee.

Mason blew across the surface to cool it slightly, licked the lip and took a sip. He took another, swallowed, and then gnawed off another chunk of jerky.

Fifteen minutes later, he had a morning constitutional, removed the hobbles from his mounts, saddled both of them and filled a spare canteen with the remaining coffee. He doused the fire with a pot of creek water and stowed the still dripping pot in a pannier.

The sun had cleared the horizon, but the wind was still gusty from the northeast. He looked to the south. *Those Comancheros have a half-day start on me…at least. Figure I can cut that down to two hours by sunset if I push it. These ponies had a hellova workout yesterday, but a good rest overnight and plenty of graze.*

Mason forked the saddle and wheeled around. He rode about one hundred and fifty yards east and picked up the trail of the Comancheros.

PALO PINTO COUNTY

After a breakfast of fried ham slices with some canned peaches, the gang and their captive saddled up and moved out, heading due south. The terrain turned from prairie to a more rugged landscape overlooking a deep flowing river in the distance.

Gomez called a halt as he studied the situation. "Any of you *hombres* know where we are? Is this a creek or a river?"

The others looked blankly at each other and shrugged.

Elizabeth Ann stared at Raoul with unhidden disgust and simply shook her head. "You tell me you do not know the Brazos River when you see it? It is one of the three largest and longest rivers inside the state of Texas."

He turned around and gave her a look that would melt steel. "I was not talking to you."

"Perhaps not. But your ignorance of topography and geography could get us all killed. That river is at least 20 feet deep after those rains yesterday."

She could tell he didn't have a clue as the what the words *topography* and *geography* meant.

"*Como se dice topography in Español?*" he asked Pedro Rojas.

The illiterate young Mexican shrugged.

Billy Satterwhite sidestepped his roan closer. "Boss, I had me some book learnin' up till the eighth grade...I know what that word means."

The leader turned in the saddle and stared at him. "Do I have to ask you, *tambien*?

Billy flushed slightly. "Naw. It just that it's about the lay of the land...You know, map readin' and such."

Gomez nodded. He turned to look at Betty. "How you know about these things? You are a woman."

"I know that I am a woman and have been one all my life." She didn't back down an inch. "I also am a school teacher and qualified to teach English, Geography and Mathematics."

"Ask her where the closest crossing is...She might know that kinda stuff," Billy blurted.

Gomez was not convinced, but he stared at Betty nonetheless. "Is *verdad*?"

"Of course it is. The closest bridge across the Brazos would be south of Mineral Wells on the Stephenville road."

She smiled slightly smugly and crossed her arms in front

of her chest. *These cutthroats and renegades are profoundly stupid and poorly educated. I shall bide my time to make good an escape.*

"I have heard of such a place, *Jefe*," Jim Bob Jones offered.

"How far?"

Jim Bob hung his head. "I said I had heard of it. Don't rightly know where it is, boss."

Betty grinned and stifled a chuckle. She lifted a slim finger and pointed southeast. "That way, about forty miles I estimate...give or take."

Gomez stared at her with a jaundiced eye, not knowing whether or not to believe her. Finally he reined that way and kicked his horse in the ribs. "*Vamos, muchachos*," he called over his shoulder.

The others followed, with Yellow Bird staying close behind Betty to insure that she didn't try to make a break for it.

The nine riders dropped off a ridge and came upon a stagecoach road from Graham to Mineral Wells, Texas. It paralleled the Brazos, but was on an obviously higher terrain. Gomez gladly took the easier path.

Betty watched the others to insure that they weren't paying too close attention to her. She transferred the reins to her right hand and snaked her left under the riding skirt hem.

Gradually she got hold of the frilly multi-layered crinoline petticoat.

She gave Penny her head as she surreptitiously tore a small strip of fabric from the undergarment. She looked to the right as if she saw something interesting. Yellow Bird's gaze followed hers. Betty dropped the clandestine marker in the muddy roadway. *"Please, God. Let my Mason find it,"* she prayed silently.

The sun broke out of the overcast skies and shone down on the lone rider with a pack horse in trail. He reined back gently and came to a halt. *That's the Brazos down there…boy howdy. She's runnin' high after yesterday's rain.*

Mason unbuttoned his jacket, quickly rolled it up and tied it to the round ring brass on the back of the McClellan.

Flynn nudged his mount forward and started down the embankment. "Easy there, Smokey. You get me and Charlie in an assholes and elbows free for all tumble and I'll sell you to the glue factory, sure as shootin'."

The sure-footed Morgan ignored his hollow threat and settled down a bit in the haunches. Flynn pushed back against the cantle as he leaned aft to keep his weight centered with the horse.

THE COMANCHEROS

Crossing over a lower ridge, he spotted the stagecoach road. "Looky there! They turned left for Mineral Wells. Even a blind man could track those brigands."

He reached the roadway and noted another set of horse tracks and wheel ruts from the north. He studied them for a moment. *Graham stage to Mineral Wells, passed through after the Comancheros. Road was already startin' to dry up a might.*

He put his heels to Smokey and brought him up to a posting trot. As the horse's right front foot was rising, he transferred a larger percentage of his body weight to the steel stirrups. That simple, but repetitive, act helped keep the ride smoother than it would have been—much less of an impact from the rising unpadded saddle. The two mounts could keep up that pace for hours, similar to a road trot, and cover a wide swath of countryside.

A few hundred yards after Flynn joined the roadway, something out of place caught his eye—a bit of white cotton cloth. He reined back as curiosity rose. "What in hell?"

Mason leaned far over in the saddle, reached down and picked up the obviously torn bit of fabric from the ground. The grim look on his face softened for a moment. *Betty! She's leaving me a trail marker. Gutsy little gal.*

He stared at the road as it disappeared into the distance. *I'll get you back, darlin'. I promise, if it's the last thing I do.*

He nudged Smoky in the ribs with his knees and continued to trail the kidnappers at a road trot.

MINERAL WELLS, TEXAS

A few houses scattered on either side of the road indicated that the nine riders were getting closer to the small town.

Gomez raised a gloved fist and reined up two hundred yards or more from the closest homestead. The others circled around him.

"I don't know if this little town has a bank, but we could use a little spending money. Right, *amigos*?"

The others readily agreed.

Three fingers spoke up first. "And some whiskey, *Jefe*. We ran out over three days ago."

Gomez grinned broadly. "I never let you down before, have I?…Burt you and the kid ride in first and check out the town. Tie up on the left side of the street…Pedro, you and Jim Bob wait four minutes and ease in on the right side. See what they have to offer, and find out if they have a sheriff. Come back and report after in one hour…*Sabe*? We'll be over in that grove of oaks." He pointed to a cluster of mature trees a hundred yard off the road.

THE COMANCHEROS

"Got it, Boss." Burt and Billy wheeled and headed for town in a road trot.

Inside the copse of trees, Gomez, Ramon, the two Indian renegades and Betty dismounted and loosened their girths. The captive woman stretched her sore back from side to side.

"You are not used to riding like we are," Ramon said as he watched her closely.

"Of course not. I am a housewife, not a ..." She held her tongue, unwilling to say what she really wanted to.

Gomez glanced over at her as he checked the tightness of his mount's shoes. He stood up and shifted his gun belt slightly. "*Mujere*...Here is the important thing for you to remember...When we are in town, you will speak to no one. Do not try to call out for help, or Yellow Bird will kill you and the person you talk to...*Sabe?*" The evil sneer on his face conveyed the threat was not an idle one.

"I understand." She tried to mask the disgust she felt for the man, but her face betrayed her emotions.

Raoul laughed. "You no like me too much now, but by the time we get to Mexico, you will. I promise."

Betty's body shook at the thought of another sexual encounter with the stocky Comanchero.

§§§

247

CHAPTER FIVE

MINERAL WELLS, TEXAS

Three Fingers and Betty followed Jim Bob through town as the rest of the gang moved into their assigned positions.

Billy sat in a barrel-back chair outside the sheriff's office, smoking a hand-rolled quirley, as he casually whittled on a green stick of willow.

Yellow Bird paced the boardwalk outside the telegraph office, continuing down past Johnson's general store, turning around abeam Hannah's Millinery. His dark, almost black, eyes darted nervously as he scanned and sized up the unsuspecting townsfolk for potential threats to the gang.

Gomez finished his beer at the Golden Eye saloon and laid two silver dollars on the bar for two bottles of rye whiskey. The barkeep lifted the unlabeled bottles from under the polished bartop and set them down in front of him. "Here you go, mister. Y'all come back and see us, hear?"

Gomez nodded and tilted his head toward the swinging batwing doors, signaling Burt to follow him.

Once outside, he placed one bottle in each of his saddle bags, separating them to prevent breakage. The two saddled up and walked their horses three blocks north to the Merchants and Cattlemen's Bank.

They casually dismounted as Ramon Diaz and Pedro Rojas rode in from the north and tied up their mounts across the street to the hitching posts with wooden water troughs beneath them. Ramon's mount drank noisily as he wrapped the lead rope into a loose clove hitch.

Pedro stared across the boardwalk into the Bluebonnet Cafe. At three o'clock, it was nearly deserted and no one seemed to pay any heed to the two young strangers.

Raoul glanced up and down the street one last time. His right hand went up to the silver *concho* on the dingy blue wild rag hanging around his sweaty neck.

"That's the sign," Pedro whispered to his friend. His heart beat faster, as he and Ramone crossed the hard-packed dirt street. They stepped up onto the well-worn wood planks and stared at Gomez.

"*Tres minutos, mi amigos. No mas*," he said in a low voice. He turned his bandana around and lifted it over his nose, sliding the *concho* up close to the back of his head to hold it tight to his face.

The other three pulled theirs up to hide their identities as well. They all drew their sidearms, as Burt pulled the door to the bank open. The four entered quickly, closed and locked the nicely paneled oak entrance door behind them.

The lone teller glanced up at the sound of the deadbolt sliding into place. The distinct clicks of four Colts being thumbed back to full cock froze his tongue. He looked down the barrel muzzle of the chunky Mexican with the huge sombrero. It seemed at least an inch across.

"What's wrong, Carl?" the only customer in the bank asked as the color drained from the teller's face.

"Mineral Wells," announced the stagecoach driver he reined it to a stop at the Cross Timbers Stage line office next to the cafe. "Ten minutes, folks…We leave for Cleburne at 3:10 sharp." He set the hand brake and wrapped the ribbons round the well-worn pole.

The guard, a young man of nineteen years, set the Greener 12 gauge side by side on top of the coach and hopped down on the left side. He moved to the door and opened it up. One very pretty twenty-five year old woman and an older businessman that had just turned forty-nine were the only passengers.

"After you, Ma'am."

"Thank you, Mister Schmidt. You are such a gentleman," she said to the well-dressed executive with the longish blonde hair and Derby hat.

"Not at all, Miss. As I told you earlier, you remind me of my dear wife when she was your age. I enjoyed our brief acquaintance." His blue eyes sparkled, and although his bushy mustache hid much of his smile, she could tell that his friendly manner and kindness were genuine.

She took the hand offered by the guard and carefully placed one high-top high-heeled boot onto the steel rung and then the other on the street.

"Mary Lou!" A gray-headed clean-shaven man dressed in a gray broadcloth suit stepped off the boardwalk.

Her head snapped around at the sound of the familiar voice. "Father!" She ran to his open arms and they hugged and held each other tight.

Eric Schmidt ducked his head as he exited. Standing six foot three and weighing two hundred twenty-five, he nearly filled the portal in the coach.

"Need a hand, Mister?"

"Not yet, son. Not yet."

"The conveniences are out back if you need to stretch your legs."

"That I do...Would never make it another three hours." He grinned and headed for the front door of the stage office.

The driver handed a small paisley carpet bag and glossy black hat box down the guard and then stepped down onto the hard-packed street next to the boardwalk.

"He said 'open the damned safe' or do you have a problem with your hearin'?" Burt pistol whipped the terrified cashier with the barrel of his Frontier six shooter.

The blow caused an inch long gash to open up on the man's forehead just under his hair line. Crimson red quickly streamed down across his eye, down his cheek and stained his starched white high collared shirt.

The man staggered to his knees and held his hands high above his head. "I done told you I cain't open it...only Mister

Cummings has the combination." He pointed at the apparently empty manager's office. The door was partially ajar.

Burt glanced in, but saw no one behind the large walnut desk. "He in there?" he demanded.

"Uh huh." Carl nodded as he shook in mortal fear.

"Get up. You ain't hurt real bad." As Carl gasped for air and made it to his feet, Burt turned to the other robbers. "Watch this weasel."

He stepped into the office and eased around the desk. He could see a man's backside and soles of pair of new shoes sticking out from the kneehole in the massive piece of furniture.

Burt kicked the man's ankle. "Get out here, you gutless wonder, afore I put a hole in you God didn't put there."

The bank president quickly complied. The portly man crawfished out and got to his feet. His charcoal gray pinstriped suit sported a new wet stain in the crotch and down the right pant leg.

Burt glanced at the brass plaque on the open office door.

HIRAM G. CUMMINGS

PRESIDENT

"Get out there with the others, *Hiram*," he emphasized the man's name with considerable sarcasm.

Cummings did so. He stared derisively at the injured cashier. "I want you to know that you are fired…effective immediately."

"So, you're the man that can open the safe for us. I suggest that you get crackin'. Ain't got all day, tubby." Burt poked him in the gut with his shooter.

"My good man, I cannot in good conscience turn over the stockholder's money. You see…"

Carl's head exploded. Bits of brain matter sprayed across the small office and splattered the stunned banker. The hapless cashier dropped like a marionette with its strings severed, hitting the polished pecan floor with a sickening thud.

Gomez smiled broadly and pulled his mask down—his single gold tooth glistening with saliva. "*Hombre*. I know you don't give a tinker's damn about him." He pointed his pistol at the body as a pool of fresh blood flowed from the head wound. "But I think you care a lot about you. *Verdad?*"

Sweat dripped from Cumming's forehead. It wasn't because the room was particularly hot. His lower lip trembled, causing his jowls and mutton chop sideburns to quiver in unison.

"I would open it if'n I was you, Hiram. We done killed one a man today…all the rest are free. They cain't hang us but once." Ramon chuckled at his small joke.

THE COMANCHEROS

Cumming's hands were shaking as he knelt before the four foot square slate colored safe. His breathing became ragged and his heart pounded as he fumbled with the tumbler. He removed his half-framed reading glasses, pulled out a folded piece of white linen cloth and wiped a bit of brain matter from the right lens.

He gasped and dropped his monogrammed handkerchief to the floor as he processed the abject horror that he had just seen. Hiram stifled a mouthful of vomit and swallowed it. On the third attempt, he heard the telltale clunk of the last tumbler lock fall into place. He turned the black handle and pulled the heavy cast iron door open wide.

The sheriff loaded two rounds of double-ought buck into his Remington double barrel shotgun and put a handful of others the outer pocket of his long broadcloth morning coat.

He snapped the barrels back up in place and headed out to investigate the sound of gunfire that had interrupted his daily afternoon nap.

He closed the front door to the office, paying no attention to the young man sitting idly in the chair outside.

A second shot rang out from the direction of the bank. The sheriff broke into a run, but slammed forward, face down on the boardwalk as a third pistol shot rang out—this time from only yards behind him.

Billy Satterwhite watched for a second as the mortally wounded man twitched twice, and then became motionless. He holstered his shooter, sprang to the hitching post and untied the lead rope, grabbed the saddle horn and swung up in a single move.

A shot came from the telegraph office. Yellow Bird emerged from the font door with his smoking sixgun in his hand. The town's only telegraph operator lay dead on the floor inside.

Eric Schmidt had barely rebuttoned his fly when the first shot rang out in the bank. He sprinted back into the stage line office and found three people staring out the front window. "What's happening?" he asked the station manager.

"Dunno. Could be a robbery over to the bank. Cain't see past the consarned stage."

"But I could have sworn that I heard three shots. There's one rider down the street heading south."

The stagecoach driver pointed out the dark-skinned man. "Y'all know that Injun fella? Seems to be in a powerful hurry."

The stranger mounted up quickly and spurred the horse into a gallop, in the same direction as the first rider. Other townspeople began to poke their heads out their doors. Eric opened the stage station door and stepped outside.

"Mister! Wait for me," called out the young guard.

"Oh, hell. I cain't just sit in here," the driver said and exited the building a few seconds behind them.

Gomez and the gang left the bank with four bags of silver dollar coins, one small one with twenty dollar gold double eagles and yet another stuffed with paper currency. He and Burt swung into their saddles as the stage guard climbed up to retrieve his scattergun.

Ramon and Pedro were sprinting across the street when they spotted the young man. They fired simultaneously, hitting him in the chest and stomach. He toppled back off the side of the stage, landing at the feet of the well dressed businessman.

Eric didn't run for cover back into the building. He ducked beside the team and moved toward the front. He reached both hands back inside his suit coat, grasping the handles of a matched pair of Remington revolvers, set in identical black reverse draw holsters. With lightning fast speed, the two guns cleared leather, his thumbs cocking each one as they became level out in front of him.

The two young Mexican outlaws spotted the stagecoach driver on the boardwalk and began firing rapidly as the neared their horses. One shot hit its mark and he went down with a wound in the side of his chest.

Gomez and Burt Wilson were already saddled up. They spurred their horses and slapped their reins against the necks of the agitated mounts.

Ramon reached his horse first—he yanked at the loose knot on the lead rope, as motion to his right caught his eye. A mountain of a man stood up steady as a rock beside the coach team and pointed two pistols at his head. He never got the chance to get off a shot before two slugs tore into his face and forehead.

Pedro screamed as his best friend exploded in front of him. His terror was short-lived. The dapper businessman put four well-aimed shots into him in the blink of an eye. He staggered back, firing one last round into the street as he slumped over.

Gomez made himself small as he hugged the saddle horn to his chest. Burt turned in the saddle and took a shot at the blond man. It flew wide and stuck one of the stage team horses in the neck. He leaned forward and made himself low as the tall man stepped back onto the boardwalk.

Eric took time to aim at the fleeing robbers. They were already close to a hundred yards away. He lined up the conical front sight with the rider's form and sent a round flying. It was a solid hit to the man's side, but he couldn't see it. The last shot he took at the galloping horse's neck. It was one like those he had made dozens of times during the bloody conflict he called the War of Northern Aggression. The Remington's trigger broke cleanly at three pounds—the 250 grain bullet struck home.

The effect on the galloping horse was electric. Its severed spine caused steed's head to droop, the front legs to collapse first—the horse and rider somersaulted violently end over end.

The wounded Comanchero broke his back when the horse crashed down upon him. He lay there stunned and bleeding as Gomez thundered out of town.

In a matter of a few seconds, the town was silent and still as a tomb. The smell of sulfurous gunsmoke wafted away with the light autumn breeze.

Schmidt holstered the revolver in his right hand without even looking down. He kept his eyes on the last two men he had dropped as he thumbed open the other pistol's loading gate, brought the hammer to half-cock and swiftly reloaded with loose rounds he kept in his outside coat pocket.

Eric scanned the adjacent buildings for any additional threats as he stowed the left and refilled the right hand shooting iron. Soot covered empty brass cartridges tinkled to the boardwalk.

Slowly and deliberately, he closed the distance to the bloody body of the second Mexican. The man's shirt was soaked in blood and frothy red bubbles emanated from his lips as he tried to speak. Eric took no chances. He fired a round into the dying man's right eye. The impact of the exploding rear of his skull rebounding off the street momentarily lifted his head a couple of inches.

Schmidt stepped off the plank walkway and into the deserted street. As he neared the wounded Comanchero, he spotted the sprawling body of a man with a shotgun lying in front of him. The sign outside the nearby office answered the question in his mind.

He approached the wounded man with caution, spotting his worn shooter lying a few feet away. *Might have another one on him. I always do.* One look at the dark blood on his shirt front spoke volumes. *Liver shot. Maybe clipped the kidney as well. He's had the biscuit.* The man's right arm was bent as an unnatural angle.

"Cain't feel my legs…Mister, can you get me some water?"

"Nope, fresh out, I reckon. What's your name?"

"I ain't gonna tell you spit."

Eric holstered his wheel gun and reached back under the left side of his coat. He drew out a razor sharp stag-handled Bowie from its sheath. "We both know you're dyin' here.

That's a given. I have some questions and you have some answers. The only thing I don't know for certain is how much pain you're willing to take before you go...It's totally up to you."

"Got to hell."

"Maybe so, but I'll likely still have all my parts together when I get there...Not sure 'bout you." He stuck the blade an inch deep into the man's broken arm. The outlaw howled in pain.

"See how that works?"

The manager of the stage line station stared down the street as he lifted his injured driver to his feet. "Let's get you inside, Jehu. You need a doctor."

"Hurts like fire. What's all that caterwauling comin' from down yonder?"

"Don't rightly know. That passenger you brung down from Wichita Falls is talkin' to one of the desperadoes that shot up the place."

§§§

CHAPTER SIX

MINERAL WELLS, TEXAS

Mason Flynn trotted into town as the sun was dropping lower in the Texas sky. The main street was jammed with people milling about. He tugged back gently on the reins, bringing the two blue roan Morgans to a walk as he approached the crowd.

"Easy there, Smokey, boy. Somethin's goin' on here." He eased though the fringes of the crowd and spotted three caskets propped up against the wall outside the jailhouse.

The editor of the local paper had a tripod set up with a long black camera atop it. He ducked his head under a black cloth and held something over his head as one of the locals posed for the picture.

Now if that don't beat all. Wonder who the...

Woof. The magnesium powder in the photographer's tray went off with a brilliant flash. Flynn's train of thought was broken with the unexpected occurrence.

Smokey reared up on his hind legs and started bucking. Mason released the lead to his pack horse, Charlie spun and headed back north.

"Dammit! Settle down, boy!" Flynn tucked the panicked stallion's nose back to his right boot and stopped his pitching after several jumps.

He wheeled him around to see a tall stranger step out of the crowd holding his arms wide. The fleeing pack horse slowed and then tried to run for daylight between the man and some onlookers.

Charlie spun around and slid to a halt when the man snatched the flying lead rope and turned his head sharply to the side.

Flynn nudged Smokey to a fast walk to retrieve his pack pony. "Thanks, Mister. Dang picture taker spooked these two pretty bad. 'Preciate you lending a hand."

Eric held out the lead rope and noticed the cavalry officer's hat. "Nothing to it, my friend. Chalk it up to one cavalry man helpin' out another." He winked.

Flynn took hold of the braided rope and nodded at the older man. "You served with Grant?"

The stranger shook his head and grinned. "Nope. General Lee...but that was a long time ago."

"It was the Derby hat that threw me off...Say, what the hell happened here?" He looked over at the stagecoach. It only had a three horses in the traces. There were drag marks leading down the street.

Schmidt took in a deep breath. "A band of Comancheros came though and robbed the bank, killin' three inside plus the town sheriff, the telegraph operator, and the young man riding shotgun on the stage...Put our driver in the sawbones office with a lung shot...through and through. He ought to make it. "

Flynn's eye flew open wide. "Damnation! Did they have a woman with 'em?"

"Don't rightly know." He motioned with his thumb over his right shoulder. "The older one died before I could finish my full interrogation...A woman, you say? Why do you ask?"

Flynn's eyes narrowed, and then rimmed with tears as he had to vocalize the cold hard truth. "They took my wife...she's with child...'Bout six months along we figure." His voice cracked and then trailed off as a single tear ran down his cheek.

Schmidt watched the emotions reflected in the rider's face. He couldn't help but think back to his youth when a Yankee patrol killed both his folks, raping and murdering his beloved kid sister.

He stretched out his hand. "Get down. Your horses need a break and you need a beer to wash down that trail dust. There's five left in the Gomez gang...You're gonna need help. I'll buy a horse...and we'll go get her back."

FARMER'S LIVERY CORRAL

The three men walked from the back of the livery office and stood next to a couple of sturdy corrals. Not a single blade of grass grew in either one.

Eric studied the large black horse in an enclosure all by himself. "I'll take that stallion you told me about. He has great confirmation and is the proper size, all right. Gonna call him Thunder."

Ken Farmer, the grizzled owner of the livery, spat out a brown stream of tobacco juice and nodded. He wiped the dribble out of the corner of his mouth on the back of his weather-worn hands. "Tell you what, Mister Schmidt. You got yourself a goodun there. Sixteen hands of fire an' brimstone. Trained him myself...Best fifty dollars you'll ever spend."

Eric handed him two gold double eagles and a single eagle. "Everybody says you got the best horseflesh in the county...We'll retrieve my rig off the stage and be back in five minutes."

The two shook hands. Flynn and Schmidt headed back into the center of town.

"Need any more supplies? Ain't much south of here for quite a ways."

Flynn shook his head. "Got plenty in the panniers. Wait a minute...Drink coffee?"

"I do. Runnin' low, I suspect?"

"The sorry bastards cleaned us out at the ranch. I'll pick up another sack at the mercantile."

"Go with you...This little city hat isn't fit for the trail."

An hour later, Flynn and Schmidt crossed the steel truss bridge over the Brazos. The muddy water churned ominously below the thick wooden planks. The setting sun was casting long shadows.

A tiny bit of cloth caught Flynn's eye, he quickly reined up, dismounted and retrieved the signal. A brief smile crossed his face. "Well, sir, we know she's still alive and marking their trail for us."

"That's good news. The bad news is we're losin' our light. Won't be enough moon to track 'em, if they veer off the road."

"But that man you questioned…didn't he say they were headed for Mexico?"

"He did…But the leader, Gomez, might have changed his mind after losing three men and three quarters of their loot."

He looked up the road as it climbed into some hilly country. "Mexico is a big place. They could cross over anywhere from Brownsville to El Paso."

Flynn sank back into his saddle as he reviewed the map of Texas in his mind. "You figured they have…what? Hour lead on us?"

"Likely. We've been making good time and their ponies are probably more tired than ours. Can't see 'em ridin' in the dark…Step on a rock, end up shanks mare, and then they're in a hellova fix. Next to nothing between here and Stephenville."

Mason nodded. "Point taken…What say we top that next ridge and see what looks like a decent campsite."

"Lead on."

Flynn hesitated for a moment. "Can't thank you enough for pitchin' in with me...sight unseen. Most men wouldn't do it."

Eric nodded and then looked him right in the eye. "Most wouldn't...I'm not most men, and neither are you....Taking off after eight hard cases all by yourself...Now that takes some sand." He took a sip of water from his canteen sloshed it around and swallowed. "We'll find her...I know it."

ERATH COUNTY

Gomez sat on a Navajo horse blanket and counted out the gold coins from the single bank bag the robbers managed to get away with. He made a tall stack for himself, much smaller ones for the four others, and then scooped his lion's share back into the canvas sack.

"With three gone, you guys get a bigger share. Too bad for Pedro and Ramon. I liked those two pretty good."

Billy had been in a somber mood at the unexpected loss of three members of the gang, but perked up at the payday. "Boy howdy! I ain't never had me that much money at one time in all my born days! How much do we git?"

"You get three hundred each." Raoul pointed at one the stacks of double eagles.

Billy eagerly grabbed up his share, his eyes glistening in the flickering campfire light. "We gonna pick up some more men?"

"*Si.* San Antonio has lots of *caballeros.* Have a cousin who lives there...We find some good ones."

After supper, Gomez stared blankly at the fire. Suddenly, he had a thought. "*Caramba!* I knew I forgot something!"

He scrambled to his feet and strode quickly to the stack of saddles near the picket line and retrieved the two bottles of whiskey.

Holding onto one for himself, he tossed the other to Yellow Bird. "Drink up, *mi amigos!* Tonight, we celebrate! Full bellies! Gold jingling in our pockets! Life is good!" He twisted the cork free, and took a healthy swig. It burned all the way down. "*Aye, Chihuahua! Es muy sabroso!*"

Betty stared at them with barely hidden disgust as a slow fire built inside her. *If only I can somehow slip away...I pray that they fall into a drunken stupor and pass out.*

She glanced out into the fading firelight at her mare, tied up on the remuda with the other mounts. *I can ride bareback if need be. My Mason is coming for me, I just feel it.*

Flynn glanced over at the big man from Colorado. His eyes were still open as he laid back with his head resting on his saddle. "Never asked you where you were headed before all this happened."

Eric smiled a wry grin. "Not a pleasure trip, I assure you, Mason. Sold my old home place east of Tyler in Smith County and was supposed to close the real estate later this week. Have to move my folks and baby sister's remains to a cemetery in town...Wouldn't be proper just to leave them out there after the place sold."

"Reckon not." Flynn tried to best to avoid thinking about such a somber task. Two days of hard riding took its toll. He drifted off to a fitful sleep.

Gomez corked the half-full bottle and stared at the sleeping figure of his prize captive. Three Fingers set another two broken pecan tree branches on the fire and drained the last of the rye whiskey from their shared fifth.

As the dry deadfall began to burn with more intensity, so did the passion in the scar-faced Comanchero. He began to crawl the fifteen feet separating him and Betty.

When he had reached her blanket, he rose up on his knees, unbuckled his gun belt and shucked the galluses off his shoulders. He swayed back and forth as he fumbled with the front buttons on his pants.

Once he had exposed his manhood, he reached down and lifted up the unsuspecting woman's dress and petticoats, exposing her young shapely legs, Gomez fell on top of her and attempted to kiss her as she awoke.

Betty's eyes flew open and she screamed, at least until his rough hand covered her mouth.

"Be quiet! There is nothing that you can do...Don't try to fight me, *Chica.*"

She ripped her right arm from the grasp of his left hand and jammed her thumb into his face.

Gomez howled in pain, as his left eyeball exploded. He rolled off of her and she attempted to cover herself as best she could.

The Mexican cursed her as he crawled back to his gunbelt and drew out a six inch blade.

"*Puta estupido!* See what you did to me?" Blood dripped down his face and across his chest.

Slashing and yelling, he came at her in a drunken rage. Betty tried to defend herself, but to no avail. The blade laid open her arms and her neck. Crimson spurted from her severed arteries.

She struggled mightily to even try to take in a breath as the horror unfolded. The man sat back for a moment and then stuck the knife deep in her pregnant belly...

§§§

CHAPTER SEVEN

ERATH COUNTY, TEXAS

The late October sun hadn't cleared the horizon when the two former cavalrymen saddled up and rejoined the search. Breakfast of coffee and beef jerky would have to make do for men on a mission. Neither man had slept well.

Flynn led the way, with Schmidt taking a turn and holding onto the pack horse. After only seven miles, the six sets of tracks broke off to the left from the stagecoach road.

"Lookie here...musta made camp down near the creek..." The sight of a sorrel mare gazing in the distance stopped him cold. "Penny?"

He wheeled his stallion to the east and spurred him into a gallop. "Betty! Betty!" he cried out as he closed the two hundred yards to his wife's favorite horse.

He was wholly unprepared for the scene that awaited him. Mason slid out of the saddle even before Smokey came to a stop. He sprinted over to the prone woman as he called out her name.

Eric rode up in time to see Flynn fall to his knees beside her and scream a cry of anguish that made the hairs on his arms stand on end. *Oh my God, no. It wasn't supposed to happen like this.*

He ground tied Thunder and swung out of the saddle. Stepping quickly to Mason's side, he squatted down and placed a strong hand on the grieving man's shoulder. Flynn held on to Betty, sobbing and shaking.

Eric glanced around the campsite. He moved to the rock ring and felt the stones rimming the camp fire. They were still very warm.

After he regained his composition, somewhat, Flynn staggered to his feet. He stared down at the lifeless figure and then spotted the bloody tear in her dress. He began to shake again as he stammered, "They killed my wife...and my...son...my baby boy."

Eric wrapped both arms around him and held him tight. "They're in God's hands now." Tears streamed down his face as well.

Mason released his hold on Eric and wiped his eyes with both hands. "I cain't just leave her here. She belongs with my family in Henrietta."

"I understand. Let me help you wrap her up."

Flynn shook his head as he looked over at the sorrel. "I can handle it. Don't let those bastards get away. Not now...Not after this."

"We missed 'em by only thirty minutes. I can pick up whatever supplies I'll need later on...Reckon I'll have to leave word for you...one way or another...with the telegraph office back in Jacksboro."

Flynn inhaled deeply, stopping the stream of tears for the time being. He nodded and stuck out his hand. "Good hunting...God speed, my friend."

The big man shook his hand firmly and placed his other on Flynn's shoulder. "I'm truly sorry for your loss. May God have mercy on her soul." Without saying another word, he swung atop his black stallion and urged it into an easy rocking chair lope.

Mason stood there for a second and watched them make the turn south onto the road to Stephenville. Suddenly, he felt more alone than at any other time in his life.

Topping a long uphill climb to a ridge, the road continued straight as an arrow down below to a creek crossing and up a shallow slope. Five dark objects were strung out in single file on the far side of the creek.

Been following the only sets of tracks left since the last rain. No doubt in my mind who those riders are. He swung clear of his saddle and unshucked a massive rifle from its custom scabbard and tied his mount to a sweet gum sapling.

The 1886 Winchester sported a twenty-six inch octagon barrel with a full length magazine tube. Studying the wind and gauging the distance to be a full 700 yards, Eric flipped the tang sight upright and quickly spun the knurled knob around until the eyepiece rested equidistant between spaces marked 7 and 8.

He stepped forward twenty yards to the summit and dropped down prone in the roadway between the wagon ruts. He jacked the lever forward and aft to send a .45-90 round into the cavernous chamber. He lifted the wide flat brim of his new hat and set it down to shade the rear peep sight and settled into a stable shooting position.

Gomez moaned as the throbbing in his head continued. "*Oww. Puta zuela.* I should have killed her the first night."

Riding just behind the injured leader of the Comancheros band, Jim Bob Jones wasn't sure what the man had said. "You say somethin', Boss?"

"Yeah…I said shut your mouth."

Jim Bob turned around in the saddle and shrugged.

Three Fingers grinned. "*El Jefe* in bad mood. White witch blind him good."

"Still say we need to get him to a sawbones, *muy pronto*. He gonna get hisself a whopper infection, iff'n you ask me." Billy Satterwhite nodded agreement to his own muttered statement, but no one else paid it any heed.

Yellow Bird rode in the last position. Out of habit, he turned around to check his back trail—a constant nagging possibility for long riders on the run. A puff of smoke almost a half mile away peaked his curiosity. His dark eyes narrowed as the gray cloud drifted with the light breeze.

Curiosity may have killed the cat, but it was a 500 grain lead slug that took off the top two inches of the renegade Comanche's skull. The dead man slumped to the left as his head snapped around from the tremendous impact.

The heavy .45 caliber projectile was far from finished. It notched the cantle on Billy's saddle before it tore through his back, blasted apart the buckle on his gun belt and severed the

276

spine of his mount. His bloodcurdling scream followed the bone crushing *thwack* the big bore's slug made when it hit flesh and bone.

Three Fingers reined his pony around at the awful sound behind him. The report of the distant buffalo gun came a split second later. He wasted no time attempting any effort to save his two compatriots. He spurred his horse back in the direction of Stephenville.

Eric levered another round into position and centered the front sight on the nearest Comanchero. He squeezed the trigger with a steady pull. The rifle bucked and belched another cloud of acrid black powder smoke. He reloaded as the haze drifted clear and quickly found another target.

Three Fingers slapped his reins at the horse's neck, only to watch a red mist explode from the steed's chest as a second slug found its mark. The mount's legs collapsed in a heap, tossing the rider over his head causing him to land badly on a rocky outcrop.

Billy screamed for help. Jim Bob looked past him at the nearly headless body of Yellow Bird. *That injun had three hundred in gold in his poke.* He rode past the hysterical white man and stepped down to gather up the dead man's share. He was rifling through the renegade's pockets when death from afar came calling. His body slammed to the roadway, mere feet from hapless Billy.

Yellow Bird's startled paint horse bolted south, running past Three Fingers. The injured Kiowa, his broken nose bleeding profusely, sprinted and leapt toward the fleeing *caballo*. His good hand grabbed hold of the saddle horn with a death grip as the momentum yanked him on board as another bullet ricocheted off the hard-packed roadway right behind him.

Eric muttered to himself as he jacked the last round into the chamber. "Take your time and make it count, dammit."

The rider he had fired at last was beginning to ride in a zig zag pattern. "Took you long enough, fool." He smiled as he watched the furthest rider reaching the ridge crest. *Eight hundred...maybe eight and a quarter*. He mentally added another four feet of drop to his 750 yard sight setting and held the front bead over the galloping man. Schmidt took in a deep breath and let it out halfway as the trigger released the sear. Gunsmoke obscured the distant ridge. When it cleared, the last two riders had disappeared.

Eric got to his feet, walked over to the slightly nervous horse and patted him on the neck. "Easy big boy. That's all the shooting for a while." He unbuckled the near side saddlebag, reached inside and retrieved a full box of

Winchester rifle ammo. He filled the mag tube, returned the cartridge box to the bag and latched it securely. "Let's go give our handy work a look see."

Billy was getting weaker by the minute. His blood loss had stanched, only because he had already lost so much. The dead horse ended up atop his right leg and his 1873 carbine. His well-worn shooter lay just out of reach behind him.

The sound of boots crunching on the dirt road puzzled him. "Who's there? Help me...I'm in bad way."

Eric cautiously stepped into view, looking for any hidden weapon the wounded man might possess. Seeing none, he lowered the muzzle of his rifle. "You must be Billy. Not old enough to be Burt."

Satterwhite looked incredulously at the huge stranger. "Mister, who told you that? I never laid eyes on you afore."

"Not important, boy. You don't have much time left, and I have a few questions to ask."

The former Confederate cavalry general collected the weapons and ill gotten gains from his three vanquished foes, as was his long time practice. He saddled up, grabbed the lead rope to the bay pony that the recently departed Burt Wilson had ridden and headed south.

JACKSBORO, TEXAS

Flynn left the Western Union office with a cryptic message and a passel of questions racing through his mind. *Why on earth would he send me a wire transfer for $900? What's in that letter that they're holding for me at the post office?*

Once he opened the large manila envelope, the four page handwritten letter explained what had transpired.

Eric apologized profusely for losing their trail in Austin. The two remaining murdering Comancheros had taken a southbound train out of Stephenville, but somehow were not on it when the Texas Rangers met it in the capital city.

A stack of freshly printed wanted posters with the presumed likenesses of Raoul Gomez and Three Fingers was included. The part about how Betty had partially blinded the would-be rapist before he killed her gave him chills.

Flynn creased the letter neatly and put it and the posters back inside the folder. He went to the bank and withdrew only $200 for traveling money. He tried to push the painful memories of Betty's burial aside as he bought tickets on the next train headed south.

THE COMANCHEROS

NUEVO LAREDO, MEXICO

It was late on a chilly Christmas Eve when Mason Flynn crossed over the Rio Grande at Laredo. Two months of tracking, asking a thousand questions and even paying for information when he had no other choice, led him to the rough border town.

His face was no longer clean shaven. A short dark beard had made the daily ritual a thing of the past. Six horses were tied up outside an adobe cantina. One of them was a paint pony—a clue that did not go unnoticed.

He could hear laughter coming from inside. *Good a place as any to start.* He tied off at the hitching post and loosened the girths on his two Morgans.

Stepping inside the swinging batwing doors, after he let his eyes adjust, he could see several tables with local men, judging from their attire.

Two young ladies of the evening eyed him as he stepped to the bar. He gave the prettier of the two a fake smile and a wink. She smiled back and got up from the table and headed his way.

"You like a little company?" she said with a distinct Mexican accent. Her cotton dress was scooped low in the front to accentuate her ample cleavage and her coal black hair reeked of cigarette smoke.

"Maybe. Need me some tequila to wash down this trail dust first."

"You buy Elena a drink, Americano?"

"You bet." He held up two fingers to the skinny bar keeper. "*Dos tequilas, amigo.*"

"*Tenemos solamente mescal.*"

"Close enough." He motioned for the man to bring it.

The man poured the shots into a pair of semi-clean glasses and slid them across the rough plank bar top. "*Cincuenta centavos.*"

Flynn dug a quarter out of vest pocket and flipped it to the young man. "Keep 'em comin'." He handed one to the working girl and then held up his glass.

She smiled seductively as they clinked the glasses together. "*Salud,*" they said in unison.

Mason downed the clear liquid in a single gulp. *That's some watered down rot-gut crap. 'Bout the worst I ever tasted. At least it's cheap.*

He turned his back to the bar and studied the crowd in earnest. One table had four men seated and one empty chair. Two were Anglos, a third was Mexican and the fourth was slightly darker, possible Indian. All wore hats and were playing poker from what he could determine.

Flynn started to turn back toward the bar when the occupant of the fifth chair stepped back in through a back door to the smoke-filled cantina. He was a heavy set Mexican wearing a black sombrero and a matching black patch over his left eye. Mason's sky blue eyes narrowed as he watched the man adjust his gun belt slightly and then take a seat.

The slight change in his facial expression didn't go unnoticed by the woman. She held up another glass of mezcal and stoked his face with her other hand. "Something wrong, my friend?"

Flynn smiled broadly as he took the proffered glass. "No, *Senorita*. I think everything is gonna be just fine." He sipped the smoky flavored liquor distilled from the agave as he formulated a plan.

§§§

CHAPTER EIGHT

NUEVO LAREDO, MEXICO

The five poker players drank from their community bottle of mescal. One by one, they excused themselves to make a trip out the back door. Flynn grinned when the plan came to him.

"Y'all have an outhouse in the back?"

The bartender gave him a quizzical look.

Oh, hell. What was it they called that thing in Santa Fe? Oh, yeah. "*Tiene un retrete?*"

The kid laughed and pointed to the back door. *"Si, como no."*

Flynn held up one finger to the erstwhile hooker. *"Un momentito, por favor."*

She grinned and reached for another round.

He headed across the room, not looking directly at the table of Comancheros, he had to pass right in front of them to get where he was headed. They were all well-lubricated and engrossed in their poker hands.

The one he took to be at least part Indian held the cards close to his chest. His left hand was partially mangled. *Three Fingers. I'll be a suck egg mule.* He glanced away for a split second as his jaw tightened and then took a quick gander at the man with the eye patch. There was a wicked knife scar on his left cheek. *That's him. Got 'em both.*

Gomez looked up at Flynn as he passed. The native Texan looked away, trying not to make eye contact that might betray his raging hatred. He couldn't miss a new scar on the Mexican's other cheek leading to a circular chunk missing from his right ear. *Damn if that's not a .45 caliber bullet graze. Eric will be surprised as hell to hear that he didn't miss him completely.*

Mason finished his business in the comfort facility and then circled around to the front of the building. He tightened the girths on both horses and stuffed some supplies into his sheared lambskin coat, and then circled to back the rear and reentered.

An hour later, Gomez laid his hand down on the table. "What in hell is taking that injun so long? It's his turn to deal."

He pushed back from the table and got his feet, more than a little wobbly from the agave nectar. He headed out back to the privies.

A man stepped from the shadows on his blind side and his world turned black in an instant.

It was past 9AM when Gomez awoke. He head ached like crazy and his body shivered to the cold. When his eyes finally focused, he realized that he was not in Nuevo Laredo any more. He tried to sit up but found strong rawhide straps bound him from hand and foot.

His sombrero was missing and he could feel the dry desert sand and rock beneath him. A green mesquite stick separated his jaws and a piece of latigo secured the ends behind his head. *Caramba! Where are my clothes?* He lifted his head and stared at a filthy saddle blanket laid across his torso. The smell of bacon and coffee filled the air.

Flynn sat cross-legged, Indian style on his sleeping roll blanket. He was sipping a second cup of black coffee from a graniteware mug, but poured it out when he saw the Comanchero start to waken. "Thought you were gonna sleep all day, you worthless son of a bitch." He got to his feet and stretched side to side.

He stepped between the two captives and ripped the blankets off of their naked bodies, exposing them both to the cold December air. "Merry Christmas."

The two struggled to get free, but their efforts were of no avail. Flynn had used in inch-wide strips that did not yield.

He watched in minor amusement as they tried to yell and only mumbled against the mesquite gags.

"What's the matter? Cat got your tongues?"

He lifted up a sheath knife he had taken from Raoul's gunbelt. He slowly pulled out the blade and stared at it. His heart turned hard as flint—his blue eyes darkened as they became little more than slits. He stood and straddled the fat Mexican. He grinned at the outlaw's shrinking manhood. "Gettin' cold, are you?"

He leaned in closer and locked eyes with the terrified Comanchero. "You don't know me from Adam's ox, do you?...Remember bein' in Jack County, Texas?"

Gomez racked his brain. *Where the hell is Jack County Texas?* He shook his head.

"Blade looks kind sharp...Is this the one you used to butcher my wife and unborn son?"

Gomez's mind suddenly recalled the picture of a cavalry officer in a ranchhouse far away. The hat was the same. The eyes were the same only they were not blue in the sepia tone photograph. His bladder let go and soaked his belly.

"Please allow me to introduce myself...I'm Mason Flynn." He knelt down and placed tip of the knife on the man's chest. "Easy name to remember, I reckon. I'll show you how it's spelled."

He pressed the blade a half-inch into the chest muscle and began drawing the letter M. Tiny rivulets of crimson seeped down the Comanchero's side and the matted hair on chest.

Gomez arched his back, writhing in pain as he fought to get away, but his efforts were in vain. His guttural screams were muffled by the inch thick mesquite stick. By the time Mason finished scribing his last name, the outlaw's eyes had rolled up in his head and he passed out.

"Yep, it's true...Pain will make a man pass out."

Flynn stood up and turned to the Kiowa. The man's eyes were wide with abject fear. His body shook and the avenging widower wondered if it was from the cold or because he had seen his fellow tribesmen torture their enemies at length.

He straddled the much smaller man and shook his head. "Bet anticipatin' what this is gonna feel like is just about as bad as the cuttin' itself." He wrote his name and then Betty's.

THE COMANCHEROS

He carved hers into the man's forehead in V shaped notches.

The vengeance lasted for hours. He gelded both men and left their bloody testicles on their chests where they could see them. Flynn then cut off their ears, saving one of Gomez's as a souvenir to send to the man who had disfigured it.

He gathered up bit of dried grass, twigs, sticks and roots growing out the steep sides of a nearby arroyo where he had hobbled his two horses. Carefully, he stacked the tinder and smaller sticks, following up with larger ones on top of their emasculated groins.

Before he set the fires alight, he cut the rawhide holding the gags in place. He wanted the last thing either man to hear to be the screams of the other Comanchero.

Flynn removed the hobbles from his mounts, and cinched them up snug for the long trip home. He led them up a draw and into the secluded clearing that he had found well off the closest road.

He pulled out the tin of waterproof matches and walked over to the two ill-fated outlaws. The bloody knife lay between Gomez and Three Fingers.

"It's written in the good book, "*Vengeance is mine, sayeth the Lord*...I 'spect he was too busy...so he sent me.""

With that, he grabbed the Mexican's Bowie and buried it to the hilt in the Comachero's lower belly—exactly where he had seen the wound on his beloved. He left the blade there as the fat man screamed and cried out for mercy.

Flynn started the fire between Raoul's legs, and then used the same match on the Kiowa. The dry desert kindling burned hot, sending only wisps of smoke heavenward.

Mason watched for only a few seconds as the screams grew louder and more shrill.

He picked up the reins, jabbed a boot in the stirrup and drew himself up into the saddle. "Take us home, Smokey."

The stocky Morgan obliged.

The sound of the two doomed and anguished men faded in the distance behind him. He began to whistle an old familiar tune that his mother used to sing him as a child. *God Rest Ye Merry Gentlemen…*

§§§§

BUCK STIENKE

Buck is a native son of Texas, hailing originally from Houston. He spent many formative years in the rural Texas Hill Country and still has family there. For a man who usually doesn't care much for hats, he's worn plenty of different and widely varied ones in his lifetime (so far!): Fighter Pilot flight helmet, Air Force Officer's wheel hat, semi-pro Football Team helmet (Offensive Team Captain, Austin Texans), Delta Air Lines Captain hat, Rancher's Stetson, Gunsmith's ball cap, Weapons Designer and Author (usually, just puts on his thinkin' cap!).

He enjoys the process of creating a tale that can draw people into an adventure and take them to another place in another time. Buck believes the author should make the reader's five senses come alive as they experience the story. If the author doesn't feel it, neither will the reader. He calls the entirely credible mixture of fact and fiction in his writing style "faction".

Buck lives in North Texas with his wife Carolyn.

Buck's Amazon page:
www.amazon.com/Buck-Stienke/e/B0057XZNKW
website: www.timbercreekpress.net

THE FIRST

BY

BRAD DENNISON

CHAPTER ONE

JACKSBORO, TEXAS

Gomer popped a lemon drop into his mouth, and leaned against a post that held up the overhanging roof overhead.

The boardwalk underfoot was old and scuffed, just like his boots. Hand-me-downs from a man he never knew—traded in at the cobbler shop down the street for a new pair.

THE FIRST

Henry Jenkins, the cobbler, knew Gomer didn't earn a whole lot of money as the deputy sheriff of Jack County, so he let him have the old boots for two dollars.

Gomer wasn't very tall, but his feet were unusually big, and the boots fit him perfectly. Now he wore them with spurs strapped on. He had to admit, he liked the way they jingled when he walked.

Slim Parker was standing on the boardwalk with him, leaning one shoulder against the other side of the post. Slim was a darkie, a term Gomer was learning to stop using. The proper term these days was *Negro* or colored. That's what people said when they were talking about men like Slim, but trying not to be hurtful. Gomer figured they had been hurt enough, and deserved to be called what they wanted to be called.

Slim was a Chickasaw Freedman, and in Texas, Gomer doubted anyone would give Slim any trouble. But to folks back East, a Negro was a Negro. More and more easterners were coming West, and bringing their so-called civilized ways with them.

Slim was taller than Gomer, and he wore an old hat with a wide, floppy brim that was pushed back on his head. He had a revolver at his hip, like most cowhands did. His legs were long and bowed a bit, and with his thumbs hooked into his gunbelt, he spat a stream of tobacco juice out into the street.

Gomer said, "You ought'a try lemon drops. Lot less messy."

Slim looked at him. "How old are you?"

Gomer shrugged. "Nineteen…Far as I know."

"What do you mean, far as you know."

"Well, I was so young when I was born, don't rightly remember it."

Slim grinned and gave a snorting chuckle. "Well, you're old enough to chew tobacky. Started usin' chaw when I was fourteen."

"Tried it onct, but I swallowed it by accident and it almost made me sick."

Slim was giving a full-on grin, now. "You ain't supposed to swallow it."

"Found that out the hard way. I'll just stick to my lemon drops."

Gomer, being a bit shorter than Slim, had a thin frame. His shirt bagged on him a little, and the county deputy sheriff badge was pinned to his left shirt pocket.

Suspenders went up and over his shoulders, and he wore a revolver at his left and turned backward for a crossdraw. He had seen the Texas Ranger Ike Hawkins wearing two guns that way.

Gomer had tried wearing two guns, but Sheriff Flynn had said he looked ridiculous. And besides, wearing two guns was heavy. So Gomer had gone back to one.

THE FIRST

He had taken to practicing his cross draw out behind the livery barn. He had to admit he wasn't very good with it, but Ike Hawkins made it look easy, and according to legend, Wild Bill Hickok wore his guns that way. Had to be something to it.

Parker was a good fella. A little older than Gomer, he was a cowhand who Flynn had hired as a deputy a while back. But lawman work had been slow lately and county funds were a bit meager, so Sheriff Flynn had let Slim go. The sheriff said he might still need to hire Slim from time to time, if no ranch hired him on.

Gomer hated to see a man go without work, but it meant Slim was still in town hanging around, and it gave Gomer someone to talk to. Not that he couldn't talk to Sheriff Flynn, but he looked up to the sheriff, and he had to admit, sometimes he tried too hard not to look stupid in front of the sheriff, and wound up looking even stupider than he had been afraid of looking. Slim was more of a regular fella.

Platt had heard Marshal Fiona Miller use the word *peer*, once, to mean someone who was your equal. That was what Slim was, as far as Gomer was concerned. A peer. He didn't care none that Slim was a Negro. Some did, but Gomer felt that was small-thinking.

Marshal Miller sure was smart. She knew all sorts of words, and could quote that Shakespeare feller all day. And dang, she weren't bad to look at. Not that Gomer would admit that to anyone but Slim.

"Hey," Slim said. "Ain't that Joe Munson?"

Slim was fixing his eyes down the street. Gomer followed the gaze. A man was on horseback, riding toward them. Sure did look like Joe.

Munson was somewhere between forty and fifty, and had the kind of lined and weathered face that can only come from years of riding into the sun and wind.

He operated a stage coach way station twenty miles outside of town, but Gomer had heard the man had scouted for the Apache, and had worked as a drover bringing herds from Texas to the railheads back in the '70s. He rode a horse like he was born to it, and the gun at his hip wasn't there for decoration.

He reined up by Platt and Slim. Joe had a look of real urgency on his face, and before Gomer could say *howdy*, Joe said, "Gomer. The sheriff in?"

The deputy nodded. "He's up to the office."

When Gomer had left the office, Sheriff Flynn had been at his desk, drinking coffee and going through a stack of dodgers that had arrived on the stage yesterday.

"Thanks," Joe said, and rode on toward the sheriff's office.

"Wonder what that was all about," Slim said, and hocked another stream of brown tobacco juice toward the dirt.

"Don't know," Gomer replied. "Come on, let's go find out."

Gomer sucked on his lemon drop while he walked down the boardwalk toward the sheriff's office. The day was hot. Texas in the summertime. The sun was harsh, and when he stepped along a section of boardwalk that didn't have a roof overhanging it, he could feel the sun burning into his shoulders.

The town's street was normally muddy from the horses doing their business, and from folks emptying chamber pots in the morning. But today, it was dry and dusty.

Gomer found the front door of the sheriff's office hanging open. As hot as it was, you left the doors and windows open hoping to catch a cross breeze.

Joe Munson was standing in front of the sheriff's desk. "The stage was late, Sheriff. I mean, really late. So I rode on up the trail...Thought maybe they'd busted an axle or somethin'."

Sheriff Flynn was a man larger-than-life in Gomer's view. He wanted to one day be like him, but he wondered if it was too tall a task. He didn't think there was a man alive who could handle Sheriff Mason Flynn in a fist fight, and there was no man alive who was faster with his guns.

Sure, Gomer had heard the stories about Bass Reeves. He was the best lawman who had ever lived. And he had heard there was no one faster with a gun than Dusty McCabe. But

Gomer didn't believe any of it. In his mind, Mason Flynn was the best there ever was.

Munson continued, "Found the stage, 'bout eight miles out of the way station...It was terrible, sheriff...Everyone was dead."

"What do you mean...dead?" asked Flynn.

"Shot. Every last one of 'em. Their bags had been gone through, and it looked like rings had been pulled off'n their fingers."

Mason Flynn got to his feet. He glanced to the doorway and saw Gomer standing there.

"Deputy Platt," he said. "Get two horses saddled. We're ridin' out there."

Joe said, "Make that three."

Slim Parker had followed Gomer to the sheriff's office.

He said from behind Platt and over his shoulder, "Make that four."

Flynn stepped out from around his desk. He stood tall, taller than Gomer could ever hope to. His shoulders were wide and filled out a dark blue bib-front shirt. He had a full mustache, and eyes that Gomer thought could pierce a hole right through you if he wanted to. He wore a revolver strapped to his right side, and his county sheriff badge was pinned to his shirt.

"That you back there, Slim?" he asked.

"Yes sir."

"I need to hire you on again, to watch the office while we're gone...Be a presence here and tell folks we'll be back as soon as we can. Be a day's pay for you."

He glanced at Gomer. "Sometime today, Paltt, sometime today."

"Oh, yes, sir." Gomer ran to the livery and got three horses saddled. He rode one and led the other two back to the office.

Flynn deputized Slim, and the Chickasaw Freedman stood in the doorway with a badge pinned to his shirt.

"I wish I was goin' with you y'all."

Gomer grinned. "Look at it this way, Slim. You been lookin' for work. Now you got a payin' job...Leastwise till we get back."

The sheriff turned his blue roan Morgan gelding down the street and clicked it to a light trot, Gomer and Munson fell into place alongside him.

Munson said, "Ain't none of my business, Sheriff...but is it wise to leave a darkie in charge of your office?"

"You're right, Joe" the sheriff said. "Not any of your business."

Gomer grinned a little. He knew that was coming.

"I'm more interested if a man has backbone. That he be someone you can rely on...Slim Parker is a man to ride the river with."

Gomer knew Munson wasn't alone in how he felt. He heard talk about efforts back east to keep Negroes from voting, and Gomer didn't understand any of it. He agreed with the sheriff. But more and more folks were coming west, and bringing their civilized notions of race and hatred with them.

28 MILES OUTSIDE OF JACKSBORO

They found the stage passengers much like Munson had described. Bodies were scattered about. Five men, and one woman.

One of the men Gomer recognized as Abel Jackson. He had a beard that was thick and wild looking, and turning a steel gray. He had been the stage driver, but now he was flat on his back and his eyes were staring toward the sky with no life in them at all. There was a dark bullet hole in his forehead.

"These people were executed," said Flynn.

Carpetbags had been opened and their contents dumped on the ground. One trunk had been opened and clothes that had been inside were now tossed about.

"Looks like whoever did this went through everything…Took their time," observed the sheriff.

Gomer had never seen anything quite like this. He had been working for the sheriff for about a year. Most of his duties amounted to walking the rounds every so often, making coffee in the morning, and pulling down old dodgers and tacking up new ones.

When they had someone in the jail cell, Gomer was usually tasked with going down to Sewel's and bringing back a meal for the prisoner.

He stared at the bodies. Each of them with a bullet to the head. He thought the sheriff was right. Them people had just been shot down. Murdered.

The sheriff swung out of the saddle and began looking about on the ground. Checking for tracks.

"How many were there?" Munson said.

"I'd say four. The sand isn't soft and the prints aren't clear, though."

Gomer was still in the saddle, his eyes fixed on the woman. She must have been mighty pretty, when she was alive. She looked about his age, with dark hair that had been tied in some sort of hairdo, but was now falling free. Probably came loose when she was shot and fell to the ground.

She was lying on her back, and her eyes were shut. There was a gash and a spot of blood at her hairline.

The skin of her right ring finger was all torn up. Them outlaws must have pulled a ring right off'n her finger, taking hide with it.

Then the woman moved. Her heard turned to one side. And she made a little groaning sound.

"Sheriff!" Gomer called out, leaping out of the saddle so fast he startled his horse, and the horse took a couple of sideways steps. "She's alive! The woman! She's alive."

§§§

CHAPTER TWO

JACKSBORO, TEXAS

They got her back to town by cutting some thin poles from a small grove of persimmon trees growing near the trail, along with some carpet they tore out of the stage, and making a travois.

Doc Mosier was an older man with thin white hair and tired-looking eyes. "That bullet cut a furrow atop her skull. She's gonna have a scar, but her hair should cover most of it. When they pulled her ring off, they almost pulled her finger off too, so I'm going to have to bandage her hand up…Maybe put a splint on it."

Sheriff Flynn and Deputy Platt were standing in the outer room of the small apartment over the dressmaker's shop that Doc Mosier used for an office. The woman was in the back room with Miz. Johnson. She and her husband ran the general store, and she helped Doc out when he needed a nurse.

"Did she tell you her name?" asked Doc.

Flynn shook his head. "She didn't really say much of anything. Slept most of the way into town. Didn't really gain full consciousness at all."

"Do you think she'll be all right?" Gomer asked.

"Hard to tell, with a head injury like that. Tell you the truth," Mosier glanced at Flynn, "sometimes medicine is more an art than a science."

Flynn said, "I always suspected you were little more than a witch doctor."

"Now you're gonna owe me a tequila, the next time I see you down at the saloon."

Flynn grinned and slapped the doctor on the shoulder.

Mosier said, "I'll do what I can for her."

"I know you will, old friend." Flynn turned to his deputy. "Let's go, Gomer…Let the man do his job."

§

Flynn and Gomer hadn't been back to the office yet. They had brought the girl directly to Doc's office.

They walked down the long wooden stairway to the street, and Gomer said, "I'll take the horses down to Mom's Livery."

The sheriff smiled and nodded. "Thanks."

THE FIRST

Joe Munson was standing on the boardwalk, waiting for them. "I want to know what's going to be done about this... Someone has to go after those men."

"Fully intend to."

"When?"

Flynn gave him a look. "I've been elected to this job, Munson, and I'll do it. Don't need you or anyone else pestering me about it."

"I'll remember that at election time. And I'll also remember the damage you did to that stage, cutting out the carpet to use in that travois."

"Bill it to the county...By the way, when you're done telling me how to do my job, you might want to get someone out to that stage to bring those bodies into town. You won't want to leave them out there overnight...Once the coyotes get done with them, it won't be pretty...And make sure and bring all of their belongings to my office...It's all evidence."

Flynn turned on his heel and started down the boardwalk for his office.

He found Slim Parker behind the desk with a cup of coffee. He also found Brushy Bill Roberts waiting for him, sitting in a guest chair in front of the desk.

Roberts got to his feet. "About time. Been waitin' here nearly all day."

He extended his hand and Flynn took it in a tight grip.

Flynn said, "What brings you all the way to Jacksboro?"

"Work. You know how it is."

"All too well."

Flynn glanced at the stove and realized it wasn't throwing off any heat.

Slim said, "We got the restaurant to make us some coffee. They made us a full pot."

Flynn went to the pot on the cold stove and found the pot still warm. He poured himself a cup.

Slim vacated the sheriff's chair and Flynn sat down.

"Last I knew, you were workin' with Marshal Miller," said Flynn.

Bill nodded. "The ranks have been spread a little thin, as of late, so she was sent down to Nueces County, to help Jericho Long escort a prisoner...In fact, they're bringing him to Jack County. I was sent here to enlist your help. Been tracking a gang of outlaws...Mostly they've been keeping themselves busy down around Harris County."

"Harris? That's a fair ride from here."

Bill nodded. "The law was getting too close to 'em. Fiona and I got near enough to take one of 'em out of the saddle...We think one of 'em might have some connection in Jack County."

Flynn told him about the stage robbery. The driver and shotgun messenger and all of the passengers either dead or left for dead. Looked like it was four men. Rifled through all of the luggage, pulled rings off of people's fingers, and took the horses.

Roberts commented, "Sounds like your job and mine just converged."

Flynn raised his brows. "Converged?"

Bill nodded. "Means come together."

Flynn grinned. "Looks like you've been workin' with Fiona too long."

Bill shook his head. "Gal as pretty as that? Ain't possible to work with her too long...But don't tell her I said that. She'd break my nose."

"Your secret is safe with me."

§§§

CHAPTER THREE

JACKSBORO, TEXAS

At sunrise, Gomer had two horses saddled and waiting outside Sheriff Flynn's office. Each saddle had a full canteen, a soogan strapped to the cantle, and a Winchester in the saddle boot.

Flynn and Bill finished a cup of coffee each in the office, and then Gomer followed them out to the horses.

Slim was with them, and he still had his badge pinned to his shirt.

Flynn turned to Gomer. "You're gonna be in charge till we get back...Sure you're up to it?"

Gomer nodded. "Yessir, Sheriff. Town will be in good hands. I've been learning a lot from you."

Flynn gave him a look like he wasn't quite sure. "Make sure and check in on the woman. See if you can get her name, and if she might be able to remember something about the robbery...Maybe identify 'em."

"Presuming," Bill said, "we bring back any of 'em alive."

Gomer said, "Yessir, Sheriff. Checked on her four different times last night."

Flynn grinned. "Only four?"

Gomer blushed, and looked down at his boots.

Flynn said, "She *is* kinda pretty, idn't she?"

Gomer didn't look up, but he nodded and said, "Yessir."

Flynn slapped Gomer's shoulder and turned to Bill. "Let's get ridin'…Daylight's a-wasting."

Gomer looked up and saw a man striding toward them. "Uh-oh. It's Mister Munson."

Flynn rolled his eyes. "I was hopin' we could be on our way before he knew we were gone."

"Sheriff!" Munson called out.

Flynn swung into the saddle and Brushy Bill fell into place.

"Sheriff! Where are you going?" Munson said. "I thought you would be gathering together a posse to go chase after those outlaws."

"Two of us will handle the outlaws."

"The two of you?"

Brushy Bill nodded. "The two of us can handle it."

"Just who do you think this man is?" Munson said. "Some great gunslinger?…Is he Johnny McCabe, or Billy the Kid or someone like that?"

Flynn gave a glance toward Brushy Bill, and Bill said, "No one ever called me *McCabe*, before."

Flynn grinned. "Sometimes a small force of men can make progress where a larger group won't."

"What's that supposed to mean?" asked Munson.

"What it means is, you stick to your job and let me do mine."

Munson didn't know what to say at that one.

Flynn looked to Brushy Bill and said, "Let's go, Johnny."

"Sure thing, Wild Bill."

They turned their horses and started down the street at a spirited walk.

Flynn said, "Wild Bill, huh? Do I look wild?"

Bill shrugged. "You sure don't look Brushy."

"How'd you get that name, anyway?"

"Long story."

Munson stood beside Gomer and Slim, watching them ride away.

Munson said, "Sometimes I just don't know what that man is talking about."

But Gomer was too busy laughing to reply.

§

28 MILES OUTSIDE OF TOWN

They found all of the bodies gone—looked like Munson had followed Flynn's advice. Even the belongings of all the passenger and the stage itself were gone. But the tracks of the outlaws were easy enough to follow.

Flynn and Brushy Bill backtracked the robbers to a small, grassy knoll within view of the trail a half mile back.

"They waited right here for the stage," said Flynn.

Bill nodded. "One thing that strikes me strange is why they took those horses. You can't saddle a wagon horse...Well, you can, but it ain't a wise thing to do."

Flynn nodded. "I was wonderin' that, myself. If you need saddle horses, there are ranches in the area that you could rob."

"Something just not right, here."

Flynn nodded again. "Half of being a good lawman is gut feeling...and the other half is patience. And my gut feeling says somethin' definitely is not right."

Roberts rubbed his bristly chin. He had been on the trail for days and hadn't shaved. "Let's utilize the *patience* part of what you're talking about, and follow those tracks. It won't be hard to follow a team of wagon horses."

"But ride with your gun loose in your holster, and keep your eyes peeled."

"Always do."

§§§

Brad Dennison

CHAPTER FOUR

JACKSBORO, TEXAS

Gomer decided it was time to go check on the girl. He had been a little embarrassed at what Sheriff Flynn had said earlier. Hinting that Gomer kept checking on her because she was pretty.

Gomer was a deputy county sheriff, and he took his job seriously. He knew a lot of people didn't take him seriously. Sure, he was often tripping over his own feet, but that was because he was trying so hard to be the kind of man Sheriff Flynn would want for his deputy. He supposed maybe he was trying too hard.

His mother had once told him that he didn't have enough confidence. He tried to compensate for that by acting more confident, but he often wound up spilling coffee on himself, or even worse, spilling it on the marshal. Or he would try to come up with a profound comment so he could add something significant to a conversation, but would make a fool of himself instead.

He felt small around Sheriff Flynn much of the time, and the sheriff indicating that Gomer was checking on the girl just because she was pretty made him feel like the backwards bumpkin he figured most people saw him as.

But she was sure enough pretty. He had to admit, it was all he could do not to think about her. He wondered what she was like. He wondered what it would be like to come home to a woman like that every day.

He wondered what it would be like for a woman like that not to look at him like a fool or a country bumpkin, like so many people in town did. Like even Sheriff Flynn did.

And so, he left Slim Parker at the office with a cup of coffee, and he headed down the boardwalk to Doc Mosier's office.

He stepped in, and he found Doc at his desk with a cup of coffee.

Doc said, "She's awake, if you want to go talk to her. But keep the visit short."

Gomer found her in bed, in a room behind Doc's office. She was in a nightgown, and her hair was hanging loose and free. Doc had tired a strip of what looked like bedsheet around her head as a bandage.

Mrs. Johnson, the nurse, was puttering around the room. Straightening things. Fixing the doily on an end table.

She said, "Now don't you bother the patient, Gomer."

The deputy had his hat in his hand. "I surely don't intend to, Miz Johnson...Sheriff Flynn needs some questions answered, and with him gone, he left me in charge."

"Lord have mercy."

He wanted to say, *thanks for the vote of confidence*. But he didn't.

He leaned forward at the young woman's bed. "Ma'am, I'm the deputy county sheriff."

She nodded and smiled. And oh, did she have a smile! It made something warm light up inside of Gomer. Her hair was dark, but her eyes were gray, and he thought at the moment that she was the most awe-inspiring vision he had ever set his eyes on.

She responded, "Yes, Miz. Johnson told me you had been in a number of times during the night to check on me."

Platt didn't know what to say. He looked down and hoped he wasn't blushing. Wouldn't do for a deputy county sheriff to blush. "Just wanted to make sure you're awright."

"I think I'll be fine."

If she did notice how uncomfortable he was, she apparently had too much class to let on. It made him appreciate her even more.

THE FIRST

She continued, "The doctor told me the bullet grazed my skull, but he doesn't think there is any fracture. And my hand...," she held up her left hand. It was wrapped from the wrist all the way down in white bandages. "It looks like they broke my finger when they pulled my ring off...It was my grandmother's."

"Hope we can get it back for you. Sheriff Flynn and Marshal Roberts are two of the best. They're trailing them outlaws, now."

Gomer then blinked with surprise. "I just realized I haven't formally introduced myself...Deputy Sheriff Gomer Platt, at your service, ma'am."

She smiled. "Elizabeth Harriman...Lately of Boston," seh said, holding out her right hand.

He didn't quite know how to shake a lady's hand. With a man, you just gripped tight to show him you were a man of character, and shook.

Gomer's father had taught him that. But with a woman, he was sure you wouldn't want to squeeze too hard. So he decided to take her hand a little gently and not shake. She smiled again, so apparently he did it right.

"So what brings you west, Miss Harriman?"

"Please, call me Elizabeth. I was on my way to Arizona. I have an uncle who runs a cattle ranch there. His name's Ben Cantrell."

Gomer nodded. "Think I've heard that name, before."

They talked about the Cantrell Ranch and about Gomer's job as a deputy, and they talked about the stage robbery. The whole time, he felt like he was getting lost in her smile. Like he could drown in her eyes.

When he got back to the office, he just stood inside the doorway, his eyes fixed on some faraway place.

Slim Parker was at the sheriff's desk. "Did you talk to her?"

Gomer nodded.

"You ask her if she thought she could identify the robbers?"

Gomer nodded again.

Slim was sitting with a coffee cup in one hand. "Well?"

"She don't remember nothin' about it. The Doc said it's not surprisin'. The way the bullet hit her, it was like getting knocked in the head by a hammer."

"Well, you was gone a long time…That's all you got out of her?"

Gomer shrugged. "We talked…And we talked and we talked."

"What about?"

Gomer shrugged again. "Can't rightly remember."

Slim looked at him with a frown. "Gomer, you all right?"

THE FIRST

"Never felt like this before. Like I'm drownin', but filled with sunshine all at the same time."

"You been down at the saloon?"

Gomer shook his head. "I close my eyes, and I can see her face...Her smile."

Slim broke into a grin. "Haw, Gomer Platt...do believe you're in love."

§§§

CHAPTER FIVE

SHERIFF'S OFFICE
JACKSBORO, TEXAS

"In love?" Gomer said to Slim. "I ain't never been in love before."

Slim shrugged. "Well, you are now…Seen it before."

Gomer looked concerned. "I ain't never felt this way before…not sure I like it. How do I get rid of it?"

"Don't know that you can."

Gomer went to the stove. The coffee kettle was still a little warm, so he grabbed a cup and filled it. "I wonder if the doc can do somethin'?"

Slim laughed. "It ain't like getting sick, Gomer."

"Sure feels like it."

"Well, that ain't the way of it. Ain't no medicine you can take for it...Has to run its course."

Gomer walked around to his desk, slid out the chair and dropped into it. "How does it run its course?"

"Well, usually goes two ways. One is the girl loves you back."

"Then what happens?"

Slim shrugged. "I suppose you get married and live happily ever after...At least, that's what they say."

"What's the other way it can go?"

"Suppose the other way is that she doesn't love you back."

Gomer didn't like the sound of that. He hadn't thought much about it either way, but now the thought of Elizabeth not loving him back left him feeling kind of empty inside.

"Does that happen often?...The girl not loving you back?" he asked.

"From what I've seen, that's mostly the way it happens."

MAIN STREET
JACKSBORO, TEXAS

No one paid much attention to the two riders. They had ridden in late the day before, covered with trail dust. Both had whiskers that were more from a lack of shaving than from a fashion statement.

One had an old, battered cavalry hat, and the other was in a gray slouch hat with a floppy brim and a hole in the crown. Both looked like cowhands who had been on the trail a long while.

When they rode down the main street, people glanced casually at them, and then past them.

A cowhand riding past nodded his head in greeting, like people will do. They nodded back.

Their first stop was the saloon. They went in and bellied-up.

"Gimme a mug-full of draft beer," the one the cavalry hat said. "To wash down the trail dust."

"Make that two," the other said.

The barkeep filled the mugs from a tap and set them down in front of the two. The one in the tattered hat dug into his vest and set two nickels on the bar.

"Don't think I've seen you boys around here, before."

The one in the dark hat said, "Name's Carson. This here is Bennett...Lookin' for work."

"There's a ranch outside of town that's short a man, last I heard. The Bar J...Where'd you boys last work?"

Bennett replied, "The Shannon place...outside of Wardtown."

"Wardtown, eh? That's a fair ride from here."

Carson shrugged. "I just git the urge to move on, sometimes...Bennett, here, thought he'd ride along."

The bartender grinned and nodded. "Know how that feels...When I was younger, I was a drover. Brought many a herd north to the railheads...When I see the ramrod of the Bar J, I'll mention you boys."

Carson nodded. "Much obliged."

§

They lounged around town most of the day. Had a second mug of beer. Brought their horses down to the livery to be tended. Stood outside the saloon and rolled cigarettes. Nodded to the country bumpkin wearing a deputy sheriff's badge as he went walking past.

Bennett said, "That can't be *the* Mason Flynn that I've heard so much about."

Carson grinned. "Ain't him...Saw Mason Flynn once."

"So you say."

"Saw him take out two men with his fists...They say he's even better with his guns."

§

They chatted with the locals. Heard about the stage robbery. They say one woman from the stage who was shot but didn't die is at the doctor's office.

"That so?" Carson said.

They were talking to an old man with stooped shoulders and flyaway hair. He was in a white shirt and suspenders, and worked as a swamper at the saloon.

He said, "That's what they tell me. And they tell me she's a right purty gal. The doc expects her to make a full recovery."

Carson looked at his partner. Bennett held his gaze a minute, and then let his eyes wander down the street.

More casual conversation led to them getting the location of the doctor's office. There was no sign because there didn't need to be. All of the local's knew Doc Mosier and where to find him.

They learned the deputy seemed to have an infatuation of sorts with the woman from the stage robbery.

"You mean that kid with a deputy's badge?" Bennett said.

They were talking to Clive Ramsey, who worked as a telegrapher. He had a green visor over his eyes, and had delivered a telegram to the barkeep.

He said, "Yep, that's him, Gomer Platt. A good boy, but one of them country boys who has two left feet and is all thumbs...We all figure Sheriff Flynn keeps him around as a favor."

"Dumb kid, huh?" asked Carson.

Clive shrugged his shoulders. "Not so much dumb as awkward, I suppose...He brings her meals to her. Spends as much time at the doctor's office as he can."

Bennett said, "Sounds like if she makes a full recovery, she might be able to identify them fellas that shot her and the others."

Clive nodded. "That's what the sheriff's hopin' for." he walked on.

Carson glanced off at the western sky. "Looks like we got a situation on our hands...Maybe we should remedy it."

Bennett looked at him. "You know how Buster is. He don't like it when we do something without clearing it through him first."

Bennett glanced at the western horizon. "We got time to go fetch our horses and ride out to camp...Find out what he wants us to do."

"Don't like it none."

"You knew what we were getting ourselves into when we signed on with Buster James...He calls all the shots."

Carson nodded. "But I know what he's gonna tell us to do. We're gonna be riding back here tonight...Don't like the idea of killing a woman. Didn't like it when he shot her out on the trail. Didn't set right with me...But it's gotta be done."

Bennett grinned. "If you want to ride on, fine with me. More money for me if Buster has one less of us to share it with."

"Fat chance of that. Let's get the horses.

§§§

CHAPTER SIX

NORTHWEST OF JACKSBORO

Flynn and Brushy Bill followed the tracks. As plain a trail as any Flynn had ever seen. Four horses being led along, single file, kicking up the ground as they went.

"Makes no sense to me at all," Bill said.

"Gotta agree with that."

"If these fellers were the ones I've been huntin', I don't see how they lived this long, leaving a trail plain as day like this…Thought Buster James was smarter'n that."

They rode along.

"Could be leading us into a trap," Bill added. "Is there any area around here that would be a good place for a sniper to sit and wait?"

Flynn shook his head. "Land's flat in all directions. Some trees, and a sniper could wait there, I suppose. But a tree don't give you a whole lot of cover. You miss your shot, and you're gonna get shot out of that tree like a coon."

The trail wound its way north. There were groves of trees, mostly leafy oaks and elm, and wide expanses of grass that were sometimes half a mile or wider.

§

Then they came to a stream that was running about two feet deep. The stage horses had been driven through it.

Flynn and Bill stopped to fill their canteens and to let their horses drink. And then they continued on.

The tracks were as they had been. Four horses being led in single file.

They followed the tracks for a mile, then another. The trail led through a patch of woods, and then back out into a grassy meadow.

When they had covered a third mile, they caught sight of the horses, all four of them idly grazing on the grass.
Flynn and Brushy Bill drew their pistols. But they found no one watching the horses.

"They just rode off and left 'em here?" asked Bill.

They scouted about, and found the trail of a single rider moving west and away from the open grassy area. They followed the through woods and then out into a dusty, gravelly patch. That was where the tracks disappeared.

"I admit," Bill said, "I'm just as puzzled as before."

"He's covering his tracks. Maybe cut a branch a while back, and now he's using it to wipe away his sign."

"But why now?"

"Come on," said Flynn.

§

The land was gravelly for maybe quarter of a mile, then became downright rocky. Then it gave way to more grass with some trees standing in the distance.

Brushy Bill said, "There's no guarantee he held to this direction. He could have turned off anywhere back there in the gravelly area."

"We could cut for sign, but there are ways to conceal tracks in grass, too. Like walking behind the horse and using a stick to stand the grass up that the horse's hooves matted down. I've seen Indians do that."

"So, essentially, we lost him."

"Maybe." Flynn rubbed his mustache. "Maybe I have a little idea starting to germinate."

"Germinate? You been listening to Fiona and her ten-dollar words?"

Flynn grinned. "What's one of the main reasons for ridin' single file?"

"So no one can tell how many are in your party by the number of tracks. One horse sort of obliterates the tracks of the others ahead of it."

"That's kind of obvious, but. I have to wonder why they would do that…We already know there were four."

"Maybe so we wouldn't know when they peeled off."

"That stream…More'n three miles back."

Flynn turned his horse back the way they had come.

§

An hour later, they were reining up at the side of the stream.

Bill said, "One rider continued on with those stage horses while the other three headed off through the stream…That water's moving fast enough to wipe away any tracks from the stream bed within a few minutes."

"The question is," Flynn said, "which direction would they go?"

"Gonna have to split up," Bill said. "You take one direction and I'll take the other."

§§§

CHAPTER SEVEN

NORTHWEST OF JACKSBORO

Flynn found what he was looking for, about a mile downstream. Three sets of tracks emerged from the stream.

To his right was a low line of wooded ridges, and that was where the tracks led.

He turned his horse away from the tracks, riding parallel, but about two hundred feet off. The land was becoming more heavily wooded the closer he got to the low ridges, and there were good spots for a man to wait with a rifle in a tree. With the woods so much thicker here, a sniper could wait until you were almost up to him so he would have less chance of missing.

Every so often, he would return to the set of tracks, to make sure they hadn't turned off.

With about an hour left of sunlight, he found the camp, but it was abandoned. There were the remains of a campfire, some empty cans of beans scattered about, and cigarette butts on the ground.

He heard a rider coming up behind him, and saw it was Brushy Bill.

"Don't shoot," Bill said. "I'm one of the good guys." He reined up. "I followed the stream for a few miles, but gave up on it. I figured you're not gonna ride far in a stream bed, with all the uneven footing...I rode back and found your trail."

Flynn swung out of the saddle, knelt by the remains of the fire and placed his hands on the ashes. "Still warm. They were here maybe an hour ago...Not much longer."

"Dang curious."

"Maybe it would help things if we knew just where they went."

"Probably east, or northeast...Toward the Nations."

"If they were gonna do that, they would likely have taken the stream in the other direction."

They mounted up and began cutting for sign. Flynn rode north of the camp, cutting a wide circle, and Bill rode south.

They met back at the camp. Bill said, "Found nothin'."

"I found a set of tracks that came from the southeast. Looked like two riders...And then four riders, including them, rode back in the same direction."

"What's in that direction?"

Flynn said, "Town."

"Why would they go right back into town when they know we're looking for them?"

Flynn's mouth fell open as the idea occurred to him. Partly because Bass Reeves had said to him once if you want to figure out how criminals think, look at how you would do things in their place.

He said, "They must have had at least one man in town. Judging by the tracks...they had two."

"But that would be asking for trouble."

"If we knew what they looked like. But we don't...Except for one person."

"That woman from the stage robbery."

Flynn nodded.

"The men in town found out she's still alive, and they rode back out to report it. Now the whole bunch of 'em is riding back there to make sure she can't identify them. And all that's back there to guard the town is your deputy and Slim Parker," said Bill.

"Come on! Let's ride!"

§§§

CHAPTER EIGHT

JACKSBORO, TEXAS

Gomer stepped into Doc Mosier's office with a tray of food.

Doc was behind his desk. He got to his feet, removed a pair of spectacles and rubbed his tired eyes. "Evenin', Gomer. Got dinner for our guest?"

Platt nodded. "Got some here for you too, Doc…Less you'd rather eat at that restaurant."

"Tell the truth, Gomer, I think I'd like to eat right here and then call it an early night. I've been sitting going over a couple of medical journals. I've got the New England Journal

of Medicine here. And now my old eyes are plumb worn out."

Doc got to his feet. "If you would leave my food on the desk, I'd appreciate it. I'm heading to the outhouse."

Gomer set a plate and a cup of coffee on the desk. "Hurry back or your coffee'll get cold."

"Won't be gone long."

Gomer found Elizabeth sitting up in bed, in the next room.

"Oh, Gomer," she said, "you didn't have to bring me dinner."

He shrugged. "It's my pleasure...Really."

"I have to admit, I'm half-starved."

"Must mean you're feeling better." He grinned.

She nodded. "I still have a little headache, but Doc says that's to be expected."

Gomer set the tray on the bed and then pulled up a chair. "I got enough for both of us...if that's okay."

She smiled. "I would very pleased if you could join me for dinner."

A red checkered napkin covered the food, and Gomer pulled it away. There were two plates of fried chicken, mashed potatoes, yams and green beans. There were also two cups.

"I got some coffee for myself, but I remember you said you liked tea," said Gomer.

"You are so thoughtful."

He was a little unsure of what to say, but he thought he would take a major leap forward. *Now or never.* "I find you're very much worth being thoughtful over."

That got another smile from her. Gomer thought those smiles were worth all the gold in the world.

He chewed into some chicken. "You remember anythin' more about the robbery?"

She shook her head. "Nothing at all. I remember getting on the stage that morning, and nothing afterward until I woke up here...I'm really sorry. I know it would be helpful if I could identify them."

"Don't you worry none. Sheriff Flynn and Brushy Bill are on their trail. They'll bring 'em in."

"Brushy Bill. What a curious name."

Gomer grinned and nodded. "A great feller, though. I don't know how he got that name...somewheres out in New Mexico, I think."

That was when Gomer realized he hadn't head Doc come back in. He glanced toward the open doorway to the outer office. "Doc said he was comin' right back. I wonder what's keepin' him?"

"Do you think something's wrong?"

"Don't know."

Often late in the evening at the office, Sheriff Flynn would talk to Gomer about law enforcement. Sometimes talking about cases the sheriff had worked on, and sometimes talking about the job in general. One thing he had talked about was gut instinct. It was the most important thing a lawman can have, Sheriff Flynn had said more than once.

Gomer's gut instinct was telling him something was wrong. He had no reason to believe it—he had seen or heard nothing out of the ordinary. But his gut instinct was going off inside like a tea pot a-whistling.

He got to his feet. "I'm sure everythin' is all right. But I've got to check…Goes along with wearing this." With one hand he tapped the badge on his shirt.

"Be careful, Gomer."

"Be right back."

He stepped into the outer office. The nagging feeling that something was wrong was pulling at him stronger than ever. The deputy drew his gun and pulled open the front door.

He went out onto the wooden stairs that led down to the street. All was quiet. Somehow, it struck him as too quiet.

Gomer went down the stairs and then cut through an alley to the back of the building, where the outhouse stood.

Doc Mosier was face down on the ground.

Platt felt a wave of fear run through him. Something had happened to Doc. He knelt down to see if he was still alive.

He had seen Sheriff Flynn touch the side of a man's neck once, to see if there was a pulse, a jasper who had gotten himself shot one Saturday night at the saloon. Gomer reached down to the side of Doc's neck, and he found he still had a pulse.

He realized there was a big dark patch on the back of Doc's head. The moon was up and providing a little light, and Doc's hair was white and clearly visible.

Gomer reached down to the dark patch and found it was wet. Blood. Doc had a bloody wound on the back of his head.

Then he realized something. Elizabeth was upstairs, alone. Somebody had taken down Doc. Maybe them outlaws the sheriff and Marshal Roberts were trailing had come to town.

Gomer turned and ran around to the wooden stairs and took them two at a time.

He charged in the front door. From the outer office, he could see through the open doorway into Elizabeth's room.

A man was standing there, his back to Gomer.

He heard Elizabeth say, "But I don't remember anything about the robbery. I couldn't have identified you if I tried."

"Can't take the chance, lady. Gonna finish the job we started."

Gomer raised his gun and cocked the hammer back, and was about to call out *Drop that gun!*

But, the man heard the gun cocking, he spun around and fired.

And Gomer fired. Two shots that blended into one roar.

THE FIRST

Gomer felt the breeze of the bullet as it whizzed past his left cheekbone.

The man caught the deputy's bullet square in the chest. He took a couple of steps backward and fell into the window frame. Glass broke, and he fell part way out the window. And there he remained, hanging out over the window sill, no longer moving.

The thought occurred to Gomer that there was more than one outlaw, and he did a maneuver he had seen Sheriff Flynn do once. He spun and dropped to one knee, cocking his gun again as he moved.

A man was standing in the doorway, his gun trained at the deputy. He fired as Gomer was dropping and spinning.

The bullet whipped past above Platt's head.

Gomer fired and caught this man also in the chest.

The man backpedaled, and then flipped over the wooden railing outside and fell twelve feet to the alley below.

Gomer looked back to Elizabeth. "You all right?"

She was still sitting up in bed, the covers pulled to her waist, and her eyes were wide. "I'm all right."

"Sit tight."

Platt ran out the doorway to the top of the stairs. The street down below was mostly lost in darkness, but he heard a man call out, "Drop your guns!"

Sounded like Sheriff Flynn.

Shots were fired from down the street. Gomer could see the flash of the guns. Two men down the street a ways, and two closer to the stairway. Then all was quiet.

The deputy cocked his gun and waited. Any one of them outlaws tried to kill Elizabeth, and Deputy Gomer Platt was going to give them what-for.

Two men stepped out of the darkness at the foot of the stairs.

"Don't shoot, Gomer."

It was Sheriff Flynn.

He realized he was holding his breath, so he let it out slowly, and he eased the hammer back on his gun.

Brushy Bill was with him, his right hand clamped over his left upper arm.

"One of 'em got me," Bill said. "Not bad, I don't think. Is the Doc in his office?"

"I'm right here," Doc said, stepping out of the alleyway. He was holding a handkerchief to the back of his head. "One of those hoodlums knocked me in the back of the head. A man can't go to the outhouse in peace around here."

Gomer said, "The one what hit you is upstairs, Doc.... Dead."

Slim Parker came running along the boardwalk, his revolver drawn. "Heard shootin'."

"It's all right," Flynn said to him. "Think we got 'em all."

Gomer led them upstairs. Elizabeth met them in the outer office and threw her arms around the young deputy.

"Are you all right?"

He nodded. "Sure enough am."

She stepped away and said, "Sheriff, Gomer saved my life. It was some of the best shooting I've ever seen."

Flynn looked at the body that was partially suspended out the window. "You did this, Gomer?"

"Yes, sir. There's another one down in the alley."

"Stepped over him in the dark," Doc said. "I checked for a pulse…He's about as dead as a man can get."

Flynn put a hand on Gomer's shoulder. "Good job, Deputy."

Gomer smiled and ducked his head. "Thanks, Sheriff."

§§§

CHAPTER NINE

MAIN STREET
JACKSBORO, TEXAS

Elizabeth was in a dress and a hat. One of those little hats women wear back East, with lots of lace pinned to it.

She was standing by the stage coach with Deputy Platt standing beside her.

"I hope you understand, Gomer," she said. "I just can't stay. Not after everything that happened. I have a sister who lives in Atlanta. I'm going to go stay with her for a while."

He nodded. His hat was in his hands, and he was trying to stand strong, even though he was feeling a pain inside that was like nothing he had ever felt before.

"Will you ever be back?"

"You never know what the future holds," she said with a smile.

He knew he might never see her again, so he had to say the words that were bottled up inside, before they burst out on their own.

"I love you, Elizabeth."

She smiled. "You're so sweet, Gomer. Perhaps the sweetest man I have ever met."

She reached a hand to the side of his face. "You'll meet the right girl, one day...When the time is right. I know there's a girl out there for you. A man a sweet as you won't be alone forever."

Gomer didn't know what to say. He was so hoping tears didn't start running. Wouldn't do for a deputy sheriff to be standing out here in the streets crying like a baby.

The stage driver was on his seat up top. Long white hair falling from under a battered old hat, and he had a white beard that reminded Gomer of Santa Claus.

He said, "Gotta be goin', Miss."

She looked up at him and nodded.

"Oh," Gomer said. "Almost forgot. The sheriff found this among the loot the outlaws took from the robbery."

He dug into a pocket and pulled out a ring with a small ruby mounted on it.

"My grandmother's ring!"

He handed it to her.

"Please thank the sheriff for me," She said.

"I'll do that."

"Good bye, Gomer." And she leaned in and kissed him on the cheek.

The man who ran the ticket office took her hand as she stepped up and into the stage, and then he shut the door.

He called up, "All set, Fred!"

And with a loud *giddyup* and a snap of the reins, the stage started forward.

Gomer stood on the street, his hat still in his hands, watching the stage roll away, knowing he would likely never see Elizabeth Harriman again.

Mason Flynn was standing back aways. He didn't want to intrude on the moment between Gomer and Miss Harriman.

But as the stage pulled out of town and was gone from sight, he stepped forward to stand beside his deputy.

Gomer wiped a tear away, and then put his hat on his head. "I wanted her to stay," he said. "I know I'm just a bumblin' fool. I know half the town laughs at me…I know you laugh at me, and I know I'm just in your way, most of the time. But I could have built a good life for her and me…I know it."

Flynn nodded. "Your first love."

"Guess so."

"And you killed your first man. A week of firsts."

He nodded. "Yup. Guess so."

"I couldn't have handled the situation better, Gomer. You made me proud, this week…And Deputy Platt?"

Gomer looked at him.

"I'm not laughin'."

Gomer nodded.

Flynn slapped him on the shoulder. "Come on. Buy you a beer."

And the sheriff and his deputy stepped onto the boardwalk and headed down the street to the Coolwater Saloon.

§§§§

BIO

Brad was born in rural New England and grew up reading Louis L'Amour, Luke Short, A.B Guthrie, Jr., and even Edgar Rice Burroughs. He knew at 14 he wanted to write for a living, and refused to give up the goal even when the odds seemed overwhelmingly against it. Now, thanks to Amazon, his stories are available. He is a member of the Western Writers of America.

Brad fell in love with the Old West at a very young age. It began with movies and old TV series like GUNSMOKE and BONANZA, and later expanded to western novels. This led to his study of western history. The pioneers, the Indians, the cattlemen, the gunfighters. His interest in history is not so much about wars and great leaders, but the people who lived on the land. And that's what he writes about. The people. He doesn't write about the old west as much as what it might have felt like to be there.

He loves contact from readers. He can be reached by email at mccabewesterns@gmail.com if you want to discuss his stories, or even just the American West in general.

Here's a link to Brad's Facebook page:
https://www.facebook.com/brad.dennison.9
Amazon:
https://www.amazon.com/Brad-Dennison/e/B00FW3R6CU

MARY ELIZABETH PEABODY

BY

T.C. MILLER

CHAPTER ONE

WICHITA, KANSAS

A gust of wind sent a cloud of dust swirling and skipping down the rutted dirt street of 1890's Wichita, Kansas. It brought with it numerous dust-devils that pursued anyone out in the open. The acrid stench of stockyards at the edge of town mixed with a low-hanging gray cloud from wood-fired cook stoves.

Mary Elizabeth Peabody used a pink and white parasol with a lace edge in one hand as a shield, in a vain attempt to protect herself. The other hand held down a small, Victorian hat trimmed with flowers and pheasant feathers. A light coating of reddish brown fell on the ivory-colored, puffed–sleeve dress and bustle that extended past her ankles to finely crafted leather boots. "What a godforsaken place!" she said to the older woman standing next to her, as a shiver of excitement coursed through her. "So different from Boston."

"Aye, that it be," her companion replied.

Mary watched a farmer turn from his freight wagon toward the saloon and waved with a lace handkerchief. "Excuse me, sir, are you going in there?"

"Ain't no law ag'in it…least ways, far as I know. Why?"

"I need to get a message to a man in there and it would be unseemly for a single woman, such as myself, to enter. Unless, of course, she was employed within, which I most assuredly am not."

"Not hardly, from the looks of you. What in tarnation er you ladies doing in this part of town, anyways? Sort of a rough and tumble area."

"I appreciate your concern, sir. We walked over from the train station to contact the gentleman who, I was informed, would be inside. We will not be deterred by a few ruffians."

The farmer rubbed his stubbled chin and replied, "Guess they ain't no harm in passin' a message. Although, truth be told, it's the kind of place what attracts miscreants and scalawags…"

"Were you not preparing to enter this den of iniquity?"

"True…that I was, but only to wet my whistle. It's a long dusty ride from my ranch. Back to the business at hand, though, what moniker does this here feller go by?"

"Rockford Whitman," she said, while clutching her purse in front of her. "I have been informed he is a skilled gambler who prefers the game of Faro. He goes by the sobriquet, Rocky."

"Sober what?"

"Nickname, is what I meant to say…"

"Well, then, why didn't you? You some kind of school marm, or somethin'?"

"Indeed, I am, sir. How did you ascertain that?"

"Ascer…there you go, again. Yer dress, and them four-bit words you're usin'."

"My apologies. I was raised in Boston and am unfamiliar with the *patois* in this…"

"Patter what?"

"French for vernacular…the language as it is spoken locally."

"That so? Have to 'member that, next time I have tea with the Queen."

"There no need to mock me, sir. I am willing to pay two dollars."

"Well, now, that throws a whole new light on the matter. Woulda done it for free, but I'll take yer money, in return for my time. What is it yer wantin' me to tell this Whitman feller?"

"That is confidential, sir. Please tell Mister Whitman I wish to speak with him."

She handed him two dollars from a coin purse in the rose-patterned arabesque handbag and snapped it shut.

"I'll see if he's in there."

"Please return if he is not," she said, with pursed lips.

"Why, you gonna take back the two bucks, if he ain't?"

"No, sir, of course not. We do not wish to remain in front of this establishment any longer than necessary."

"Reckon y'all don't fit in, at that...be back in two shakes."

"Very well...by the by, what is your name?"

"Henry Johnson, but most folks jist calls me Hank."

An irate young cowboy brushed past them into the saloon, mumbling about getting his money back, no matter what it took. Less than a minute later, he flew head over heels into the dirt street.

A burly man wearing a burgandy brocade vest under a long black morning coat stood in the doorway. "Next time you accuse me of cheating, you'd best be packing, or be ready to meet your maker."

The cowboy stared up from a prone position in the dust. "Who says I ain't?" He pulled a derringer from his boot.

The man in the doorway drew a Colt Peacemaker from under his coat and fired two rounds in quick succession into the cowboy's chest, with sickening thumps.

The lifeless man shuddered and collapsed to the dirt like a wet newspaper.

The firearm returned to the holster so fast it looked like one continuous movement from start to finish. The shooter turned to go back inside and yelled as he pushed through the doors, "George, get somebody over to haul this body off before it starts stinking up the street."

The women shrank back from the violence and held white lace handkerchiefs to their faces.

Henry Johnson stepped gingerly over the lifeless body and pushed through the batwing doors into the dark interior. He paused to let his eyes adjust. A blue-tinted cloud of smoke from cigars and a woodstove swirled near the fourteen-foot tall ceiling. The sour smell of stale beer and urine filled his nostrils. A small stage with faded, royal-blue curtains that sagged from the staircase landing above was empty in the early afternoon. Later, it would contribute to a cacophony of raucous noises. For now, the upright piano next to the stage was silent.

MARY ELIZABETH PEABODY

It was so quiet in the dank interior that Hank could hear the man in the vest speaking to four card players at an oval table with a cutout for the dealer.

The gambler's sleeves were gathered at the wrists and mid-arm by garters, to show he was not hiding cards. They took attention away from hidden slit pockets in the vest that concealed a few spares. His black, pencil-brimmed Mississippi gambler's hat sat squarely on his head.

"Seeing as how you gentlemen have never played Faro, I will offer instruction for your edification..."

"Our edi...what?" queried a thin young man across the table.

"Edification...think of it as learning of the adult kind," the dealer replied. "The deck is known as the Faro Bank and I am the banker. You gentlemen are the punters, or players. In order to participate, you must purchase checks, otherwise known as markers, or chips, from the banker...in this case, me.

He pointed to a board in front of him that had an entire suit of a deck glued near the top. "You place your bets by putting a check on one of these cards. I draw two cards, the first one being the banker's card. Placing a bet on any card that is the same, no matter which suit loses and the money goes to the banker.

"The second card is the player's card. If you've bet on the same denomination, you win a 1-1 return, unless you have a card that is higher than the banker's, for which I pay 3-1. There are more subtleties, but we should start with the basics. Now, in order to provide recompense to me…"

One of the young men had a puzzled stare.

"It's like schooling younguns," the banker mumbled to himself. "It means payment for services rendered. In this case, I will keep the stakes low…let's say, fifty cents per check. How many do you fine men desire?"

Hank took the opportunity to interrupt while the four dug through pokes and pockets. "Beg pardon, sir, you be Rockford Whitman?"

"Might could be, depending on who's asking."

"Didn't get her name, but a woman needs to talk…"

"Tell that no-good, two-bit, soiled dove there ain't no talking to be done…I never pay more than two dollars…"

Hank interrupted, "Ain't likely we're talkin' 'bout the same lady. This here one's dressed like a school marm."

"Oh…what does she want?" His thoughts went to a dozen or more men he had relieved of valuable's and, on occasion, their lives at the Faro table.

"Didn't say."

Rockford was intrigued, but reluctant to leave the four marks alone, lest they lose interest. "Please purchase your checks," he repeated.

Rocky collected their money, dispensed the chips with a flourish and stood. "I have a brief bit of business to attend to and will return forthwith."

"Now, hold on there just a durn minute, Slick," one of the older players said. "I was born at night, but not last night. How do we know you ain't gonna skeddadle?"

"A point I hadn't considered, sir. Perhaps, one of you could hold the money until I return." He looked at one of the young men, who took the cue.

"No offense, fellas, but I'm just passin' through...don't know any of you. You could be in cahoots with him."

Whitman turned to the message bearer. "What did you say your name was?"

"Johnson, sir...uh...Henry Johnson. But...but, most folks calls me Hank."

"Hank, how would you like earn a quick buck?"

"Fer what?"

"Standing here with these fellas holding this money, while I talk to the woman outside."

"Sure." Hank could already taste whiskey, instead of watered-down beer.

Rockford handed the money to the rancher. He wasn't worried about him sneaking out the back door.

Whitman squinted as he stepped into the afternoon sun, stuck his toothpick in a vest pocket and pulled the rolled brim of his felt hat down. An attractive woman with tight blonde ringlets, who appeared to be in her early twenties, stood off to one side clutching a handbag.

Her prim posture was testament to training from an eastern boarding school. A middle-aged woman in a plain brown travelling dress stood hesitantly next to her.

He tipped his hat. "Ladies, allow me to introduce myself, I am Rockford Whitman, at your disposal."

The manners he learned from his mother often smoothed the way into higher levels of frontier society than his background would dictate.

"I am Mary Elizabeth Peabody, and this is Agnes Whetherby, my maid and chaperone." She extended her hand and offered a slight curtsy.

Rockford brushed her gloved hand with his lips as he bowed. "Pleased to meet you. To what circumstance do I owe this opportunity to make your acquaintance?"

"I am on a journey to settle the affairs of my late brother, who met an untimely demise at the hands of another. The culprit may be of interest to you. I was informed that you occasionally engage in the profession of, I believe the correct term is, bounty hunting. Is my information correct?"

Whitman breathed a sigh of relief. This petite woman was apparently not going to draw a pistol from her bag and shoot him.

"I have been known to assist the judiciary in apprehending criminals of any ilk. Although, I must tell you, my services are available only if the remuneration is adequate."

"I offer you, then, a two-part proposal. The first task would be to simply accompany us to Fort Sill. Would a thousand dollars be sufficient?"

Rockford paused to allow his heartbeat to return to normal. "It would, Miss Peabody...I assume it is, Miss?"

"Indeed. I will pay for travel through Oklahoma Indian Nations to Fort Sill, Oklahoma Indian Territory, to include lodging, transportation and three meals a day. You are responsible for any personal entertainment you require.

"The second part pertains to the capture of his assassin. I have been informed there will be a substantial reward for his capture, easily two thousand dollars or more. That matter would be between you and the authorities. I will not personally participate in the pursuit of the evil person. I would prefer he face the eternal justice of the Lord, sooner, rather than later."

Whitman salivated as he considered the payment, but also thought of the easy marks sitting inside. "When do you propose to commence this journey?"

"The next train to Gainesville departs on Wednesday at midday. I would think that would offer adequate time for you to prepare."

That gave him two more nights to fleece the local card players. "Yes, it would."

EMPIRE HOTEL
WICHITA, KANSAS

The Tuesday morning sun shone through lace-curtained windows and burned holes in the gambler's eyes. Whitman stumbled to a pot in the corner to relieve himself, sprinkling spots on the flowered wallpaper in the process. He poured water from a white Ironstone pitcher into a basin and splashed some on his face. Rocky preferred the comfort of fine hotels and was confident the school marm would, too.

The hotel dining room was quiet at ten in the morning as Whitman joined three men at a table. "Mornin', my scalawags...you ordered, yet?"

"Jist now, boss," a scruffy, middle-aged man named Nigel answered. His boiled cotton shirt was buttoned to the collar, with a gray wool vest over it. The two younger men wore similar apparel and all sported gun belts.

Whitman called the waitress over and ordered a hearty breakfast with a pot of coffee. He turned back to the table after she left and leaned in. "I found an easy job, but we don't have a month of Sundays to go over the plan, so listen up."

§§§

CHAPTER TWO

MISSOURI, KANSAS & TEXAS DEPOT WICHITA, KANSAS

"May I assume you have a clear understanding of our arrangement?" Mary Elizabeth asked the obviously hungover and surly gambler.

"…not a half-wit," Rocky snarled as forcefully as his pounding head would allow. He softened his tone when he saw her reaction. "I get you safely to Fort Sill and then capture or kill this outlaw, once he's identified. You get justice…I get a thousand dollars and the reward. That sum it up?"

"Yes…yes, I believe it does."

"Good, now I'm having a nap." He slouched in the seat and pulled his hat over his eyes. "Wake me when it's time to eat."

Mary had wondered if Whitman was the right man for the job of capturing one of the most ruthless outlaws in the west. His current demeanor and killing of the man in Witchita proved he was capable of extreme violence. Whether or not he had the skill to track down a vicious criminal was still an open question.

Using Whitman to exact revenge was not a Christian reaction to her older sibling's murder, but it was what she needed…she hoped God would forgive her.

GULF & COLORADO DEPOT
ARDMORE, CHICKASAW NATION

"I thought the instructions in my telegram were quiet clear, Mister Farnsworth," Mary said, in as civil a voice as she could muster. "I requested a horse and buggy be made available for my use, as well as a riding horse. Where are they, sir?"

"Well, Miss Peabody, that there's the problem…I never got no telegram. Could be it got lost, or could be Jorgenson tore it up before he quit and run off. I'm the new Freight

Master…been here three days and still sortin' out the mess he left…"

Rocky shouldered Mary aside and poked the hapless railroad employee in the chest. "Listen up, Slick, if you don't want to end up as buzzard bait, you better come up with something fast. Get off your dead rump and give me an answer…"

"Mister Whitman, if you please! This is my affair and I will negotiate with him," Mary said. "What would you suggest I do, Mister Farnsworth?"

The shorter than average employee wiped his forehead with a stained handkerchief and kept his eye on Rocky while he replied, "Pap Smith's livery's just down the way. I'm sure he'll do whatever he can to help."

"Thank you, sir. I would be much obliged if you would see to my luggage and we will return, forthwith."

"Luggage? You have luggage?" Rocky said as they walked away.

"Yes, I had the hotel deliver it to the train depot in Wichita. I am aware this is the frontier, however, there are certain standards of appearance to which a Boston lady must adhere. That requires a wardrobe and accoutrements."

Whitman scratched his head and replied. "I don't understand why we came all the way to Ardmore, when we could have gotten off at any one of a number of rest stops along the way."

"I was told that Ardmore was the most likely place to find a suitable hotel, as well as a livery from which to hire a buggy and horses. Please, do not question my decisions."

"I wasn't," he mumbled. "This is your circus, and you are the ringmaster."

"I hope you shall not, again, forget that," she crisply stated and walked off, with Agnes in tow.

"Oh, believe you me, I won't," Whitman mumbled, as he trailed behind the two woman.

SMITH'S LIVERY

"Love to help you folks...truly would," Pap Smith said, while bending over to clean a horse's hoof with a pick. "Problem is, got no buggies of any kind...buckboards is all I got."

"A common workman's conveyance?"

"Most of my customers work for a livin'," he replied with a sour look. "You want one, or not?"

"I suppose I have no choice. I would be most appreciative if you have the buckboard harnessed and ready in the morning, as well as a mount for Mister Whitman. Would you kindly provide directions to the Whittington Hotel? I have been informed it is the best in Ardmore."

"A fair description." Smith smiled. "Seeing as how it's the only hotel in town. Go thataway to the second street and turn left. It's about two hundred feet down on the right…can't miss it."

"Thank you, sir. Come, Mister Whitman."

"Yeah, sure," Rocky mumbled. He was getting tired of the haughty attitude of his temporary employer. He might have to give her to the boys for their amusement after her money was safely in his poke.

WHITTINGTON HOTEL
ARDMORE, CHICKASAW NATION

Mary sat in a wing back chair and surveyed the parlor. The furnishings represented a tasteful, although somewhat eclectic style, ranging from Queen Elizabeth to Chippendale. The guests who gathered for dessert after supper were as varied as the furnishings.

An elderly pastor and his wife had chosen to rest for a few days before continuing their journey to Fort Worth to join their son, who had established a sizable congregation.

A history professor who had secured a position with the recently established Saint Edward's College in Austin was discussing the opportunities for advancement in the recently affirmed capitol of the State of Texas, after years of political haggling. A land speculator from Kansas City, who was also seeking a new life and fortune, sat quietly in the corner.

The air was charged with the excitement of people looking for a fresh start in a new place. Mary was needle pointing a design of a wren sitting on a branch and thought how different she was from them.

Her only desire was to reconcile the death of her wastrel older brother, conclude his affairs, and return to Boston. She longed to be back on the Commons in the springtime and would even welcome winter there, instead of the parched dusty landscape that surrounded her.

Eldon Barkley, the history professor, sat his coffee cup on a saucer and spoke to Mary, "Are you one of the Boston Brahmin Peabodys?"

"A *non de guerre* coined by the physician and writer Oliver Wendell Holmes, Senior," she replied. "We prefer to think of ourselves as the educated elite who are attempting to improve the social environment."

"Ahem…of course. My apologies, young lady, if I offended you."

"No apology is necessary, sir, and I took no offense. It is a popular term these days, employed far too often by yellow journalists and those of limited intellectual capacity. It helps them to reconcile their circumstances. But, as to you, sir, from whence does your family hail?"

Barkley hesitated before answering the simple inquiry, "We are from Chicago, by way of Baltimore."

Mary Elizabeth replied, without thinking, "Our family has never had much use for either place. One is an inferior seaport to our own, and the other is a packing town with little culture. It must be a challenge, living on the edge of structured society."

"I suppose you might say we are attempting to improve educational opportunities on the frontier," the professor noted. "Therefore, the hardships are a small sacrifice."

"Then, I wish you and them well in your endeavors," Mary said, with a wan smile.

The professor was relieved to return to his conversation with the pastor emeritus.

Mary absentmindedly continued her needle work and imagined what Fort Sill would be like. Members of her family told her it was a primitive installation populated primarily with soldiers and Indians, with few cultural pursuits, if any. They tried to dissuade her from traveling there. She listened to their arguments and weighed them against the desire to inject adventure into her life.

MARY ELIZABETH PEABODY

Mary Elizabeth had long ago surrendered to the notion that she would, in all likelihood, die a spinster. It was a sobering notion, since she was still in her early twenties.

She thought back to her coming out party, and how she considered the idea of pairing with any of the gangly, callow young men as being too much to bear. Consequently, she followed the example of many women in her family and dedicated her life to the education of other people's children. She did not rule out the possibility of marriage, but did not embrace it, either.

On the other hand, there was a steadily increasing desire in her for soul-stirring adventure before she settled down to the quiet life of a Boston socialite. The news of her brother's passing offered an opportunity with purpose, and she embraced it.

Her mother had quietly encouraged her to open her mind to new worlds. She insisted that Agnes, a trusted family retainer, accompany Mary Elizabeth as a maid and chaperone.

Agnes said she would welcome a change of scenery for a few months. She had cared for Mary since childhood and would be of great comfort on the trip.

SHERIFF'S OFFICE
JACKSBORO, TEXAS

Mason Flynn, the duly-elected sheriff of Jack County, stretched his six-foot two-inch frame with his hands over his head and yawned. His two hundred and ten pounds of hard muscle belied the fact that, at forty-years old, middle-age was staring him squarely in the face. The knowledge that many lawmen his age had passed on to their reward, mostly due to injuries inflicted by miscreants and perpetrators of various misdeeds, was a constant reminder to be on guard.

He sat down in the wooden rolling chair behind his desk and began the transfer paperwork for Johnson Peterson, a deserter from Fort Sill, the Army post in Oklahoma Indian Nations to the north. Peterson was apprehended after a drunken knife fight in a local saloon the week before.

A Deputy US Marshal would normally escort a deserter back to his post for trial before a military judge. Unfortunately, the Marshal's Service was shorthanded at the moment, which was the subject of the telegram on the desk in front of Flynn.

He reread it and commented to Slim Parker, one of two deputies who worked under him, "Looks like I'll be taking a ride up to Fort Sill to return Private Peterson to his unit."

The black Chickasaw freedman looked up from the stack of wanted dodgers he was studying. He was fortunate to have learned to read in a Quaker school he attended in his youth.

"That so, Boss?"

"Telegram says they want him back soon as possible."

"Want me to do it?"

"'apreciate it, but no...has to be a Federal agent. US Deputy Marshal F.M Miller deputized me when we were chasing down Davis Trotter's gang. Marshals service appears to think it's permanent. Shouldn't take more'n a week...putting you in charge while I'm gone..."

"Well, now, that ain't fair!" The protest came from Gomer Platt, Flynn's other deputy, as he stood in the doorway to the holding cell area.

"Give 'em hell," Johnson Peterson yelled from behind bars and laughed.

"Shut your mouth, you deserter scum," Platt ordered over his shoulder. He stepped into the office and slammed the door before continuing, "Been here seven months and two weeks longer than Slim. I should be in charge."

"Parker's older and more experienced," Flynn replied, with his head down as he wrote.

"But, Sheriff..."

"Not open for discussion...isn't it time for you to fetch dinner?"

Gomer recognized the tone of finality in Flynn's voice and knew from experience the futility of arguing with his boss once his mind was set.

"Guess I best be on my way," he said as he left and slammed the door behind him. It bounced open, and it took the hapless deputy two more tries to get it properly latched.

"Door needs to be fixed," Slim observed.

"I'll have Gomer look at it later," Flynn replied.

"Say, Boss, you sure you ain't concerned about putting me in charge while you're gone?"

"Not a bit…why?"

"Just thought, me being colored and a Chickasaw might upset some folks."

"Their problem. Hired you 'cause I thought you were the best man for the job. Haven't changed my mind. Besides, it's only a week…they'll get over it."

"And, if I run into trouble?"

"Handle it like I was sitting right here."

PAP SMITH'S LIVERY

"It appears he took my words to heart," Mary Elizabeth said to Agnes, as they approached the livery.

Whitman was loading the last of the necessary supplies behind the women's luggage. He covered the provisions with the canvas material for a tent and lashed an oilskin cover over the back of the buckboard to protect the cargo.

"Good morning, Mister Whitman. I trust you had a pleasant rest last night?"

"About as well as to be expected," he replied. Rocky chose not to tell her that he spent half the night playing cards in a saloon down the street from the hotel, and most of the remaining time with a painted lady, before getting a couple of hours sleep.

He got up at sunrise to ride a few miles out of town to meet with his men.

"Wake up, you dunderheaded saddle tramps," he demanded as he rode into a camp along a creek. "It's time for some dirty work."

He had picked the spot a few years before when he was on the run from a failed stage coach heist in Texas. It was a low spot protected from the wind and, better yet, from being spotted by anybody traveling the road into town.

Three tousled heads slowly poked their way out from under woolen blankets. "Hells bells, Boss, sun ain't been up no longer'n a fawn's tail. We rode hard gittin' here last night...ain't had but a few hours sleep," Nigel whined. "Ain't that right, Virgil?"

Virgil scratched his head first, and then his crotch, as he answered, "Didn't hardly sleep none...think they's sand fleas here."

"Not surprised," Rockford replied. He looked at the last member of the hapless trio. "How 'bout you? Got any gripes?"

Gabe poked at the smoldering fire in a vain attempt to rekindle it as he replied. "Well, I am a might peckish...guess I'll go round up some wood to fix some victuals,." he replied.

"Ain't time," Whitman noted. "Grab some Arbuckle in town. I expect that she-devil of a woman to be chomping at the bit, ready to hit the trail...need to get back and round up supplies before we do. Just wanted to say a quick how-de-do."

"Tell me, again, which road we goin' on?" Nigel asked.

Whitman sighed and slowly shook his head before answering, "The Ardmore to Duncan stage road where it meets up with the Ft. Arbuckle to Ft. Sill road. How many times do I have to go over it for you half wits?"

The three hung their heads until Nigel answered in a quiet voice, "Got it, Boss. We stay a mile or so behind and wait for your signal."

"Right. I want to wait til we're in Commanch country, so they get blamed for the massacre of two white women. That'll keep the soldiers from Fort Sill busy for a good while chasing down ghosts. We'll be deep in Texas before they figger out what happened, if they ever do."

"That's a right smart plan, Boss."

"Glad you like it," Whitman sarcastically replied. "Like I said before, I need to get back to town. Break camp and try to keep up with me...and don't try anything bright. You ain't got one brain twixt the three of you, so stick with my plan."

"Yes, Boss," they said in unison.

Rocky shook his head and spurred his mount.

§§§

CHAPTER THREE

ARDMORE TO ARBUCKLE/FORT SILL ROAD

"I fail to see why we are going north, instead of straight west, Mister Whitman," Mary Elizabeth asked.

"I believe I explained it earlier, Miss Peabody, The Arbuckle range is difficult to travel this time of year on horseback, much less by wagon. It would also be prudent to avoid some towns on the southern route."

"I will trust your judgment, sir, since you are more familiar with the surroundings than I."

Agnes waited until the conversation concluded before asking a question, "Mister Whitman, not meanin' to be a harridan but, since you are the grand pooh-bah in this godforsaken land, can you tell me why there be three men a followin' us? For aught we know, they could be meanin' us harm."

"Many men come this way to better themselves."

"Aye, and that may be the case, indeed, but what if they mean to waylay us?" Agnes raised one eyebrow.

"Your concern is not unwarranted, madam. I will wait until we stop for the night and reconnoiter their camp."

"A most excellent idea, Mister Whitman," Mary Elizabeth commented. "Be sure to remind them of the wrath of the Lord against those who sin."

"I most certainly will," he mumbled. *It'll also give me a chance to tell those worthless scum knuckle heads to fall back a little further. How'd I end up with men like them?*

NEAR THE TEXAS/OKLAHOMA BORDER

"Hey, friend, you really think you're gonna get me back to the fort without being bushwhacked?" Peterson Johnson posed the question to Sheriff Flynn as they rode the trail north.

Flynn ignored him and searched the hilly terrain ahead, looking for signs of unwanted company. Renegade attacks had tapered off since cavalry patrols from Ft. Sill were increased, and even outlaws had learned to avoid the main roads. But, it was still a good idea to be alert.

Johnson repeated the question.

Flynn answered through clenched teeth, "Get this through your thick skull, deserter···I'm not your friend...never could stomach yellow-belly scum. I mean to hand your worthless carcass over to the Provost Marshal and wash my hands of you. So, shut your mouth and think about your future, grim as it might be."

Peterson lowered his head, slumped in the saddle and mumbled something.

"You got something to say?" Flynn demanded.

Johnson nodded his head to indicate no, but thought to himself, "Wait til my kin shows up, yer a dead man and don't even know it."

ARBUCKLE TO FORT SILL ROAD

"This is a distinct improvement over the rutted trail we just left," Mary Elizabeth noted. "Although, I must say, I am surprised at how muddy they both are, since I was told this was parched prairie."

"Indeed it is, most of the year," Rocky replied. "There are a few wet months, however, and this appears to be worse than the last time I traveled this way."

He had welcomed the rain and mud during the previous trip, two years before. It had greatly reduced the posse's ability to track him after he robbed a train near Pauls Valley. They eventually gave up and returned home.

The bandanna he wore during the robbery meant he had not been identified, and no one was hurt badly enough to require revenge from family members. The stolen money was a payroll destined for Fort Sill, so none of the locals cared enough to do more than a cursory search.

"I do pray the road ahead is passable," Mary Elizabeth said.

Her remark brought him out of his reverie and he replied, "The Federal government paid copious sums to contractors to ensure travel during times of flooding."

"A judicious use of taxes."

"Yes, it would appear so, and another reason we came this way. The station master in Ardmore received reports of flooding to the south and west. This trail has bridges over creeks and rivers."

"Very well, then. I will allow you to lead," was her haughty reply.

He pursed his lips. *I'll be glad when I rid myself of them. Perhaps I'll take a little pleasure before I pass them on to the boys. They'll welcome death after that."*

She noticed his smile and queried, "Have I said something that amuses you, Mister Rockford?"

"No. I am taking pleasure in the beautiful scenery."

RED RIVER STATION, TEXAS

"Don't believe I've ever seen the Red this high," Flynn remarked to John Gilbreath, the ferry operator.

"No, sirree, Sheriff. Been here nigh on to five years and this beats all. Asked old man Heaton if he'd ever seen it this deep and he said not that he could recollect."

"How is he?"

"Crankier'n a hobbled bull ever since he retired."

"He ever say how he lost his leg?"

"Naw…'spose it was during the War of Northern Agression," Gilbreath replied. "You see action in it?"

"Me? No, I'm a little young for that. Did fourteen years in the cavalry, though. Mustered out and began ranching in Jack County."

"What called you to the law?" Gilbreath regretted asking the seemingly harmless question when he saw Flynn's reaction. "Never mind...none of my business…"

"No, it's a fair question," Flynn replied. "Renegade Commanch murdered my pregnant wife half–a-dozen years ago. Hunted the murdering savage down and took my sweet time killing the heathen. Not long after that, townspeople in Jacksboro urged me to become town marshal.

"Later on, Special Deputy US Marshal F.M. Miller commissioned me as a Deputy US Marshal to extend the boundaries of my authority. I take on occasional jobs for them when they're shorthanded, like taking that coward back to Fort Sill."

He spit a stream of Brown's Mule toward the shade of a pin oak where the shackled Peterson Johnson was sitting.

"Thought you might be headed toward Fort Sill," the ferry operated said. "Guess you ain't heerd 'bout the road..."

"What about it?"

"Cache Creek and Beaver Creek been over they banks nigh on a month. Washed the road out wider'n a section of land in half a dozen places. Best bet is to follow the Rock Island tracks up to ol' man Duncan's trading post and pick up the Fort Arbuckle road on to Fort Sill."

"Add's a day and a half to the trip," Flynn noted.

"Sure does, but you'd get there," Gilbreath agreed. "And it's still faster'n swimming."

"Good point," Flynn replied. "Guess I better cross now."

"Shore thing. That'll be four dollars."

Flynn reached into his vest pocket for money. "Only half as much last time,"

"Only half as deep then," Gilbreath said, with a grin.

Flynn handed the affable ferryman the coins and walked over to fetch his prisoner.

"You have a trip, Marshal."

"My intention."

"How long ago'd you say that marshal feller came this a way?" the large man in overalls asked the ferry operator.

"Didn't," John Gilbreath answered, as he prepared the ferry to take the motley group of four men north.

"But, you did take them across," another man said.

Gilbreath had already surveyed the rough-looking quartet and determined they might be trouble. He had an old Civil War pistol under his shirt, but that might not be enough. He casually walked toward the small, wooden tool shed where he kept his shotgun and tried to measure his chance of success against four men.

"Don't want no trouble, friend," he said as he entered the shed and grabbed the scatter gun from the wall rack. He turned around with the weapon in hand and addressed the group, "Now, what bid'ness would it be of yourn when he came through here?"

"Whoa there, fella, ain't you jumpin' the gun jist a mite? We don't mean you no harm. What cause you got to draw down on us?" The big man asked, as he reached into his overalls. "We're kin to Peterson Johnson..."

"And who might he be?" Gilbreath asked.

"My son, and I fully intend to make sure he makes it to Fort Sill alive," the big man replied. "And our cousin there means to go with us."

Gilbreath glanced to his side and saw the fifth member of the group step out of the trees. He lowered his weapon when he realized the odds were overwhelmingly against him.

A bead of sweat broke out across his forehead and there was a tremor in his voice, "Look, friends...don't mean no harm to none of you...jist a man tryin' to make a livin'. How 'bout I take you 'cross for free, since you be lookin' out after kin?"

"Right neighborly of you." The big man smiled and nodded to the others. "Git on the ferry."

They complied and he joined them, while keeping an eye on Gilbreath as he followed them.

The wooden conveyance bumped against the other side a few minutes later and the passengers disembarked. The big man reached into his overalls and Gilbreath wondered if he had made a mistake by not opening up on them with both barrels.

"Cain't no man never say William Johnson took somethin' from another man," he said, as he leaned down and handed the ferryman five silver dollars. "Like you said, you're tryin' to make a livin', and I jist want to make sure that worthless son of mine ain't killed by no trigger-happy marshal. Thought lettin' my boy join the Army would straighten him out some...guess it ain't. He will pay the piper and maybe get home to his mama some day."

Gilbreath took the coins and looked Johnson in the eye. "If it makes you feel a mite better, Mister Johnson, I know Mason Flynn. He's a God-fearin' man what won't let no harm come to yer boy."

"Sweet words to my ears," Johnson said. "But, I got a notion to follow along behind them anyways, jist to be sure he's safe."

§§§

MARY ELIZABETH PEABODY

CHAPTER FOUR

DUNCAN'S TRADING POST
OKLAHOMA TERRITORY

"I understand, Mister Whitman, that you are inclined to complete our journey to Fort Sill as quickly as possible, but I have never seen an authentic Indian trading post," Mary Elizabeth said.

"This isn't precisely an Indian trading post," Whitman answered in a dry tone. "And the proprietors could barely be considered Indian. Duncan's wife, who is white, was married to an Indian, which put her on the tribal roles. He passed away unexpectedly a few years later, leaving the property to her. Duncan, who is also white, married her and gained access to the roles through her previous marriage."

"An intriging set of circumstances. Nonetheless, I wish to peruse the offerings. Unless, of course, you think it unwise."

"Not at all, Miss Peabody. this is your shindig."

Rocky actually welcomed the delay. His men were supposed to come into the store to confirm their presence in the crossroads community.

Whitman watched the two women admiring handmade Indian clothing on a shelf while he strolled to a table stacked with beaver hats. He glanced toward the entrance door and noticed a tall, broad-shouldered man enter with a dejected rail-thin man in tow. Something about the taller man seemed familiar and, as the two passed by, Rocky noticed the star pinned to a bib-front shirt under his open duster.

Whitman's three men came in shortly after the two and paused to let their eyes adjust to the darkened interior. They walked slowly toward the hat table and Nigel made eye contact with Rocky.

Without warning, Virgil pushed both men aside, his eyes focused on the two men at the other end of the store. He pointed his finger at the imposing figure and yelled, "Hey, ain't you the bushwackin', low-down, egg-suckin' law dog what dry-gulched an kilt my brother Cabe?"

You could hear a mouse sneeze in the silence that gripped the store. Some patrons crouched behind whatever cover they could find, while others froze in place. Specks of dust floating in a shaft of sunlight were the only things that moved.

William Duncan, the hearty Scotsman owner, reached under the counter for the breakover eight-guage shotgun he kept for situations like this and addressed Virgil, "Noo jist haud on, there, laddie. I'll brook no violence in me establishment. Keep your heid on straight and take the beef ootside, or I'll be inclined to intervene."

Flynn brushed back his coat and placed his hand on the butt of his Smith and Wesson Peacemaker pistol. "Depends. Where did this happen?"

"You know damned well where, you worthless sidewinder…down in Jack County, Texas."

"Was he shooting up a saloon in Jacksboro?"

"How 'n hell would I know? Weren't there," Virgil answered in a slightly less confident tone.

"I was," Flynn said, "He sliced up a sporting lady and killed a cow hand who tried to stop him. Did my duty, and I only shoot people who need it."

"An' now I'll take my revenge," Virgil said through clenched teeth. He glanced toward Whitman before he followed that comment up with, "Slap leather, law dog." His right hand slid down to the holster on his belt.

Virgil's weapon barely cleared its holster before the .45 caliber slug burrowed a neat hole between the outlaw's eyebrows. A second slug tore a hole in his throat and a gurgling breath was Virgil's last testament before he joined his brother.

A pale-blue cloud of smoke hung in the air as one of the women shoppers screamed and another covered her little girl's eyes.

"Anybody else after revenge?" Flynn asked.

Nobody stepped forward, not even the two men who entered the store with Virgil. They looked to Rocky for guidance, but he turned away and joined his female charges.

"Come, ladies, I believe it's time we continue our journey," he said, while keeping his eyes on the two remaining gang members.

"Don't shoot," Nigel cried. "Ain't got no quarrel with you, Mister...don't even know this here feller. He pointed to Virgil. "Honest, we met him on the trail a ways back...figured three of us stood a better chance ag'in Indian attacks."

"Then get out of here and don't darken those doors again," Flynn muttered in a low growl.

T.C. Miller

Nigel and Gabe looked at each other, then to Whitman, before returning their gaze to Mason.

"Now!" he said to the hapless duo.

They joined the rush of store patrons, including Whitman and the ladies, out the doors.

"Sorry about disturbing your business," Flynn said to Duncan.

"Ah dinnae ken you had a choice, Marshal. The skinny malinky longlegs was itchin' to dance with the devil, himself."

The puzzled look on Flynn's face prompted Sally Duncan to explain, "Sorry, Marshal, my husband's command of the King's English slips a little when he's excited. What he said was, he didn't think you had a choice, since the outlaw seemed to be in a hurry to die."

"Thank you, ma'am…figured it was something like that. Anyway, where is the closest law to this town?"

"Wynnewood, but the Lighthorse Police are due here tomorrow on their weekly patrol. We'll turn the body over to them and give a report. I'm sure they'll contact you if they have questions, or if there's a reward for the miscreant. He appeared to be the kind that attracts trouble."

"Much obliged, ma'am. Say, do you folks know the man who was with the young blonde lady and the older dark-haired woman?"

"Naw, kinna say I do," William answered, as his wife shook her head.

"Looks familiar...course, when you've been a lawman awhile, they all begin to look alike. Anyway, I'll be on my way with my prisoner."

"Lang may yer lum leek," William said.

"Which means, 'May you live long and stay well,'" Sally translated.

"Same to you," Flynn said over his shoulder as he led Johnson to the door.

FORT SILL ROAD
WEST OF DUNCAN'S STORE

"Sure as shootin', I can't figure you out, Sheriff," Peterson Johnson said. "First, we hurry away from Duncan's like demons was chasin' us, and now we're just a sittin' here off trail, hidin' in the trees like bushwackers. Sun's gettin' low, 'n I need to rest my sore bones."

Mason leaned down and spoke softly to Laddie, his horse, "Something about that man with the two women stuck in my craw...don't seem like the type either woman would travel with. Swear I've laid eyes on him before, just can't recall where."

"Sittin' right here, you know...you kin talk to me..."

"Prefer my horse, he's smarter."

"Well, don't that ring the bells on a Monday...almost rather be back in the stockade, 'stead of toleratin'..."

"Shush, there's a wagon coming."

Peterson wasn't sure why he obeyed Fynn, but he did. *Man's a natural-born leader. If he'd been my troop leader, instead of that brayin' ass, Ledbetter, I might not be in this here trouble.*

As Flynn predicted, a buckboard with the two women passed by a few minutes later, followed by the dark-haired man on horseback.

Mason let them get a good distance ahead, then turned to his Johnson. "Still two or three hours of daylight. We'll follow them at a safe distance. I figure they'll stop for the night at Lil' Beaver Creek. Something's off-kilter...those three nabobs at the store seemed to know the hombre travelin' with the women. Stay quiet, and I promise I'll put in a good word with your commander."

"That's the most you've said to me at one time."

"Right."

JUNCTION OF LIL' BEAVER CREEK AND THE FORT ARBUCKLETOFORT SILL ROAD

"May I be of some assistance?" Mary Elizabeth asked Agnes, who was preparing supper.

MARY ELIZABETH PEABODY

"Are you saying I'm a slamkin and not earnin' me coppers? I work hard as a body can, what with poor sleep and sittin' on that torture rack," Agnes replied, as she nodded toward the buckboard. "Not once has an offer of help fallen on me ears all the years I've known ye, so why now?"

Mary Elizabeth's face turned bright red. "I meant no offense..."

Agnes noticed the young woman's embarrassment, and quickly added, "I know the limits of Boston Society are lackin' in this God-forsaken place, but, saints preserve us, you should not be doin' me work."

"You are right, of course, dear Agnes, and have always been a faithful companion. I have unbosomed many a worry to you..."

"So, what is it now that would be speakin' to yer heart?"

"I am not sure. Perhaps it is what newspapermen refer to as the frontier spirit. The fiercely independent spirit of the local women inspires me to experience more of this land."

"I understand, me little Molly-bug. Truth be told, me weary feet would welcome a wee bit of help. Would ye mind fetching a half-stone sack of flour from the wagon?"

A broad grin spread across Mary Elizabeth's face. "I would be honored." She was walking toward the buckboard when the two men from Duncan's Store rode into camp.

Mary Elizabeth looked around for Whitman as she scurried back to Agnes and the fire.

"Change your mind about helpin'?" Agnes said without looking up. She heard the horses and looked up. "Faith and begorrah, 'tis the scalawags from the trading post."

Rocky returned with a load of firewood in his arms as the two men dismounted.

"We have visitors, Mister Whitman," Mary Elizabeth announced, while trying to keep her voice steady. At least they had Rocky to protect them.

"I am aware of that, Miss Peabody, since it was I who invited them."

"Why, in the name of all things holy, would you help these rapscallions?"

"Because they work for me. I intend to relieve you of your valuables, as well as your virtue." An unmistakable leer spread across his face.

Nigel pulled the front of Agnes's dress down nearly to her waist as he slapped the cooking knife from her hand and pushed her to the ground. He began fumbling with the buttons on his trousers.

Gabe held the woman's shoulders down as she wiggled and squirmed to get away.

"Unhand me, ya worthless scum," she screamed.

MARY ELIZABETH PEABODY

Mary Elizabeth slipped a single-shot derringer from her boot and pulled the trigger. The round caught Gabe squarely in the chest and he fell back with eyes open wide in a death stare.

Agnes seized the opportunity and broke free from Nigel, who was caught with his trousers around his knees. She had taken only three steps when Whitman fired a round squarely into her back that sent her sprawling to the grass.

Mary Elizabeth fled to the trail and ran in the direction of Duncan's Store. *I cannot outrun a man on horseback, but I refuse to stay and face the indignities they have in mind.*

"It's useless to run, you simpering little highbrow tart," Rocky said with a laugh. "I'll have my way with you before I slit your throat." He mounted his horse and nudged it into a slow walk. The chase excited him, and he imagined the agony he would soon inflict upon her.

Mary Elizabeth had no idea where she was going, or what she would do when Whitman caught up to her. She only knew she had to escape. Her hair fanned wildly around her terrified face and her arms flailed about like an out of control windmill as she ran headlong down the trail.

Each breath became harder and harder to draw in. Her lungs burned and her stride became uneven. She was losing momentum when she tripped over a rock in the road. Mary

Elizabeth fell toward the hard-packed clay with her hands in front of her.

The sound of horses hooves behind her signaled the arrival of her tormentor. He sat astride his mount, hands crossed over the saddle horn.

"Now, we'll have some fun," he needled her. "May as well take off your clothes and lay down. Make it easy for me and death'll come faster for you. You'll no doubt welcome it."

Whitman started to swing his leg over the saddle, but stopped with his foot hanging in midair over the horses rump when a .44-40 slug slammed into his chest. A second slug arrived close behind it and knocked him off the horse in a macabre, twisting dance.

Jack County Sheriff and duly deputized US Marshal Mason Flynn chambered another round into his rifle and waited for Whitman to hit the dirt. The wretched evildoer landed with a sickening thud and stared at the darkening sky with unseeing eyes.

"One less miscreant to deal with, Laddie. Let's go check on the other woman. A dazed and weary Mary Elizabeth stood in the middle of the road. He reached down and pulled her up with one hand.

"Thank you, sir," she said between gasps for air. "You surely saved me from humiliation and death." She sat behind the saddle clinging to him and sobbed.

§§§

CHAPTER FIVE

OFFICE OF THE COMMANDER
FORT SILL, OT

Lieutenant Colonel Edgar R. Kellogg stood ramrod straight and, in a Midwestern voice that was just as stiff, said to Mary Elizabeth, "I want to begin by offering my most sincere condolences for the loss of your maid…"

"Agnes was more than my servant, sir. She is…was a lifelong friend."

"I beg your pardon, Miss Peabody, I was not aware of her status," the mildly flustered officer replied.

"Of course you were not. I do appreciate your assistance in arranging for a suitable burial in the post cemetery. She was an only child whose last relative died years ago."

Colonel Kellogg hesitated, cleared his throat, and spoke, "Again, my condolences. Now, to the matter of your brother's estate. The land upon which he established his ranch was leased, since white men are not allowed to own land here. That is but one of the reasons I am returning to Toledo when I retire next year.

"In the meantime, the rightful owner has terminated the lease and taken back the land. My Provost Marshal did a careful inventory of your brother's possessions, including livestock and tools. Everything, except his personal items was auctioned off, and here is a bank draft for the proceeds."

"This barely replaces the money I have spent on this trip," Mary Elizabeth quietly said, as she stared at the check. "Surely, there was more than this, was there not?"

"With no disrespect intended, Miss Peabody, your brother had quite the reputation as a gambler who imbibed heavily. He was known to lose hundreds of dollars…occasionally thousands, in an evening. I am afraid you are looking at the sum total of his estate."

"Sixteen hundred and ten dollars? My family gave him five thousand dollars to establish his ranch," she said. There was a moment of silence before she spoke again, "Still, I am sure you and your people did a commendable job of liquidating his property."

"Sheriff Flynn was stationed here with the Second Cavalry and can attest to the fact that we are guided by the Federal Code. Furthermore, this is Indian Territory, so our actions are carefully overseen."

Mary Elizabeth turned to Sheriff Flynn. "Does this sound proper to you?"

"Not a lawyer," Flynn replied. "Might talk with one, though, or consult your family."

"I sent a telegram to them this morning, and expect a reply forthwith. In the meantime, Sheriff, I wonder if I could impose upon you to accompany me to Jacksboro? Colonel Kellogg has informed me that all of his troops are occupied searching for renegade Indians, and there are none to escort me back to Ardmore. I know no one else here and am hesitant to travel alone, in light of recent events."

"Be glad to, but what about the buckboard and horses?"

"I purchased them from the livery in Ardmore, and planned to dispose of them before returning to Boston. It seemed like a sound investment," she replied.

"Shrewd move," he noted.

"Well, then, Colonel, I suppose that concludes our business. Sheriff Flynn, I am prepared to depart whenever you desire."

MARY ELIZABETH PEABODY

SEWELL'S CAFE
JACKSBORO, TEXAS

"Oh, my, how is a young lady supposed to maintain a slim figure?" Mary Elizabeth exclaimed, as you looked at the spread, Molly, their waitress, had placed in front of her.

A slab of breaded meat nearly the size of the dinner plate was liberally covered by a rich, cream gravy, as was a bowl of mashed potatoes. Serving bowls of green beans garnished with fatback sat next to platters of fried okra.

"What did you say this entreé is called?" she asked Molly.

"That? Why, it's chicken-fried steak, of course. Guess you don't have it back east."

Mary Elizabeth daintily cut into the meat. "Oh, I see. We do have similar fare, but it is known as breaded cutlets. I believe it is French in origin."

"Don't know about that, Miss. Recipe comes from my German grandmother. She called it *Schnitzel*, and usually made it with veal. Chicken's easier to find, and cheaper. It's on the menu for folks who're a little light in the poke."

A quizzical look crossed Mary Elizabeth's face as she absorbed the information before replying, "So, this is common fare?"

"Sure is, at least in these parts."

"This has been an educational trip, to say the least."

There was little conversation as she and Sheriff Flynn finished the meal. Mason had noticed her watching him on the ride from Fort Sill, trying to determine if she was husband-hunting. Flynn was almost old enough to be her father, although, that didn't mean much on the frontier. Besides, he felt some stirrings in his heart that had been absent since his wife was killed in '92.

Flynn pushed his chair back and put his hands on his belly. "I will say this, nobody leaves Ruth Sewell's restaurant hungry. Don't know if I could eat another bite."

"Does that mean I should throw this to the dogs?" Molly asked as she came out of the kitchen carrying a tray with two bowls of blackberry cobbler and a pitcher of heavy cream.

"Well, er, I 'spect those dogs are getting a mite heavy in the middle. Maybe we should save them the trouble and eat that cobbler," Mason replied.

"Thought so," Molly said, as she placed the bowls and pitcher on the table.

Mary Elizabeth reached for the small clutch she carried. "Perhaps we should settle the bill, since it appears your midday patrons are arriving…"

"I got this," Flynn interrupted. "Not proper for a lady to pay for her own meal." He handed a gold coin to their waitress. "Keep the rest, Molly."

MARY ELIZABETH PEABODY

"Thank you, Sheriff."

Mary Elizabeth leaned toward him after Molly left and commented in a low voice, "I am not questioning your generosity, but was that not quite a bit more than the cost of our meals?"

"More'n likely, but she's a widow with three growing younguns. She can use the help."

"I see." Mary Elizabeth looked at the tall, rugged man sitting across from her. He was the kind of man she would be seeking, if she were inclined toward marriage.

They finished the meal a quarter-hour later and left the tidy restaurant for the short walk across the hard-packed dirt street to the Sheriff's office.

The sound of a shotgun blast stopped them halfway and they glanced toward the bank at the other end of town in time to see a figure fall from a line-back dun. Nineteen-year old Gomer Platt, Flynn's deputy, stood with a wide-eyed stare, his sandy hair waving wildly in the wind. He took aim at the other two bank robbers headed straight for Flynn and Mary Elizabeth and hesitated, since they were in the line of fire.

The bandits whipped and lashed as they fired wildly at whoever had the bad fortune to be on the wooden sidewalk.

Women pushed children down and covered them with their bodies. Two farmers loading a wagon took cover behind it.

Flynn assumed a shooting stance, and, as if by magic, a stag-horn handled .45 caliber Colt SAA appeared in each hand. He drew a bead on the onrushing riders and fired. The bandit on the right was slammed back against the cantle of his saddle and fell end-over-end off the back of his horse, dead before he landed face first in the dirt.

The rider on the left took a slug in the chest, but managed to get one round off before he slumped sideways in the saddle and was dragged unceremoniously down the street by a foot caught in the stirrup.

Flynn heard a whimper on his right and turned. Mary Elizabeth had a trickle of blood dripping from her mouth onto the pink lace of her dress. She looked down at a red stain spreading across her bosom from the stray round that had pierced her heart. Her knees buckled and she began a slow-motion collapse.

Mason caught her before she hit the ground and cradled her in his arms. She took one last gurgling breath and stared up at him with lifeless eyes.

"Damn," he softly said, "I'm so sorry."

§§§§

Bio

T.C. MILLER

T.C. Miller came of age during the turbulent sixties and avoided the draft by serving twenty-four years in the Air Force; including six-and-a-half years with Air Force Reserve Recruiting Service.

His writing career began at nine years of age when a poem he wrote was published in the *Toledo Blade*. Freelance writing in the seventies and student manuals, police and self-defense courses for *Hakkoryu Jujitsu* classes he taught added to his resume.

Retirement from the military in 1993 led him and his wife to demonstrate products at countless commercial exhibitions across the country. A workplace accident eventually resulted in four back surgeries, and, while recuperating over a three-year period, T.C. returned to his first love-writing. The result was the successful *BlackStar Ops Group* series of spy-thrillers and the beginning of the *Antarrean Dilemma* science fiction trilogy.

Mary Elizabeth Peabody is his first foray into the Western genre, but certainly won't be his last.

Many thanks to Ken Farmer, for including the work in this anthology.

T.C. Miller's Amazon Author page:
www.amazon.com/T.-C.-Miller/e/B008SHDTY6
Website:
www.blackstaropsgroup.com/index.html
Facebook:
Https://www.facebook.com/profile.php?id=10000409688033